The Las Vegas M… g.
A MODERN DAY AMERICAN MASSACRE

The Las Vegas Mass Shooting:

A MODERN DAY AMERICAN MASSACRE

By Mark Tozer

Paperback ISBN: 9798874255411

This book is dedicated to all the victims of the Las Vegas Mass Shooting.

Table of Contents

Introduction

Over 13,000 people were in the grounds of the Route 91 Concert in Las Vegas on the night of October 1, 2017, when 64-year-old Stephen Craig Paddock opened fire on them from across the street, high upon the 32nd floor of the Mandalay Bay hotel.

For ten minutes, Paddock who would later become known as the infamous Las Vegas gunman, fired over 1,000 rounds at the unsuspecting concertgoers that night. The wave after wave of unrelenting shots fired into the venue would leave 58 people dead, over 500 wounded, and thousands of others suffering from mental scars due the actions of a sick and twisted individual. Then, over the course of the next few years, two more people would die as a direct result of their wounds, bringing the total number of deceased victims to 60 people.

In the days and weeks following the attack; the media were a buzz with myths, conspiracies, and blatant lies that all claimed to unlock the secrets to who the gunman truly was, and what forced him to commit his heinous and monstrous act. All the while, supplemented by confusing statements and personal theories being interjected from senior members of law enforcement, who were tasked with overseeing the investigating into the deadliest mass shooting in modern America history.

This was combined with the fact that to many people, it seemed that the parent company of the Mandalay Bay Hotel and Casino, MGM Resorts International (MGMRI), were somehow dictating certain elements of the law enforcement investigation, for their own gains. These claims surfaced due to the constant revision in the timeline for the wounding of the unarmed hotel security guard, close by the room the shooter was firing from, on the 32nd floor of the hotel. Later, the Las Vegas Metropolitan Police Department would use MGMRI's timeline, in place of their own.

Due to so many apparent issues with how the case was being conducted and the fact that MGMRI were seemingly trying to bend the truth, to their own advantage. The Detectives from the Las Vegas Metropolitan Police Department, who were working tirelessly to answer so many of the questions relating to the incident, were branded as incompetent. All the while, behind closed doors they were fighting a losing battle with their own senior officers.

Sadly, though, the true victims of the attack were left wondering if they really mattered at all. Because on the one hand you had what seemed to be a bungled police investigation, then on the other, you had the world's largest casino company trying to countersue the victims when they asked to be compensated for their injuries and suffering.

Then, close to the first anniversary of the attack, LVMPD released their final case report into the Las Vegas Mass Shooting titled: LVMPD Criminal Investigation Report of the 1 October Mass Casualty Shooting. The main body of the report was nothing short of a carefully choreographed Las Vegas show, and comparable to a whitewash of epic proportions.

In short, after an extensive investigation, all that LVMPD could conclude was the gunman acted alone, the unarmed security guard was a hero, and there was never any real motive for what the deranged gunman did that night.

Now, though, it is time that the thousands of victims are told the truth of what really drove a seemingly ordinary man, to subject them to such hatred, though no fault of their own. It is also important to show how a small team of dedicated detectives battled against the odds, to give the victims what justice they could. All while being handicapped by their own senior officers, who seemingly had some type of agenda they were working to.

Chapter One:
The Las Vegas Gunman

"Monsters are real, and ghosts are real too. They live inside of us, and sometimes, they win."

-Author, Stephen King.

Prior to the attack on the Route 91 Concert, Stephen Craig Paddock was seen as a loving son and big brother, that made his mother and youngest brother wealthy. To the casinos he frequented, he was viewed as a low-risk high roller, who always paid his debts on time and caused no trouble while staying in the hotels. And, to the outside world and law enforcement, he was truly an irrelevant nobody who was never given a second glance.

All that changed, though, a little after 10:05 p.m. on the night of October 1, 2017, after Paddock raised an AR-15 rifle to his right shoulder while he stood in front of the window in room 32-135 that he had broken out just moments before, high on the 32nd floor of the Mandalay Bay Hotel and Casino.

Then he fired his first shot into the defenseless crowd of concertgoers, enjoying the Route 91 Concert across the street. From that moment on, he ceased being Stephen Paddock, the once astute businessman and methodical accountant, and became known as the infamous Las Vegas gunman.

In the time that has come to pass, since that fateful night in Vegas; there have been countless misconceptions, misrepresentations, and conspiracies surrounding the man who Paddock once was. This has led to mismatched facts and lies masking how it was that a seemingly ordinary man could plan the deadliest mass shooting in modern American history, without coming to the attention of law enforcement or hotel security.

Now, though, it is time to break down the facade that has surrounded the Las Vegas gunman since that fateful night, which will show the evolution of Paddock from the person he once was, to the monster that he would become.

Stephen Craig Paddock was born on April 9, 1953, at Lamb Hospital in Clinton, Iowa to Benjamin Hoskins Paddock Jnr. (1 Nov. 1926 to 17 Jan. 1998) and Dolores Irene Hudson (Jan. 1928 to Jan. 2021). Steve, as he was more commonly known to his family, was the eldest of four children born to Dolores and Benjamin.

Paddock's mother and father were complete opposites and were married in Reno Nevada, on July 16, 1952, some nine months before Stephen was born. Many people have speculated that Benjamin's and Dolores's marriage, was more comparable to a shotgun wedding then then a well-planned loving affair. Years later, after Steve had made his fortune, he would own a property close by the church in Reno, where his parents were wed.

Due to Benjamin Paddock's colorful life and criminal past, he featured prominently in countless news articles published after the attack. It was even claimed by the Federal Bureau of Investigation's (FBI) Behavioral Analysis Unit (BAU) that one of Paddock's motivations to commit the mass shooting, was to become more infamous than his estranged criminal father. But that theory would later prove to be false.

A few weeks after Stephen's birth, in May 1953, Benjamin was arrested for his involvement in a check cashing scam, which netted him just over $90,000 ($945,003 in 2023). For his crime, Benjamin was sentenced to three years in the Illinois State Penitentiary. But this was not the first time that Paddock's father was incarcerated, nor would it be the last.

In late 1946, sometime before Benjamin met his future wife and mother to his four children, he was sent to prison for the first time, after being arrested for selling stolen military vehicles. His punishment on this occasion was five to eight years in the State Penitentiary. Within a few weeks of his release from his first prison sentence, in April 1951, he met Dolores.

Shortly after Benjamin was sent back to prison for the second time, Irene as she preferred to be called, and the young Stephen were forced to move in with her father, Ralph Hudson who at the time lived on the outskirts of Chicago. To pay her way and provide for her young son, while her husband served his sentence, she worked as a typist for a local printing company in Chicago. While his mother was away at work, Stephen was cared for by family and friends.

In the aftermath of the attack, Irene was interviewed by two FBI Agents regarding the mass shooting. During the interview she told the agents that the last communication she had with her eldest son before the attack, was when he called her to see how she was coping after Hurricane Irma. She also told the agents that Paddock was non-violent, good with numbers, and highly intelligent.

Irene also could never recall her eldest son having any religious beliefs nor was he associated with any political parties. When one of the agents asked her why she thought he committed the attack, Irene stated she did not know, but she believed that he may have had a brain tumor, which could have caused him to act and think differently.

In mid-1956, Benjamin was released from prison and rejoined his wife and young son in Chicago, which was to the disapproval of his father-in-law, Ralph. However, not wanting to see his daughter and grandchild out on the street, Ralph allowed Benjamin to stay at his house, under the provision that his son-in-law would change his ways and support his wife and child. Irene also gave her husband a firm ultimatum, turn away from crime, or lose his wife and child for good.

Within a few weeks of Benjamin moving into his father-in-law's home, the situation became untenable, as Benjamin was unable to abide by Ralph's strict rules. With very few options open to Benjamin, he packed up his wife and young son and headed to his father's house in Oregon.

The reception Benjamin and his family received from his father, Benjamin Senior, was less than welcoming. This was due to the fact when Benjamin Jnr. committed his first string of offenses in 1946, he used his father's position in the US Army reserve to gain access to blank military documents to enable him to steal military vehicles.

After staying with his father for a few days, Benjamin then took his young family to his mothers' house, in Tucson Arizona. Benjamin's mother Olga welcomed her only child and his young family with open arms, to her home. She did the same thing when Benjamin was discharged from the U.S. Navy, just over a decade before.

For the first few weeks, Olga was excited about having her young grandson staying with her. However, she made it known to Benjamin that he and his young family could only stay until they found their own place to live, and that had to be sooner, rather than later.

A month after moving to Tucson, Benjamin purchased three properties in cash. The first was a modest single-story four-bedroom ranch style house at 1122 North Camino Miraflores, which he purchased for $5,000 ($52,500 in 2023). The second and third purchases, which he acquired a few days after he bought the new family home, was two gas stations on East Broadway for a little over $15,000 ($157,5000 in 2023). Both gas stations also had a used car lot attached to them.

Shortly after purchasing the family home and the two gas stations, the local police department paid Benjamin a visit. Because it had come to their attention that this recently released convict had just purchased three properties in cash, in a short space of time. Benjamin assured the officers that he and his wife had been saving hard for several years and were also helped with the purchases of the properties, due to a modest family inheritance they had just been left.

The truth was, though, Irene could hardly afford to live when Benjamin was in prison, so she was not able to save any money, whatsoever. Neither had anyone recently died in either of their families to leave them an inheritance. In reality, the money that Benjamin used was from his illicit check scam, because after he was captured law enforcement were only able to recover a small percentage of cash.

Within a year of moving to Tucson, Stephen was joined by his first of three younger brothers, Patrick, in September 1957. In the aftermath of the attack, like Irene, Patrick was questioned by law enforcement. During his interview he stated that he only learned of his brothers' actions, after a co-worker asked if they were related, because he bore a striking resemblance to the shooter, and they shared the same last name. Patrick was of little use, though, as he had not spoken to his brother for over two decades.

All Patrick knew for certain was that at one point, his older brother worked for the IRS and may have had a pilot's license. He did confirm that he never knew his brother to be violent or to seek revenge, but he was motivated by what benefitted him personally. Unlike most of Paddocks family, Patrick also spoke to the media, and again he echoed that he only discovered what his brother had done, arriving at work on Monday, October 2, 2017, when a colleague asked him if he was related to the shooter.

He told the reporter that it was hard growing up in a single-parent low-income household, as money was tight. He also recounted was that it would be commonplace for he and his brothers to argue at breakfast time, over who was going to get the fresh milk for their cereal, and who was going to get the powdered milk.

After two years of being in Tucson, Benjamin seems to have become quite an entrepreneur and was easily able to support his wife and two young sons. He had also expanded his business empire, as by that point he owned a contracting company and a garbage disposal business. Meanwhile, the young Stephen, was blossoming into a smart and articulate child, who also took regular piano lessons.

In mid-1958, the Paddock family business empire grew once again, when Benjamin and his brother-in-law, Howard Ayers, went into the entertainment business together. They purchased a night club on the 2800 block of North 1st Avenue in Tucson, which was named Big Daddy's.

Irene, meanwhile, had become the quintessential 1950's homemaker, and made sure the house was kept in good order and the children were cared for. It was not all hard work and no play for the Paddock parents, though, because Benjamin and Irene would regularly head down to Big Daddy's on a Saturday night, while a family friend from Chicago, Mary Jacobs, who had moved in with the Paddocks, babysat Stephen and Patrick.

By early 1959, it seems that the Paddock family business empire had run into financial trouble. Because at around 11:40 a.m. on Thursday February 19, 1959, Benjamin committed his first robbery at the Valley National Bank on 18th Ave. and Van Buren in Phoenix. In less than ten minutes, the smooth talking and confident bank robber was able to make off with $11,210 ($107,073 in 2023) in cash.

A few months after the bank robbery, in June 1959, Stephen and Patrick were joined by another brother, Bruce. In the aftermath of the attack, Bruce learned of his older brothers' murderous act, while in hospital recovering from back surgery. After being woken up by a nurse to take his pain medication, he saw a report on TV about a mass shooting in Vegas, and a photo of someone who looked like his older brother Stephen. Bruce called his mother, Irene, to ask if that was Steve and she confirmed that it was.

Just like Patrick and Irene, Bruce was also questioned by law enforcement in the aftermath of the attack. He claimed that he thought his brother was suffering from a mental illness, as he was paranoid and delusional. He also confirmed that his brother was never known to be violent and did not abuse drugs or alcohol. Bruce speculated that not only would have Paddock methodically planned the attack, but also, he must have been very pissed off to commit such an act of violence.

Shortly after Bruce was interviewed by law enforcement, about his brother. It came to light that there was an active warrant for his arrest, relating to the possession of child pornography and child exploitation charges, dating back to 2014. However, Bruce was never tried for his crimes, as the case was later dismissed by a judge, due to a legal technicality. Bruce passed away in 2020.

In 1960, the Paddock family would have its fair share of ups and downs, with not only the arrival of the fourth and final child, but also, the patriarch would disappear from the family. On Jan. 29, Benjamin committed his second bank robbery at the same bank as the first, but unlike the previous occasion, he only netted $9,285 ($87,031 in 2023).

Then in March 1960, Stephen, Patrick, and Bruce were joined by their youngest Brother, Eric. In the aftermath of the attack, Eric would be one of the first family members to learn of his eldest brothers' horrific crimes, after a detective with the Las Vegas Metropolitan Police Department (LVMPD) called him on his cellphone at around 2:00 a.m. Eastern Standard Time (EST) on the morning of October 2, 2017. Once Eric was told of his brothers' heinous act, he took it upon himself to become the family spokesperson and gave countless interviews to the media.

While being questioned by law enforcement he stated Stephen was the only brother he spoke with, as Bruce was a sociopath and Patrick had mental issues. Eric also confirmed Paddock was non-violent but was passive aggressive to anyone that angered him. He also told law enforcement that despite his brother appearing unkempt, he was very detail-oriented, and he would have meticulously planned the attack.

Shortly after Eric's birth, Steve won first place in a piano competition held in Tucson. The young Stephen was not just a talented piano player, though, as seemingly he was gifted at making pottery. One piece of pottery he made for a school project was a gift for his mother, which was an astray in the shape of a tennis court. In his teenage years, tennis would become one of Paddocks many passions, until he left high school. Irene kept the ashtray until the day she died, in January 2021.

On July 26, 1960, Benjamin would embark upon his third and final bank robbery. This time though, he committed the robbery at the 19th Street and McDowell branch of the Valley National Bank in Phoenix. It seems that someone may have tipped Benjamin off to increased security procedures at the W. Van Buren branch. But unbeknown to Benjamin and his insider person, the increased security was rolled out at all the Valley National Bank branches, and not just the one he had robbed on the two previous occasions.

Due to the new measures in place, he only escaped with just over $4,620 ($43,304 in 2023). This was not the only misfortune, though, which Benjamin encountered during his third robbery. Because, within seconds of Benjamin walking out of the bank, the assistant manager, Mr. Schmidt, was able to follow closely behind Benjamin and spotted him drive off in his get-a-way car.

Then, with the help of a passing motorist, the bank manager was able to follow Benjamin as he drove away from the bank to a parking lot, several blocks away where he had parked his own vehicle. Based on Schmidt's description of Benjamin's car, which was claimed to be either a Buick or Olds Mobile, with two long radio antennas on the roof, and armature ham radio plates. The FBI were easily able to trace the vehicle to Benjamin.

Due to the time-consuming investigative process employed at the time, though, Benjamin was able to drive the 113 miles from Phoenix to Tucson, alter the look of his car and spend time with his family. Then visit his mother and give her $500 ($4,686 in 2023). Before he would head out to Vegas and lay low for a few days.

The first time that Irene knew of her husband's wrongdoing was when four FBI agents arrived at the family home, early on the morning of July 27, 1960. After the agents informed Irene of her husband's bank heist, she confirmed that he had left the day before headed to Las Vegas, on what he claimed was a business trip. The FBI then searched the single-story ranch style house but found nothing.

The Tucson Daily Citizen published several articles in both the Thursday and Friday evening editions of the newspaper, on July 28 and 29, 1960. One of the headlines in the Thursday evening edition stated, "Little Children Underfoot As FBI Agents Move In." In the Friday evening publication, one of the taglines read, "A demure wife, four bouncing children and a four bedroomed ranch house made it hard for neighbors to believe 'Big Daddy' Benjamin H. Paddock could be accused of being a bank robber."

In the Thursday edition, it stated that when Irene was asked to make a comment about her husband's arrest and the FBI searching her home, she refused. However, a neighbor, Mrs. Eva Price, and the family friend; Mary Jacobs who was still staying with the Paddock's at the time, both spoke to the reporter.

Mrs. Eva Price, who lived across from the Paddock family, stated that it was her husband that had sold the house to the Paddocks, some years earlier. Eva also described how both Benjamin and Irene minded their own business and seemed respectable. She then went on to say, "We're trying to keep Steve from knowing his father is held as a bank robber. I hardly know the family, but Steve is a really nice boy. It's a terrible thing."

Mary, who had been staying with Irene and Benjamin for a little over a year babysat Patrick, Bruce, and Eric as the FBI searched the house. Mary told the reporter, "This is terrible," and then went on to describe how Benjamin was a nice man, attentive to his wife, and how kind he was to his children while always doing things around the home.

True to her word, though, shortly after the FBI finished with their search of the family home, Irene confided in her friend Mary that from that point forward, she would class herself as a widow. With Stephen being the eldest child, he was told shortly after the house search that his father had died in a work accident. Then, as each of the other children became older enough to understand, their mother would tell them the same story.

In the aftermath of the attack, several theories emerged that claimed one of the motives for the Las Vegas Mass Shooting, was that the son was trying to avenge the father in some way. This was claimed because Paddock not only took his own life with a revolver that was like the one his father used to carry. But also, in the wake of the third bank robbery, Benjamin was apprehended in Las Vegas, in what was later described as a long police pursuit involving violence.

In a bizarre twist, the spot where Benjamin was arrested in July 1960, was close by where the Ogden hotel is now located. In the days prior to the shooting, the gunman rented three rooms at the Ogden. However, there was never any evidence that the gunman knew where his father was arrested. Neither was there any proof that the shooter visited the area close by the Ogden where Benjamin was apprehended.

Despite there being no connection between the fathers' arrest and the sons' heinous attack, to dispel the rumors and conjecture, which claims the shooter committed his sickening act to avenge his father, it is worthwhile noting the circumstances of Benjamin's arrest.

On morning of July 27, 1960, a Las Vegas Sheriff's Deputy was conducting a routine patrol when he spotted a car matching the description belonging to a person of interest, parked on East Fremont Street. The deputy reported the vehicle, and two FBI agents from the Vegas field office were sent to take a closer look at the car.

Just as the agents pulled up and parked on Fremont St., FBI Agent John T. Reilly who was an eight-year veteran of the Bureau, spotted Benjamin as he exited a nearby restaurant and was heading towards the suspect vehicle. Both Reilly and his partner then got out of their vehicle and followed Benjamin on foot, to see exactly where he was heading. After following Benjamin for a few moments, they realized that he was heading to his car.

Without hesitation, Reilly shouted for Benjamin to stop and place his hands on his head. However, after Benjamin took a quick look back at where the voices were coming from, he ran to his vehicle and jumped in the driver's seat, started the engine then tried to drive away. To prevent Benjamin from escaping, Agent Reilly stepped into the middle of the road, but it quickly became apparent that the suspect was not going to stop the vehicle.

With very few options open to Reilly, he pulled out his service issued revolver and fired a shot at the passenger side of the windshield. Benjamin immediately slammed on the brakes, and the car stopped just feet from where Reilly was standing, at the intersection of E Fremont St. and 4th St. The unphased Reilly then shouted commands at Benjamin to place his hands on his head, exit his vehicle and walk towards the Agents. Without hesitation, Benjamin complied with Reilly's instructions. The whole incident was over in less than two minutes.

Once the suspect was placed in handcuffs and sat in the rear seat of the Agent's vehicle, they set about searching the suspects' car. On the front passenger seat, they discovered a black leather jacket, a newspaper with a .38 caliber snub-nosed revolver hidden under it, along with a brown paper bag containing $2,975 ($27,885 in 2023) in cash. The agents then inspected the roof of the vehicle, where they discovered two areas that had been patched over, where the holes for the antennas used to be.

Benjamin was then taken into custody and driven to the Clarke County Jail and held, until he could be transported back to Arizona. However, shortly after being placed in a cell, Benjamin discovered that the cell door was unlocked, so he tried to escape; but he was quickly apprehended. Benjamin's failed escape attempt led to his bail being set at $25,000.00 ($242,476.00 in 2023), which Irene refused to pay.

In the aftermath of Benjamin's arrest, both Mary and Irene continued to run the family businesses, but they were seemingly no longer as lucrative as they once were. To help his daughter and young grandchildren, Ralph Hudson sold his home in Chicago and moved to Tucson. While the women worked hard to try and make the businesses profitable, Ralph looked after his grandsons.

In January 1961, Benjamin, who had bitterly protested his innocence, stood trial for the three robberies in Phoenix. After several weeks, he was found guilty of the bank heists and was sentenced to a minimum of twenty years in federal prison and was sent to the federal penitentiary in La Tuna, Texas to start his sentence. Shortly after Benjamin was sent to prison, he signed over the family home and businesses to his wife.

Irene now faced a dilemma, should she stay in Tucson, or leave town? However, because they were both well known, it had become common knowledge that Benjamin was now a felon. This caused Irene to feel ashamed. More importantly, though, she had another issue to contend with. If she wanted her sons to truly believe their father was dead, then they had to leave Tucson. Because by staying in the city, there was a chance that one day, someone may tell her boys the truth about their father.

After liquidating the business assets and selling the family home to her father, she netted just over $22,000 ($206,213 in 2023), for her and the boys to start a new life. Within no time at all, Irene and Mary had packed up their belongings, the children's clothes and toys, and moved to Sun Valley California, where Irene's older sister Olga lived with her husband. The new family home for the Paddock's was a modest single-story house, located at 11914 Snelling St., Sun Valley California.

Shortly after moving to Sun Valley, the young Stephen was enrolled at Fernangeles Elementary School, which was only a short distance from the family's new home. After the mass shooting, a picture surfaced of the young Paddock, from his time at Fernangeles. The photo shows him lying on his stomach and propped up on raised elbows with his head resting on his hands smiling at the camera, proudly showing off his prized rock collection.

During his time at elementary school, Paddock was seen to be gifted in mathematics, and socialized well with his peers. However, due to the family finances being strained, he was no longer practicing piano.

After graduating from Fernangeles in 1965, Paddock then attended Richard E. Byrd Middle School. According to former classmates, Paddock could be rebellious, but he was a very bright child that was still good with numbers. However, some reporters tried to connect the actions of a rebellious teenager, as a precursor for signs of a would-be mass shooter.

One story, which many tried to claim showed early signs of Paddocks eventual evil, related to a physics class project. Based on information from students who were in the class, they were set a project to construct a bridge from certain materials. Unlike his peers, though, Paddock completely went against the rules and used strong bonding agents and disqualified materials. When Paddocks 'cheating' was discovered by the teacher, Stephen along with his fellow students found it funny.

This story does not single Paddock out as someone who had the potential to become the deadliest mass shooter in modern American history, instead, it shows he was being a typical teenage boy and trying to flaunt the rules.

While in middle school, mysterious rashes started to appear on Paddock's hands and various parts of his body. Irene was so concerned, she took her eldest son to the doctors, where it was discovered that he had overly sensitive skin. The doctor believed that he would grow out of the alignment, but as he got older, his skin issues caused him several problems in his day-to-day life.

By the time he was 50 years old, the condition was so severe that Paddock took to wearing black cotton gardening gloves, on an almost daily basis. Along with his overly sensitive skin complaint, Paddock also developed a heightened sense of smell, which would also adversely affect him. By the time of the mass shooting, his sense of smell was so heightened that certain perfumes and chemicals, caused him to feel nauseated and gave him headaches.

In 1967, Paddock graduated from middle school and moved to Francis Polytechnic High School. Just like before, former classmates recounted that for the first few years in high school, he was intelligent and good at mathematics. However, he was not without issues, because a former friend and fellow classmate of Paddocks, Joseph Klotchman, told the Las Vegas Review Journal; "He was quiet, very kind of mild-mannered. I did sense, though, that he was a little bit troubled. It seemed like under the surface there was something bothering him. But he was quiet, mild-mannered." Joseph Klotchman was not the only one that noticed this change in Paddocks' behavior.

Around late 1969 to early 1970, other classmates also recall that Paddock started to eat his lunch alone. Along with Paddock seemingly alienating himself, his teachers also noticed that his grades had started to drop. The normally straight A student was now becoming a loner with disastrous grades. With such drastic changes in Stephens' behavior, over a short period of time, in mid-February 1970, the school called Irene in to discuss the matter.

According to various accounts, Irene told the school that Steve was going through a rough time at home and was still trying to cope with his father's death. She also told the school that she was trying her best to help him, but with being a single parent with no male role model in his life, he was not getting the right parenting balance. But Irene was not telling the full story.

In late-December 1968, Benjamin escaped from federal prison in La Tuna, TX. In efforts to find the escaped felon, FBI agents went and interviewed Irene, in early January 1969. At some point during this meeting with Irene at the family home, Paddock came home from school and walked in on his mother talking to the agents. At the time, Irene downplayed the meeting with the FBI, and she told her eldest son that they were there discussing an incident at her work.

This was a plausible story, because Irene worked at an engineering company, which held contracts with several defense companies. However, unbeknown to Irene and the agents, Stephen arrived home from school earlier than they realized, and he stood by the front door listening to what was being said in the kitchen.

Shortly after this incident, Stephen went around to Mary, who by now was married and living just around the corner from the Paddock family. After arriving at the house, Paddock began to ask her if she knew what the FBI were doing at his home, as he did not believe his mother's story. Unsure of what to do, Mary downplayed the incident, as best she could. Then, Stephen dropped a bombshell, as he claimed to have heard one of the agents tell his mother that his father had recently escaped from jail.

Mary was shocked by this remark and told the young Stephen he must have misheard what was said. It seems that after almost an hour, Mary was able to convince Paddock that he was mistaken, and he left shortly after. Once Stephen had left her house, Mary immediately called Irene to warn her about Paddock's visit. Irene told her old friend she would take care of the situation.

After several days, Irene told Mary that she had spoken to Stephen on his own and reassured him that the FBI were at the house to discuss an issue at her work. Seemingly, to Irene at least, the talk appeased Stephen. But evidently, Steve did not fully believe his mother.

A few weeks later in February 1969, a police officer who knew Irene went around to see her and told her that Stephen had been at the local police station, asking questions about a Benjamin Paddock. Luckily enough, the desk sergeant on duty that day was aware of who Stephen was and that Irene had told her sons that their father was dead.

Seemingly, the police sergeant played along with the request and appeared to look through some paperwork, before informing Stephen there were no records relating to a Benjamin Paddock. However, the lie about Benjamin was soon to unravel.

Nine months later, on the evening of November 2, 1969, Paddock sat down to watch one of his regular TV shows, The FBI. The show was a dramatized version of real FBI cases, which had been previously solved.

That night it was episode eight season five, titled The Challenge. As was customary with the show, at the midway point, a section was designated to people who were on the FBI's Most Wanted List. The wanted felon featured on this show that night was fugitive # 302, Benjamin Hoskins Paddock, who had been on the most wanted list since June 10, 1969, after escaping from federal prison.

The then 16-year-old Paddock must have been horrified after seeing his fathers' picture on TV, because for nine years, he had believed his father was dead. What was worse, though, when he suspected his father was still alive. Everyone who Paddock thought he could trust, had seemingly been lying to him.

Benjamin was the talk of Paddock's high school, the following day, as the show stated that the wanted felon had family in the Sun Valley area of California. Several of Paddocks classmates asked him if the wanted felon was any relation to him. According to several people who witnessed this incident, it was evident that Stephen was affected by the questions and seemed very embarrassed and visibly upset. But he stated that he did not know the person who was on the most wanted list.

After Paddock discovered the truth about his father, he did not confront his mother right away. Instead, he left it for several days, as it seems that he wanted to speak to her alone, so he waited for the opportunity to arise, and when it did, he took it. What ensued was a bitter argument between mother and son.

Stephen told his mother that she should have been honest with him and his brothers, about their father, as they had a right to know that he was alive and a convicted felon. Irene quickly argued back, telling her oldest son he had no idea the type of man that his father truly was. Paddock responded, telling his mother that irrespective of what his father was like, they still had a right to know about him being alive.

But Irene was not backing down, and with little to no choice, she told Stephen exactly what type of man his father was. Not only was he a compulsive gambler, but he also seldom told the truth. Worst of all, Benjamin's only motives for the robberies, was so that he could go to Vegas and spend the money on other women and gamble it all away.

The argument went on for close to twenty minutes, but once Irene told her son exactly what his father was like and the horrible things, he did to people, the family included, Paddock backed down. Irene now had a new problem, as she did not want her other son's finding out the truth about their father. So, she swore Stephen to secrecy, which he complied with, providing Irene agreed to her eldest son's request.

In exchange for his silence, he wanted his mother to support him financially, in his endeavors. Such as buying Stephen his first car, and paying for him to take flying lessons, so he could get his pilot's license. Despite how costly this would be to Irene, for many years to come, she reluctantly agreed to the deal.

At the age of seventeen, In August 1970, Paddock started flying lessons so that he could obtain his private aircraft license to fly single engine planes. According to FAA records by September 21, 1970, he had logged a total of 54.4 hours of dual and solo flight time. This allowed Paddock to obtain a temporary airman's certificate, which was set to expire on November 30,

1971. The address on his pilots' license was the house the family first moved to in early 1960, after leaving Tucson Arizona.

Paddock graduated from Francis Polytechnic High School in 1971 with a grade point average (GPA) of 3.1. Shortly after graduating, he enrolled at San Fernando Valley State College, which would later become California State University Northridge. His area of study was business administration and accounting. Based on information from his college enrollment paperwork, under the section for his father, Stephen simply wrote deceased.

To help pay his way through college, Paddock had several jobs as a source of income. Initially, he worked as a security guard at both Van Nuys private airport and for a movie production company. However, neither of these positions paid very well, so Paddock became a part-time mail carrier for the United States Postal Service (USPS). Shortly after being employed by the USPS, he not only had an increase in salary, but he also had access to health benefits and a government pension.

His employment as a mail carrier may not have been what it seemed, though, because Paddock had a side hustle while in college. According to various sources, he grew and distributed marijuana. To evade any possible trouble, he used fake IDs to rent several apartments, in and around Sun Valley, and if the smell became too obvious, he simply took what he could and closed his operation and moved to another apartment.

Within no time at all, Paddock was one of the main marijuana sellers on campus to his college-friends and anyone who would buy from him. Also, it was rumored that he offered a delivery service to select customers on his mail route.

While at San Fernando Valley, Paddock's college records show that he was typically a straight A student, who even made the dean's list for academic achievement. However, there were notes that show from early December 1971 to late January 1972, he took a leave of absence from Northbridge, for unspecified health reasons. Coincidently, this period corresponds with a renewed effort by the FBI to find Benjamin, which was specifically aimed at the Los Angeles area.

It turns out that in early December 1971, the FBI went to Stephens college and spoke to several of his teachers to see if Benjamin had ever been on the campus, or if Paddock had even mentioned anything about his father. The FBI drew a blank, as none of the people they spoke to could recall seeing Benjamin, nor could they ever recall Paddock speaking about his father, other than stating he was deceased.

A few days after the FBI visited the college, one Stephen's teachers happened to mention to him that they had had a visit from federal agents, asking questions about his father. The teacher told Paddock that he thought it was strange for the feds to be asking about someone, who Stephen was claiming to have died years before. Paddock told the teacher that there was some confusion, as it was not his father they were looking for, but it was someone from his dad's side of the family who he had never met.

After leaving his teachers' classroom, Paddock immediately left the camps and went home and told his mother about the FBI visiting his teachers. Irene felt that the FBI were invading the family privacy and preventing Paddock from having access to an education. So, she filed a complaint with the FBI headquarters in Washington D.C. and spoke with her Senator. Within a week or two, the Paddock family were no longer of interest to the FBI. Over the next few years, Paddock was a model student, but that did not last long.

In the summer of 1975, Irene was forced to tell her son's the truth about their father. It is not clear what prompted her to confess, as there are conflicting stories. But evidently, when the truth came out, it had a profound impact on Stephen. However, Irene tried to keep it a secret that her eldest son had known for several years, about Benjamin being alive.

Somehow, Patrick found out that Stephen had known for some time, and shortly after enlisting in the US Air Force, Patrick ceased regular contact with his family and hardly ever spoke to Stephen again.

Not long after the truth came out about Benjamin, even though he was still on the run from authorities. Stephen and his brothers started to communicate with their father, and even went to visit him on occasions. However, within a few weeks of Stephen seeing his father for the first time in some fifteen years, he abruptly cut contact with Benjamin and never spoke to his father, again. In Paddock's eyes, his father was nothing more than a piece of crap that should have reminded dead.

In 1976, Paddock graduated from college with a degree in business administration and accounting, with a GPA of 2.97. According to his college records, Paddock should have graduated with a much higher average, but in his last semester his grades drastically dropped. With the prior changes in Paddock whenever his father's life encroached on his, this drop in grades can be attributed to the family rift created by the truth coming out about Benjamin still being alive.

Within a few months of leaving college, Paddock and his college sweetheart, Sharon Brunoehler married on July 17, 1977. The marriage only lasted for three years and ended childless on December 29, 1980. Despite the divorce, though, Sharon and Stephen parted ways as friends. Sharon was never interviewed by law enforcement in the aftermath of the attack, because after the divorce she had very little contact with Paddock.

Both Brunoehler and her brother did speak to the media after the incident. She stated that she could not foresee any reason as to why her ex-husband would commit such an attack, because Paddock was never violent when they were married. Her brother stated Paddock was a fun-loving guy, who never showed signs of aggression or violence towards anyone.

There is evidence though, that Paddock certainly knew how to handle himself and could be aggressive when he wanted to be. One story relates to a family friend of the Paddocks, who was skilled in mixed martial arts. He and Stephen would regularly spar, and surprisingly, it was typically Paddock that won the sparing sessions, and not the friend.

Paddock's first professional job after leaving Northbridge and getting married, was working for the Internal Revenue Service (IRS) as an auditor. His role consisted of sitting behind a desk from 9 to 5, Monday through Friday, scrutinizing both business and personal tax returns looking for any evidence of irregularities. Despite widespread speculation, though, Paddock was never a revenue agent. This means that he would not have received any type of firearms or tactical training.

Within a year of Paddock starting work at the IRS, his father was finally captured by federal agents, living under the name Bruce Warner Erickson in Oregon. However, Benjamin had been removed from the FBI's Most Wanted list over two years before, in 1975, as the FBI changed the guidelines as to who could be on the list; and Benjamin's escape from federal custody did not fall within the new rules.

While working for the IRS, Paddock would take his foray into the world of gambling, by joining his work colleagues for regular poker nights. It seems that Paddock was a skilled player, often winning most of the hands. It was also shortly after starting work with the IRS, Paddock purchased his first firearm on June 14, 1982, which was a Charter Arms .38 caliber undercover snub-nosed revolver. His second firearm purchase came the following year, on April 19, 1983. This time, he purchased a Beretta Model 20 .25 caliber compact pistol.

By mid-1984, Paddock was growing increasingly disillusioned with his work at the IRS and the small weekly paychecks. The only bonus his job offered was an insight into the US tax system and how to get favorable tax returns. So, he sought a new job within the US government that would enable him to move from government employment into the more lucrative private sector.

After looking over his options, he found that his best course of action was to apply for an auditor's position at the Defense Contracting Audit Agency (DCAA), who specialized in scrutinizing the accounts of various companies that held defense contacts. He started at the DCAA in December 1984. While working at the DCAA, Paddock would purchase at least four more firearms, which were a mix of pistols and revolvers in various calibers.

In 1985, Paddock married his former classmate from Francis Polytechnic, Peggy Okamoto. Just like his first marriage, though, Paddock and Peggy would separate in the early-1990s, and the marriage ended childless. Stephen and Peggy would remain good friends until the Las Vegas Mass Shooting, as they invested in various property deals together.

While Peggy never spoke to the media in the aftermath of the attack, she was interviewed by law enforcement. Just like his family members, she was unable to give any information as to what motivated him to commit such a horrendous act. She also confirmed that he was not violent, and never showed any malice towards anyone.

Not long after marrying Peggy, Stephen along with his mother and youngest brother, Eric, went into the real estate business. The first property that the family purchased was a small 11-unit apartment complex in North Hollywood, which was in the final stages of foreclosure and valued at $407,000 ($754,428 in 2023).

In the aftermath of the attack, there were countless reports that Paddock and his family were able to buy the property, as he used his access to single engine planes to smuggle drugs into the United States, for the Medellin Cartel. However, as exciting as this story sounded, it was just that, a story. The source of the capital was far more mundane and boring, then most people could imagine.

For several years prior to the purchase of the 11-unit complex, Paddock had been filing the family's tax returns. And, due to his insight into allowances and how the system worked, he made sure the family obtained healthy returns and favorable deductions. Despite the strong financial position, which he had put the family. When they came to purchase the apartment complex, they found themselves short of the necessary funds.

So, both Stephen and Eric paid a visit to the bank that owned the property. Unlike Benjamin, though, they never went to rob the bank at gunpoint, they went to cut a deal on the foreclosed apartments. Due mainly to Stephens' skills in negation, he was not only able to get the purchase price lowered by a few thousand dollars, he was also able to convince the bank to loan them the short fall in money they needed to purchase the property and to make repairs.

Ever the businessman, Stephen convinced his brother Eric that they should undertake the daily maintenance jobs and renovations of the property, instead of bringing in a contractor. However, as their funds were tight, they both maintained their day jobs and doubled as repairmen and contractors on the evenings. Due to Eric's job at the time, and the fact that he had a young family, it was mainly Steve who did the work on the apartments.

Within a few years of the family purchasing their first rental property, Paddocks' day job at the DCAA combined with his work in the evenings at the apartment complex, was taking a toll on him. But due to the financial commitments of the family, he was unable to quit. So now, he started to explore his options of moving from government employment, into what he thought would be the more lucrative private sector.

A short time after making the decision to move into the private sector, he secured a job at McDonnell Douglas, as an internal auditor. At the time, McDonnell Douglas was one of the largest defense aerospace contracting companies in the United States.

Despite moving into the private sector, though, Paddock found that his income did not increase by a vast amount. This meant that he still had to work two jobs. Now, though, the family not only owned one property, but they owned and operated several apartment complexes in Los Angeles, which were mainly in impoverished areas.

By early-1988 the financial strain on the Paddock family real estate business was starting to show, because according to L.A. tax records from the time, there was a longstanding tax debt of $85 ($220 in 2023) owed on one of their properties. Despite the amount being a minor amount, as the debt had been owed for some time, the city placed a lien against the apartment complex.

Around late 1989, Paddock had reached his breaking point, as he never seemed to get ahead. So, he decided that either the day job had to go, or the apartment complexes did. To help Stephen make up his mind, he resorted to his tried and tested decision-making method.

He sat down with a piece of paper and wrote pros and cons at the top, then drew a line down the middle. He then wrote out what would be the pros and cons of him quitting work and keeping the apartment complexes, or what would be the benefit of staying with his employer and selling the family's property holdings.

After a short time, he arrived at the conclusion that his best option was to quit his job and focus on the property business, full-time. Because while he may be losing a steady paycheck, he would have more time to refurbish the apartments they owned, which would make them more desirable to rent. In turn, this would mean that while he may experience a drop in income for a short period, in the long run, he would make more money.

Once he made his decision, he handed in his resignation at McDonnell Douglas and worked his two-week notice and never looked back. When Paddock left the company, he had acquired 0004% of the company's shares, through the employee share scheme, which had a cash value of roughly $40,000 ($59,048 in 2023). But despite Paddock being in desperate need of money, he chose to keep the shares and not redeem them for cash, as based on his projections they would help towards a higher return, further down the line.

The 1990s would be the start of a rollercoaster decade for Paddock, not only on a personal front, but also on a business level as well. First came his divorce from Peggy in early 1990. Then the family property portfolio was experiencing even more cash flow problems than before, which nearly resulted in the Paddock property empire crumbling. However, despite the family's financial woes, Paddock was still able to acquire several more firearms, mainly pistols and one Colt CAR 15 rifle chambered in .223.

Then, when all hope was seemingly lost, and the Paddock's were on a collision course with financial ruin. A cataclysmic event occurred in Los Angeles, which was catastrophic for the city, but would have a positive rebound effect for the Paddocks and L.A. as a whole.

In April 1992, tensions within the L.A. area came to a head, when several LAPD officers who participated in the Rodney King incident were found not guilty of assault. This literally lit the fires ablaze in L.A. for five days; from April 29 to May 4, as there was mass rioting in the city. By the end of the riots, over one billion dollars of damaged had been caused to businesses and homes, 63 people had been killed, with another 2,383 injured, and over 12,000 people arrested. This incident came to be known as the 1992 L.A. Riots.

Like so many events that transpired in Paddocks' life, in the after math of the mass shooting, an incident that occurred during the riots was twisted to make it appear that it had an influence on how he planned his attack in Las Vegas.

Due to the destruction being caused by the thousands of rioters, countless property and business owners close to the area of the riots, took to the rooftops of their buildings to stand guard over their investments.

Just like hundreds of other people in the L.A. area, at the time, Paddock also took to defending one of the family's investments, as one of their apartment complexes was just a stone's throw from the epicenter of the riots. Wearing a bullet proof jacket and armed with his CAR 15, Stephen kept watch on the roof of the building, for several days.

Unlike the other property and business owners in the area, though, the Paddock's had an advantage. By chance, Eric's office overlooked the area of the riots and the apartment complex the family owned. So, Stephen decided to run a phone line to the roof of their building, while Eric would routinely watch from his office window with binoculars and relay time sensitive information to his brother. The riots were quelled just three blocks shy of where the apartment complex was located.

In the aftermath of the riots, the federal government stepped in and instituted a series of projects to improve the area and create jobs for residents. This caused property values to soar overnight, which benefited the Paddocks tremendously. Because now, all their low-income apartment buildings, were worth more than double then what they were before the riots.

The Paddocks were unlike other apartment complex owners, though, because when the property values soared, the Paddocks never got greedy. Instead, they increased the rent by a small amount and made sure that tenants had a secure and well-maintained area to live.

This boosted their business considerably because their apartments were affordable, well maintained, and in an up-and-coming area of the city. Now, 99% of the apartments were rented out at any one time, and there was also a long list of people that wanted to move in.

This gave the Paddocks a steady stream of revenue and boosted their reputation as being honest and decent landlords. Furthermore, Steve knew that one of the secrets to being a good businessman was outstanding customer service. So, when he could, he would help tenants who fell behind with rent payments and gave them a longer grace period then most landlords would have.

However, this tactic sometimes did come back and cause issues for the family, as some tenants would abuse Stephen's good nature. One incident with a tenant stands out the most, and shows that while Paddock may have appeared passive and easy going, when he was pushed, he could flip a switch and defend himself.

A former tenant, who Paddock had evicted for not paying their rent for several months, despite the tenant promising Steve, he would pay. Began to cause trouble for the family business, and started to make false claims as to why they were evicted. To appease the tenant and maintain the reputation of the family business. Stephen reached out to the former tenant, to try and calm the situation.

The offer that Stephen put on the table, was that Paddock would either allow the tenant to move back into the apartment complex, with a slightly reduced rent. Or the family business would give the tenant around three months' worth of their rent back. However, this offer did not please the tenant in question, and they wanted more than the Paddock's were willing to pay.

When Steve pointed out to the former tenant that this was in effect, extortion, the tenants' response was to cause damage Steve's car. Frustrated and angry with the tenant, Paddock retaliated by damaging the former tenant's vehicle, then he used his imposing size to intimidate the person to stop any further reprisals.

This incident alone, goes to show that while Paddock may have been a person of imposing size, violence was never his first cause of action. Instead, he preferred to work through a problem as amicably as possible, before resorting to more drastic measures. And that was consistent with Paddock as a person because there are countless incidents in his life, where he tried to resolve matters, before he flipped the switch and became violent.

In August 1997, Paddocks personal fortunes took a turn for the better, when Boeing and Lockheed Martin entered a joint venture to purchase McDonnell Douglas. Paddock's modest 0.004% shares he had obtained in the company under the employee share scheme, back in the late 1980s. Suddenly ballooned in value from $40,000 to an impressive $500,000 at the time of the sale. Like most employees, Paddock sold his shares.

One of Paddocks first investments after he sold his stock in early January 1998, was the purchase a house on Keswick Lane in Mesquite, Texas. Paddock would retain ownership of the house until he sold it in March 2010, for $134,518. Coincidently, at the time Paddock started the paperwork to purchase this property, his estranged father Benjamin lived in Arlington TX, which was less than an hour away from the house Paddock was buying.

This raises the question as to whether father and son truly did reconcile their differences? According to family sources, Paddock truly detested his father for countless reasons, and after the mid-1970s they never spoke again. But does this mean that the family are mistaken? As why else would Paddock buy a property in a State that he seemingly has no connection to, as his main business interest was in California.

However, his purchase of the property was twofold. Firstly, the property gave him an address in Texas, which does not have a state income tax. Secondly, Paddock had invested in several commercial and industrial properties in Mesquite TX, and while in the town on business, he would stay at the house. Basically, Paddock purchased the property for tax reasons and for business use.

So, the purchase of the house was not connected to a reconciliation with his long-lost father. Also, Benjamin died just days before the purchase was completed, which meant that Paddock would have no reason to keep the house, once his father passed away, but he did. To further confirm that Paddock and his father never reconnected, Benjamin's obituary only lists Patrick Paddock as his son, and not the other three boys.

Based on various records relating to Paddocks life, it was around late 1998 when he started his journey into the world of serious gambling. It seems that during the first 12 months of his venture, he played a mixture of table and computerized games, which is not out of the ordinary for rookie gamblers. As many professional gamblers will test a variety of games before they settle on one specific game to play.

After several months, Paddock found that most of the table games were slow, and you were not only playing against the house, but also other people at the table and the variables were far harder to control. He then focused on computerized gaming and experimented with a variety of computer-based games and slot machines.

By late 1999, it seems that Paddock had found that video poker offered him a better return than any other game. And like most financial investments Paddock undertook, he not only wanted to increase his income, but he also wanted to reap as much profit as possible.

For several months, Paddock immersed himself in studying video poker to find his optimal winning strategy. He even went as far as to purchase a machine like the ones used in casinos and bought countless books on video poker playing strategy. After months of research, he found that there were three factors that would drastically increase his chances of winning.

First, he would have to vary his bets between $25 to $250 per hand. Secondly, he would have to select a machine that had a higher win to play ratio. Third and finally, he found that if he gambled with a steak of around $25,000 per night, at the same machine, the odds shifted in his favor.

There was a flaw in his strategy, because initially he only needed $25,000.00 per night to increase his odds of winning, when he first started gambling. However, for every year that he gambled, this amount would go up. By the time of the Las Vegas attack, he needed at least $250,000.00 per a night of play, to maintain his favorable odds.

To further perfect his strategy, and really learn the game, he started playing in the lessor known gambling region of Reno, Nevada. This was mainly because Reno was closer to his home in Sun Valley. But also, had he commenced his training in the bright lights of Vegas from the get-go, there was a chance the house would have beat him and suck his funds dry.

With in no time at all, it seemed that Paddock's winning strategy was starting to work. Initially, the casinos in Reno did not suspect anything untoward, and thought that it was just beginners' luck, and he was on a winning streak.

They also made sure that they took the best care of their new high roller and gave him outstanding customer service and perks. Because in their mind, sooner or later, his run of good luck was going to end, and they wanted to make sure that it was their casino who would reap the rewards of his misfortune.

Like all professional gamblers, Paddock kept a very accurate record of which machines offered him the best odds at each casino, along with how much he would put into the machine, and what his return would be. This enabled him to know exactly when to play and how much to play with, to get the best return.

While using Reno as the proving ground for the development of his player strategy, he also did stray to the bright lights of Vegas, on occasion. Usually, he would visit Vegas when he would receive complimentary stays after spending a certain amount of money at the Reno casinos. Paddock's very first stay at the Mandalay Bay was in April 1999, shortly after the property opened. At the time, though, the hotel was owned by Circus Enterprises.

Paddocks first big win at video poker came in May 1999, when he won an impressive $35,000.00 in a single night. Then the following evening, he won another $25,000.00. These wins seem to have confirmed that his winning player strategy was viable. However, much to the dissatisfaction of Paddock, despite having two impressive wins, and countless years of continued success in the world of gambling, he would hit two stumbling blocks.

First, he would never realize his full potential, simply because he did not have enough money to gamble with. Because despite countless myths circulating about Paddock's wealth, his peak net worth was $10 million in the mid-2000s. And for his strategy to be effective, he would need at least $25 million to reap astronomical amounts of cash. Secondly, comes the adage, the house always wins. When Paddock did start to win on a regular basis, casinos downgraded his packages, which meant he had to pay to stay at the casinos.

However, in true Paddock fashion, he calculated how much the cost of the stays were costing him, and how much it was truly impacting the overall amount that he was winning. And it turned out, that if he booked a low to mid-range room and paid close to full price, as they would offer him a loyalty discount, he was still ahead of the casino. Surprisingly, though, while the casinos downgraded his overall comp packages, they still waited on him hand and foot, while he played.

After a short while, though, casinos got wise to the fact that even while paying for his rooms, he was still winning more than they were. By 2001, Paddock was starting to come the attention of the casino bosses in Reno, for his above average win rates. So, to curb his play even more, they hit him even harder. Now, they would not allow him to book a low to mid-range room, they forced him to book premium rooms, which did impact his total income from gambling, but not by very much.

In a further bid, to push Paddock away, the casinos in Reno gave strict instructions to floor hosts, not cater to his every whim while he was playing. This did not bother Paddock, though, as he started to split his casino visits between Reno and Vegas, to take extra heat off him.

With spending increasing time in Vegas, Paddock joined multiple reward programs. One was the MGM Resorts International (MGMRI) rewards program, Mlife, which he joined on September 13, 2001, while on a trip to Las Vegas. Initially, though, he was seen as a low-level player at MGMRI casinos. But as time went on, his credit limit and comp level increased.

By the time he committed his dreadful act, he was able to access a $100,000.00 credit line while playing at MGMRI resorts. Paddock's winning strategy, though, was about to be his undoing in Reno, which would lead to him not gambling in Reno for a while, and Vegas would be his preferred choice.

One of the casinos that he played at on a regular basis in Reno, took a closer look at his win and loss statement and spotted what they believed to be some highly unusual win rates. The casino surmised that Paddock was somehow rigging the machine in his favor, which led to the management ordering an internal investigation.

After several months, the security team at the casino could not find any evidence to support the theory that Paddock was cheating. So, they got drastic. They removed all of his comps, while also making him pay full price for the premium rooms they were making him book, during his stays.

On a short-term basis, this did not impact Paddock too much, but as time went on, his level of gambling income began to take a major hit. By early 2003, Paddock was becoming frustrated with the casino and how he was being treated by them. To get even, for what he saw as unfair treatment, he used his tried and tested methods of negation to get back at the Reno casino.

He convinced his VIP host to allow him and a group of people to stay at the resort and have one of the best comp packages the casino had to offer. For this, the group had to gamble a certain amount of money during the stay. But Paddock and his group, who were mainly his family members, had other ideas. They indulged more in the comps than they gambled. This meant that by the end of the stay, the casino was the true loser and not Paddock.

After he pulled this stunt, the casino instantly barred him, and it took a few years for the casino to allow him back through their doors. And when they did allow him to play at the casino again, it took several years for his comp level to increase. In a further blow to Paddock, when the other casinos in Reno learned of his actions, very few casinos in the area would allow him to play. This forced Paddock to change his gambling venue to the bright lights and glitz and glamour of Las Vegas, for several years.

By the time Paddock changed his preferred gambling venue to Vegas, his real estate investments had increased to include properties in California, Texas, and Florida. This meant that now, he was incurring increased costs and travel time when he wanted to gamble, as he either had to drive across the county or fly commercially, which caused Paddock to reevaluate his mode of transport.

After exploring his options, Paddock calculated that it would be cheaper for him to obtain his instrument rating private pilot license, which allowed him to fly at night and in various weather conditions. He then rented a plane to fly between his destinations, rather than driving across several states or flying commercially. By November 17, 2003, Stephen Paddock had passed the instruments test.

Around 2004, the family real estate holdings in L.A. stood at just over $5 million, and with Paddocks solo business interest and investments, his wealth stood at just over $10 million. However, the family's operations in Los Angeles were on yet another uncertain path, as California began to adopt more stringent rental property regulations and placed extra taxes on apartment complex owners. So, the Paddock's called it quits and sold off their properties.

But the family were not quite done with their days as real estate moguls, just yet, and Paddock knew of just the right property they should set their sights on. A 111-unit complex called Central Park Apartments, in Mesquite TX, just a short distance from the house that he owned in the town.

There was a minor issue, though, as after they paid back the small number of mortgages on the properties, they were left with a little less than $4.6 million. The price tag on Central Park was $8.4 million, which meant they needed to raise close to $4 million to buy the apartments.

By this point in time, the Paddock family property business was in good standing with the bank. So, Steve went to meet with the bank manager and arranged a line of credit for the extra money. After a very brief meeting, Paddock left the bank with an agreement for the shortfall in funds. Once the line of credit was secured, he then flew to Mesquite TX and met with the agent for the property to take a tour.

In the aftermath of the attack, the property agent told various media outlets that when Paddock first approached him, he did not take him seriously, because initially Paddock came dressed in shorts and flip-flops. This caused the property agent to be skeptical of him, as he did not think he was a serious buyer.

However, after conducting the necessary financial checks, the agent discovered that the Paddocks had an exchange account with a little over $4 million, and a line of credit with the bank for the remaining balance. So, negations were started and after a few short weeks, the Paddock family were the proud owners of the 111-unit Central Park Apartment Complex.

In true Stephen Paddock style, when the deal was concluded, he was the clear victor in the negotiations. Because not only had he been able to get the purchase price reduced by a few hundred thousand dollars, the sellers had to pay both theirs and the family's closing fees, along with the first year of property taxes.

After the sale of the apartments in L.A., Irene moved from Sun Valley, as by this time Eric and his family were living in Florida and Stephen was spending very little time in California. So, Irene decided it was time to call it quits and moved to Mesquite TX, to a house close by the apartment's they now owned.

Just like in L.A., Paddock would manage the apartments and oversee the family business interest, while flying away on weekends to spend time at various casinos. But within two years of purchasing Central Park Apartments, Paddock decided that it was now time for him to step back from running the family business full-time and enjoy life a little more.

So, he employed a property manager, named Lisa Crawford. Like most people that admitted to knowing Paddock in the aftermath of the attack, who spoke to the media. Lisa recalled her former boss as a kind and thoughtful person, who was always ready to help people, and not the monster that laid waste to the innocent concertgoers.

Shortly after hiring Lisa as a building manager, in 2006, Paddock took close to 12-months off and spent much of his time playing video poker. To many, this would be unthinkable, but to him it was his second job. Based on information from his own testimony in a 2012 lawsuit, which is corroborated by his financial records from the time, Paddock did gamble large amounts of money during this period. According to his estimates, at the peak of his play, he was gambling with close to $1 million per night.

From looking over various documents, Paddock was not telling the whole truth, but nor was he lying. In 2006 alone, he gambled a total of $945,476.35 but he lost $56,160.18. But with continued play throughout the night, his balance would fluctuate. So, in theory he would run a million dollars through the machine, just not physically.

Then, when you add in the comps that Paddock received during this time, he was not a loser by any stretch of the imagination. Because the cost for the rooms, food, and beverage packages, along with other extras he would receive, he was up by at least $139,000.00.

At around the time that Paddock stepped back from running the family apartment complex, he recalculated the true cost of renting a single engine plane to fly between the casinos in Vegas and his business interest. Based on his evolution, it was cheaper for him to buy his own plane. So, on June 2, 2006, Paddock purchased a 2004 Cirrus fixed wing single engine aircraft, with tail number N5343M, for a little over $500,000.00.

While he was in Vegas, he would store his plane in a hangar at the North Las Vegas private airport, or at an airfield in Henderson. When he was not in Vegas and visiting one of his homes in either Texas or Florida, he would pay daily hanger fees at the closest airfield to his properties.

During Paddock's years long gambling vacation, one of the hotels he stayed at for a prolonged period, was the Mandalay Bay; by which time had been purchased by MGMRI. While staying at the hotel, an incident occurred, which caused Paddock to put in a formal complaint to the casino managers.

On Friday 14 September 2007, Paddock lodged a complaint with hotel security after a hotel employee entered his room without permission. According to Paddock, he left the room about 1:00 p.m. and placed the

Do not Disturb sign on his door. However, upon his return at 3:00 p.m., he noticed that the sign was removed, and the room had been cleaned.

The reason Paddock was angry was because when he checked in, he specifically requested that his room was not to be cleaned while he was staying at the hotel. However, due to hotel policy that stated if a guest stayed over a certain amount of time, hotel staff would enter the room to clean it. It seems that this requested was not fully complied with and, housekeeping went in and changed the bed along with removing trash.

Towards the end of Paddocks marathon gambling spree, though, in the latter part of 2007, disaster struck. The global economy crashed, which wiped out much of his paper wealth, as his net worth was tied mainly to property investments and the stock market. In the space of a few months, his wealth dropped by over $6 million. Despite such a large drop, he was not impacted too much, as he had a steady stream of income from his rental properties.

Between the end of his gambling vacation to when his finances picked back up in the early stages of 2010, he gambled just over $1.9 million in the three-year period. However, it seems that his playing strategy had started to wane slightly, because his level of wins was started to decrease. Not by a vast amount, but he was still down $95,000.00. Again, though, when you factor in his comps, he was still breaking even.

By 2010, with Paddock spending increasing amounts of time in either Vegas or Reno, his single-engine plane was rapidly becoming surplus to requirement and a burdensome expense. So, on February 13, 2010, Paddock sold his aircraft to a private broker and allowed his pilot license to expire.

A year after selling his plane, in 2011, Paddock would have two minor health issues, while staying in Vegas. The first was on October 11, 2011, when he slipped on a wet floor at the Cosmopolitan Hotel and Casino, badly injuring his leg. Due to the extent of the injuries, Paddock was taken to hospital for treatment.

Then, a few weeks later, in November 2011, while staying at the Aria Hotel. Paddock called hotel reception shortly before 11:40 a.m., claiming he felt unwell and a hotel medical team was sent to his room on the 17th floor, to check on him. By 11:47 a.m., Paddock was lying on his stomach on the bed in the master bedroom, with an oxygen mask on.

According to the report filed about the incident, Paddock was suffering from pain in his left leg and arms and claimed that he felt exhausted. With no clear explanation of what was causing Paddock's issues, shortly after 12:05 p.m., paramedics had taken him to Saint Rose Hospital Siena

Campus, in Henderson. However, doctors could not find anything wrong with him, and simply said he was fatigued.

Towards the end of 2011, Paddock was allowed to play at the casinos in Reno, once again. This brought a love interest into his life, named Marilou Danley who was a VIP casino host at the Atlantis Casino, in Reno. However, at the time Danley and Paddock first met, she was still married to her husband. But based on various people who worked with Danley, within no time at all of Paddock and Danley first meeting, she became his main host, while he was at the casino.

Just over a year after Paddock slipped on the floor in the Cosmopolitan, on September 17, 2012, he sued the hotel company, for the cost of his medical bills. According to the court filing, he was asking for $10,000.00 in compensation. However, after a short court battle Paddock lost, and the hotel owners were not found liable. This was because, shortly before Paddock slipped, security cameras had recorded other patrons in the hotel walking over the same area, without falling over.

After owning Central Park Apartments in Mesquite TX, for close to a decade, in 2013, the family partnership decided that it was time to retire. The apartment complex was put on the market for a little over $9 million and in no time at all, Central Park was sold to another property company for $9.1 million.

Once the small mortgage on the property was paid back, and they settled their taxes Steve, Eric, and their mother netted just over $2.5 million each. Combined with the other assets that Paddock had sold by this point, his cash wealth now stood at close to $8 million. Irene decided that it was time to move once again, and purchased a house in Florida, close by where Eric and his family.

At around the time of the sale of the apartment complex, Paddock and Danley's relationship became more permanent, and Paddock asked her to quit her job so they could spend more time together. With hardly any reluctance, in April 2013, Danley separated from her husband and quit her job and begun a full-time relationship with Paddock.

Prior to quitting her job, Danley wanted to make sure that Paddock would take care of her and give her some type of income. With this, they entered into an agreement that in return for Danley moving in with Paddock, he would pay her a monthly stipend of around $3,000.00 per month, along with covering all other expenses and purchasing her a vehicle every two to three years.

There were also conditions of financial compensation for Danley, should they break up, or Paddock was to pass away. In the event of a separation, she would be paid around $50,000.00 to make sure she could take care of herself. However, in the event of his death, she would be given $150,000.00 from his estate.

Shortly after Danley and Paddock began a relationship, Eric paddock noticed that Stephen treated Marilou much differently than most people he was close to. Because while he would not do many things for Danley, he would do small gestures that he would not do for anyone else. Because by this time, Paddock was accustomed to being waited on hand and foot, by those around him.

In June 2013, Paddock decided it was time for another change and purchased a house in the Del Webb retirement community, on the outskirts of Reno. At the same time, he put his condo up for sale, which finally sold in December 2013 after he cut the asking price by some $20,000.00.

When Danley divorced her husband in February 2014, her registered address was at the condominium that Paddock owned in Reno, close by the Atlantis Casino.

At the time of the attack, Danley was visiting her family in the Philippines, as Paddock had sent her away on a 'surprise' vacation. She first learned of the incident, while she was on her way to have dinner and a family member called her, saying that they had seen her photo on the local news, as a person of interest in a mass shooting in Las Vegas.

Danley returned to the United States on October 3, 2017, and landed at LAX airport in L.A. She was then taken to her daughter's house for the evening before meeting with the FBI at their field office in L.A. on October 4, 2017.

During the interview she claimed that she knew nothing of the attack but did state that in the months leading up to the incident, Paddock's behavior changed considerably. Danley claimed that he was starting to experience severe nightmares, and he was also becoming increasingly aggressive. Furthermore, his physical health and memory was declining, and he was becoming less sexually active.

She also told law enforcement that she had fired some of the weapons owned by the gunman and helped him load magazines some weeks prior to the attack. Then she went on to say that while staying with the gunman for the final time at the Mandalay Bay hotel in early September 2017, in room 60-235. She witnessed Paddock looking out of the windows towards the concert venue.

By mid-2015, Paddock purchased another property, this time it was in Mesquite Nevada. Now, both Paddock and Danley split their time between the two properties, with their primary residence being the house in Mesquite. This enabled them to frequent Vegas on an almost weekly basis, typically on a weekend. Also, they would take around several overseas vacations a year, along with visiting Danley's family in L.A., the Philippines, and Australia.

But all was not as it seemed, with Paddocks finances. Because after the sale of the family property business, Paddocks steady monthly income ceased. And, by late 2015, cracks were starting to show. Based on various financial records, Paddock seems to have over speculated, and his wealth was starting to dwindle. Along with this, his win rate dramatically decreased.

By October 2016, Paddock had just over $3 million left in his bank accounts. As to where the other $5 million had disappeared, it is reasonable to assume that it was mostly to casinos, and the rest on keeping Danley by his side.

There were periods, though, where Paddocks winning formula seemed to be paying off. But his wins verse loss ratio seemed to be ebbing flowing at an unusual rate, as if someone was controlling as to when he would win and lose. But how could that have been, as even though gambling machines are programed in favor of the house, there are laws which prevent outright cheating by the casinos.

The answer to this question was simple, and neither did it strictly involve cheating. After looking into Paddock's play and his win streaks, countless casinos in Vegas discovered what the casinos in Reno could not. They figured out how Paddock picked his machines and what his gambling strategy was.

So, they would allow Paddock to have a good run of wins, then they changed out the winning machines, for ones that had less favorable odds for Paddocks type of play. To ensure Paddock played the replacement machine, they would take the floor number off the old machine and place it on the new unit.

Paddock obviously knew there was an issue, but it took him a while to figure out exactly what was going on. And when he did, he would try and get even, just like he did in Reno. But the more he did this at the casinos in Vegas, the more they pushed back. This was confirmed by his former VIP host at Caesars Palace.

When the host was interviewed by LVMPD in the wake of the attach, they confirmed that it was not unusual for casinos to change out machines on Paddock. Nor was it unusual for Paddock to book a stay at the hotel and convince his host to give him an outstanding comp package. However, when he came to check out, the casino saw that Paddock did not gamble to the required level. So, he was told not to return unless his play improved.

But certain casinos were not just content with changing out the machines to make him lose money. They would also alter his comps around, which was also a frustration to him. One of the worst casinos for this were the ones owned by MGMRI, more specifically, the Mandalay Bay.

Typically, Paddock would be contacted by his host at MGMRI, and offered a particularly decent comp package. At check in, though, Paddock would be told that his offer had been rescinded, as the level of room he was offered was no longer available. So, for him to stay, he would have to pay a small upgrade fee.

But this was not the only step the Mandalay Bay would take, to bleed Paddock dry of his money. Because when there were special points promotions on offer, where players got three times the points per play, Paddock would not.

Another tactic employed against Paddock, was when he would enter video poker and slot tournaments. When he won, instead of taking the luxurious prizes, he would exchange it for the cash equivalent, which he was allowed to do. The casino, though, considerably undervalued the item and give him a much lesser amount, than what they usually would.

While this may seem like cruel and unusual treatment, this is a commonality in casinos, because if winners exchange the prizes for cash. Typically, the amount of money they are given, is far less than the value of the physical item. However, apparently in Paddock's case, they penalized him even more than most people. As he had been a winning player for nearly two decades.

By the start of 2016, Paddock's play at the Mandalay Bay, and his winnings picked up. However, it is reported by various sources that in early September 2016, while playing at the hotel he lost over $200,000 in a single evening. On this occasion, he made his feelings known to a manager. It seems though, that the manager was not really interested in what Paddock had to say, but he did offer Paddock extra comps for the next time he stayed at the hotel.

When Paddock came back on his next stay at Mandalay Bay, from September 29 to October 2, 2016, the offer was rescinded. However, Mandalay Bay only informed him of this when he checked-out, and he was made to pay nearly the full price for his and Denly's hotel room. When Paddock confronted the front desk about this, he was told that his level of play was not where it was expected, so there was nothing anyone could do.

The day after this event occurred, the gunman purchased his first round of firearms, which he planned to use in his attack. Then, over the course of the next year, the gunman would devote significant time and effort to planning and preparing for his attack.

He amassed thousands of rounds of ammunition and some fifty-two firearms, which were mainly rifles, along with bump-stocks and other rifle accessories. He also took steps to distance himself from Danley, to a point, she thought he was trying to break up with her.

Then, on the night of October 1, 2017, there was no more planning and preparation for Paddock to do. So, he unleashed his deadly and sickening attack, on people enjoying the final night of the Route 91 concert. The once kind landlord, who was loved by his mother and idolized by his youngest brother, Eric. Became the monster the world now knows him as, the infamous Las Vegas gunman.

In the aftermath of the mass shooting, the coroner decided that the victims would take priority over the gunman. This meant that the perpetrator of the attack was not pronounced dead until noon of October 2, 2017. His body was autopsied on the late afternoon of October 6, 2017.

Shortly after the shooters' body was examined, sections of his brain was sent to Stanford University, for closer examination, which concluded there were no abnormalities. The corner listed the gunman's cause of death as a intraoral gunshot wound of the head.

Shortly after the gunman's body was examined, officials in Clark County Nevada decided that they would cremate his remains at their own expense. There is no official date as to when the cremation took place, but it is believed to have been performed around the latter part of October 2017. The gunman's family were given his remains in January 2018, after Eric Paddock flew out to Las Vegas to take custody of the ashes and then return them to their mother, Irene.

Chapter Two: Planning, Preparation, Attack

"We have no idea what his belief system was. I can't get into the mind of a psychopath."

-Sheriff Joe Lombardo, LVMPD Press Conference, Oct. 2, 2017

While researching the Las Vegas Mass Shooting, I encountered a team of people who had been investigating the incident, since just after it happened. The group consisted of former law enforcement and armature sleuths, who felt there was something more to the attack, than what the public was being told.

The group of dedicated researchers, were right to have those suspicions, as there have been several areas where it was found LVMPD did not include certain aspects of evidence, in their final case report and the construction of the timelines. But what was interesting about the group of investigators, was that they claimed to have found the illusive missing hard drive, which the shooter disposed of sometime before the attack.

According to the group, they found the hard drive after they obtained the cellphone signal data, from one of the gunman's cellphones. How exactly it was they gained access to this information is not readily known, nor were they willing to talk about it. But after reviewing the information on the hard drive, it did appear that they had truly discovered the missing drive.

It was also claimed by the group that they did inform several law enforcement agencies about the discovery, along with several news networks. But either the officials nor the media took them seriously, or they were not interested. What the drive contained, though, if it is genuine, is the blueprint for the deadliest mass shooting in modern American history.

With the discovery of the hard drive and the information it contained, debunked the theories which have speculated that the gunman discarded the drive to either protect his family from possible charges of tax evasion, or to hide the fact that he was also a pedophile.

But when you consider either of these theories and compare them to the evidence relating to the incident and the gunman's life, neither of them makes any sense.

Firstly, if the gunman truly discarded the hard drive to protect his family, as he was the person that prepared and filed their taxes. He would have been aware that even by disposing of the drive, it would still not protect those that he loved. Because being a former employee of the IRS, he would have known that all the IRS needed was a copy of the family tax filings, which they had. And access to the bank accounts owned by the family, which they could easily get with a court order.

Secondly, if the gunman had mistakenly disposed of the wrong hard drive, then he would have known this fact within a few hours. Mainly because, he viewed the sickening images of child pornography several times after he disposed of the missing hard drive. So, again, under closer scrutiny, the second theory also falls apart.

Where the team of researchers discovered the drive, also fits with the character traits of the gunman, as he would have likely disposed of the missing drive in a place where there was very little chance of someone finding it. Along with a place that he could easily access and would not have aroused suspicions if he was seen in that area.

The location of the missing drive was on the crest of the southwest riverbank of the Muddy River, in thick brush. Coincidently, the gunman was very familiar with this place, as he crossed over the river, on an almost weekly basis, when he drove from his home in Mesquite to either the casinos in Vegas, or his Reno property. Because the Muddy River runs under Interstate 15, before it meanders south and drains into the Overton Arm basin on its way to Lake Mead.

It appears, based on the cellphone signal data, when the shooter stopped his vehicle on the I-15 bridge that spans the Muddy River, at around 2:39 a.m. on the morning of October 1. He was parked on the section of the bridge closest to the top of the riverbank, and not the section that is directly above the river itself. So, when he threw the drive over the side of the bridge, it landed in the bushes and not in the water.

After examining the information contained on the drive, it does fit with how the shooter would have meticulously planned and prepared for his attack, based on his known character traits, and known incidents that occurred in the days and weeks leading up to the mass shooting.

Furthermore, there were several documents contained on the drive, which also fit with information of how the gunman used to record and analyze data. But if this drive is a fake, then someone went to extreme lengths to produce this data, and had insights, no one else ever had.

Overall, of all the data contained on the hard drive, only around 95% of it could be recovered. All the recoverable data only contained information that related to either mass shootings or the Las Vegas attack. No sickening images of children were contained in the recovered data, and neither was there any indication of images of this type were contained in the unrecoverable data.

Planning

Officially, it is believed that the gunman started to plan his attack, around a year prior to the Route 91 Concert. This was determined from his increased firearm purchases, because according to this information, he started to buy weapons with increasing frequency from October 2, 2016. However, it seems that the gunman may have been thinking about an attack of some type, since at least June 2016; at around the time of the Orlando Nightclub incident.

Because, from June 13, 2016, the day after the Orlando incident, he began to take a very keen interest in the nightclub attack. This is unusual, as the Las Vegas gunman was never known to take a particular interest in news articles of this type. He may have read one or two stories, just to get a better understanding of the attack. But he would not have read over thirty articles in two days.

While this type of behavior was out of place for the gunman, as an aspiring mass shooter it was not. The reason that it is not unusual, though, is because most mass shooters get the idea for their attacks from other incidents.

Although the Las Vegas Mass Shooting and the Orlando Nightclub attack are vastly different, mainly because the Orlando incident was designated as a terror attack, whereas the Las Vegas Mass Shooting was not. Furthermore, the Las Vegas gunman fired from an elevated position, while the Orlando shooter actively walked around the nightclub. Where they share similarities, is that both incidents occurred at entertainment venues.

According to the information pulled from the hard drive, by late-September 2016, the Las Vegas gunman had ended his research into the Orlando nightclub attack, which mainly focused on the reasons the attack was not more deadly. He then began to focus on two other mass shootings, the 1966 University of Texas (UT) Clock Tower Attack and the 1999 Columbine High School Massacre.

This type of research may not have been in keeping with the gunman's known character traits, but again, it is indicative of mass shooters. Because based on published data of mass shooter pre-attack behaviors, over 21% if not more of mass shooters, actively researched other mass shootings of a similar nature, before undertaking their own attacks.

Again, though, the Las Vegas Mass Shooting was different to the UT attack and the Columbine Massacre, in as much that the UT and Columbine attacks took place at educational institutions. While the Las Vegas Mass Shooting took place at a live music event, in the gambling and live entertainment capitol of the world. But there are a lot of similarities between the Las Vegas incident and the UT and Columbine attacks.

Firstly, the Las Vegas attack compares to the UT mass shooting, as both the Las Vegas gunman and the perpetrator of the UT attack fired from secluded elevated positions. Because the UT shooter, fired from the clock tower observation deck down into the street and public areas below. While the Las Vegas gunman fired from the 32nd floor of the Mandalay Bay, into the concert venue and the road directly in front of the hotel, on the west side of the venue.

Furthermore, the UT gunman used multiple rifles during his attack, just like the Las Vegas gunman also did. At least one of the rifles used by the UT shooter was fitted with a rifle scope, while several of the weapons used in the Las Vegas attack was also fitted with rifle scopes. Lastly, both the Las Vegas and UT gunman had more than 700 rounds of ammunition and countless magazines, with them for their attacks.

The similarities between the Columbine High School Massacre and Las Vegas attack, are also evident. Again, the perpetrators of the high school incident used multiple weapons, but these were shotguns and small caliber firearms, such as 9 mm TEC-9. However, when the firearm purchases of the Las Vegas gunman are examined; between October 2016 to early March 2017, he seems to focus on rifles, shotguns, and handguns. Then from mid-March 2017 to September 2017, the gunman purchases only rifles.

It could be assumed that with the earlier firearm purchases, the gunman intended to throw anyone who was looking into him, of the scent, as to what he was truly planning. However, it seems that this is not the case. Because he seems to have figured out, as to why the shotguns and small caliber weapons were not suitable for his attack. As these weapons are only used for shooting at targets close to the shooter, and not for any long-distance shots.

Based on evidence found in the Las Vegas gunman's vehicle after the attack, he planned to incorporate a mixture of Tannerite and homemade explosives (IED), during his attack. As to how he planned to use them, it is not really understood. But there was evidence found on the missing hard drive, which suggests he planned to use both the Tannerite and IED's as not only a way to inflict more casualties. But also, to draw the attention of law enforcement away from the area of the main attack to another part of Las Vegas before he launched his main assault.

This was the same tactic used by the Columbine High School perpetrators, as they planted diversionary IED's some distance from the school, which was timed to go off prior to their attack. Then, they also placed two propane bombs in the school cafeteria, which were set to go off at around the start of their attack. In addition to these devices, the shooters also rigged their cars to explode after they had concluded their attack.

According to the missing hard drive data, the gunman had reviewed information on using cell phones as a detonation device, along with how to detonate Tannerite with something other than a high velocity projectile. After the Las Vegas attack, there was a large quantity of Tannerite and chemicals to make IED's, found in the gunman's vehicle. So, there is both physical and digital evidence, which does show he had intent to use explosives, he just never did.

The behavior displayed by the Las Vegas gunman of researching prior mass shootings, which had occurred during his living memory and incorporating elements of the attacks, in to his own, is indicative of other mass shooters. Because studies have found that over 70% of active shooters will review material from prior incidents, which happened in their lifetime, and add elements from these attacks into their own.

Considering the gunman was 64 years old, at the time of the Las Vegas Mass Shooting, his memory of attacks would have been more extensive than someone in their early 20's to 30's. At the time of the UT Attack the Las Vegas gunman was around 13, and when the Columbine Massacre occurred, he would have been 46 years old. So, he would have been able to recall both events, for his research of the attack he was planning.

Chillingly, on the night of October 1, 2016, while the gunman was staying at the Mandalay Bay, he searched the internet for the dates of the Route 91 concert in 2017. At that time, though, the dates were not confirmed, but he did read an article where it stated that the event would occur around the same time as the 2016 concert. Then, a day later, on October 2, 2016, which was the last day of the 2016 concert; the gunman began his purchase of firearms and ammunition.

By mid-October 2016, the gunman's internet searches began to focus on whether hotels kept a record of how many bags a guest takes with them, during their stay. Also, what the reaction of hotel security would be, during certain emergencies, such as a fire or terrorist attack. A few days after researching this information, the gunman then began to research online for ways to test for security vulnerabilities, specially at hotels.

It appears that by mid-December 2016, the gunman was becoming increasingly paranoid that someone in law enforcement may have been watching him and securitizing his online activity, along with his increased firearm purchases. Because his internet searches started to focus on how law enforcement and federal agencies monitor online activity combined with firearms purchases.

Also, he began to research counter-surveillance methods, and how to determine if someone is being covertly watched by law enforcement, both online and in person.

There were also searches in the internet cached file, which shows that he tried to become as tactically proficient, as possible. Because not only did he read tactical manuals that he found online. He also searched YouTube for videos that focused on tactically clearing houses and large buildings, such as hotels.

According to the Microsoft account information, which was not under the gunman's name, and had been paid for with a voucher and not a credit card. The Microsoft OneDrive contained an excel workbook, saved under the file heading, 'Gambling Account 2'. In the workbook were several spread sheets, which not only gives a very good insight to the level of planning the shooter undertook, for his attack. But also, it reveals some sickening aspects of his true desires for how many people he wanted to kill or wound.

The first sheet in the workbook, named wins verses losses, related to how long it would take a person to go from one point in the hotel to another; using different routes. Such as from the main lobby or parking valet to a suite at the end of the hallway on floors higher than the 31st floor. He also calculated how long it would take a person to move between floors, via the stairwells.

While the second sheet, was far more sinister and harrowing, and named video poker machine floor numbers. It appears that he timed how long it would take to change magazines, along with how many rounds he could fire before the weapons started to encounter issues, such as overheating barrels and feed jams.

However, the most sickening sheet in the workbook was the sheet tilted points per play. This focused on his intended kill/wounding ratios, while firing into the venue, along with estimating how many casualties would be caused by igniting the fuel tanks.

As time drew closer to the attack, the gunman's internet searches began to focus on several key factors that may have caused him issues during the attack. One of these areas was the volume of noxious gas that would accumulate in the hotel room, with firing over 7,000 rounds.

To counter the buildup of the gas, he initially looked at using a military style gas mask, but quickly determining the filters on a military respirator are not designed to filter smoke, only chemical agents etc. He then looked at a breathing system like the ones used firefighters, but he seems to have quickly determined that the weight of the oxygen tank may arouse suspicion. Also, he may have encountered mobility issue, while wearing the oxygen tank.

Finally, he chose to make a breathing system, based on a design he found online, on a website for preppers. This breathing system was very crude and used a mechanical fan, length of hose, and a mouthpiece from a diving snorkel. It worked by securing the fan to one end of the tube and placing this below the smoke layer. Then, the other end of the hose was secured to the mouthpiece of the snorkel, to ensure an airtight seal was made with the mouth. To counter the effects on his eyes, he wore diving goggles.

By early September 2017, the gunman's plan was almost complete. All that was left for him to focus on was his firing positions and determining the distance from the 200-wing of the Mandalay Bay to various points he was going to fire at. Based on his assessment, the 200-wing not only offered the better chance of not being quickly detected from anyone looking at the building during the attack. But also, it was forty feet closer to the fuel tanks than the vista suites on the 100-wing of the hotel.

As an added layer of security, and to create confusion for anyone that may be watching him, the gunman began to actively look at other venues and public places. Because, other than a few internet searches on the Route 91 concert, he never actively looked too much at the event, online. This was because while he was staying at the Mandalay Bay in the months leading up to the attack, there was enough information on public display, for him to gain information from.

Along with the digital evidence on the missing hard drive, in the days and weeks leading up to the attack. The shooter also used the three other laptops found in either 32-134 or 32-135, to research various aspects of the attack or to create more of a smokescreen and to mask his true intensions and target.

The searches conducted on the other laptops, either focused on law enforcement tactics or researching other public events or open areas and making reservations at other hotels, both in Las Vegas and other areas of the United States. But by early September 2017, the gunman would have fully mapped out his plan, in his mind.

Preparation

One of the first steps taken by the shooter in preparation for his attack, was the purchase of a second laptop that was identical to the one that both he and Danley used, on an almost daily basis. He purchased this laptop in September 2016 and the reason for this was twofold.

Firstly, it would prevent anyone asking questions about his search history or accidentally stumbling across information that he wanted to keep secret. Secondly, should he come to the attention of law enforcement, and they confiscated the shared laptop. Not only would Danley be able to confirm that she had witnessed the gunman using the shared laptop on multiple occasions. But also, law enforcement would not find anything incriminating on the shared laptop, relating to the attack.

Once the gunman had a workable plan and a target, he then began to purchase his arsenal of weapons. His first purchases occurred on October 2, 2016, which consisted of two 12-gauge (12G) shotguns and a single semi-automatic rifle chambered in 5.56 mm. Then, a little over a month later, between November 17 to 30, 2016, he purchased five more firearms.

This time, it was two pistols chambered in 9 mm, a single rifle chambered for .223 and 5.56 mm, along with a 12G shotgun and an AR-10 .308 rifle. During this period, the gunman also started to obtain his large number of ammunition, magazines, and other weapons related accessories he intended to use.

Most of his firearm accessories, such as his bump-stocks and extended magazines were ordered from various sellers on Amazon. In the aftermath of the attack, Amazon began to prevent sales of firearm related items on their sales platform. In addition, former President Trump also banned the manufacture, sale, and use of bump-stocks.

Between December 2016 to March 2017, the gunman purchased another slew of weapons. During this time, he purchased three more 9 mm pistols, fifteen rifles in various calibers ranging from .223 to 7.62 mm, and three more 12G shotguns. However, after March 22, 2017, the gunman ceased purchasing pistols and shotguns and only focused on rifles.

By the end of March 2017, the gunman had amassed thirty-one firearms, over 4,000 rounds of ammunition, some eight bump-stocks, over 60 extended magazines that could hold between 30 to 100 rounds each, and various bi-pods and optical weapons sights.

From mid-April 2017, the shooter then started to lay the groundwork at the Mandalay Bay, should security be keeping a record of how many bags each guest took to the hotel. With this, he started to take an increasing number of bags with him, when he and Danley stayed at the hotel.

Interestingly, when he started to take an increasing number of luggage items with him on his and Danley's stays at the hotel, some of the bags contained the rifles and ammunition he would use in his attack. As an excuse to Danley, he would tell her that he did not feel comfortable with leaving the weapons in the car, while they were at the hotel.

On April 16 and April 22, 2017, the gunman purchased two Slide Fire Bump-Stocks online from Cabelas, which were delivered to his Mesquite address. A few days after these purchases, he acquired several other firearm accessories from Amazon, to be delivered to his home in Mesquite.

What was strange though, is that in April 2017, the gunman never purchased any firearms. The reason this is strange, is that from October 2016 to March 2017, the gunman purchased an average of six firearms per month. However, one possible reason for no firearm purchases in April, was in March 2017, the gunman purchased 10 weapons. So, there is a possibility that he wanted to avoid suspicion.

During May 2017, he purchased five rifles that were a mix of 5.56, .223 wylde, .308, and 7.62. Around mid-May 2017, the shooter then started to commence his in-depth look at how he was going to unleash his attack on the concert venue. One of his first steps, was to calculate how long it should take for a person to get from certain points in the hotel, such as from the main lobby and up to the vista suites at the end of the hallways.

He also took an extra precaution of timing how long it would take for someone to get from the fire door in the stairwell, back to the foyer close by the suites, using either the elevators or stairwells on the floors above or below the floor he was staying on.

Along with his research at the Mandalay Bay, in May 2017, he was also conducting countless online searches looking at various concert and sporting events. Again, this was his way of creating a smoke screen, to hide his true intensions, should he be under any type of surveillance.

In June 2017, the shooter started his counter-surveillance phase of the attack. One of the methods he employed was by sending several emails between two of his email accounts, while staying at the Mandalay Bay. The wording of the emails was "Try an AR before you buy. We have a huge selection. Located in the Las Vegas area." Also, "We have a wide range of optics and ammunition to try." And finally, "For a thrill, try out bump fire AR's with 100 round magazines."

In the mind of the gunman, he believed that by sending emails containing key elements of his impending mass shooting, such as the weapons he had been purchasing for the attack, while staying at the location he intended to launch his attack from. If anyone was watching him, they would have no choice but to either arrest or question him, mainly due to the wording of the emails.

Also, in June 2017, the gunman purchased two more rifles that were multiple calibers, which were rifles capable of firing 5.56 and .223. Then, in July he only purchased one rifle, which was another multi caliber weapon.

Around late July 2017, the gunman started to increase the number of bags he took into the hotel, containing firearms and ammunition. During one of his regular stays, based on the digital evidence contained on the missing hard drive, there was a Word document that appeared tot be a to-do list. One of the items on the list stated, 'more filler material'. It appears that the gunman was trying to muffle the sounds of the weapons in the bags. Along with padding out the bags, so if anyone touched them, they would not feel the firearms inside.

In August 2017, the gunman's preparations took another step forward, when he paid a visit to a hardware store in St. George Utah. The store in question was only a forty-one-minute drive from his home in Mesquite NV, and to mask his purchase he paid with several gift cards, which he obtained from his credit card rewards program.

Many of the items he brought during this visit to the hardware store would later be found, in either 32-134 or 32-135. Amongst the items he purchased were several rolls of packing tape, a small sledgehammer, a pack of twenty corner brackets, and two packs of #5 1-inch flat head wood screws.

A week or so after the gunman's purchases from the hardware store, he then placed orders from several online retailers. The items he purchased was a security camera and the webcams he planned to use to create his security network, in the hallway outside of his hotel rooms. Along with an endoscope camera, which it seemed he planned to insert through a wall close by the doors to the room he intended to fire from, close to floor level.

It seems that his idea was to not only cover the area looking down the hallway, but also, to cover the blind spot between the donors to the main room and the door in the hallway to the adjoining room. To do this, he would place a webcam on the inside of the doors, which would allow him to see anyone standing up between the back of a room service cart and the door. Then the endoscope close to the floor, would be to see anyone crawling along the floor towards the main doors of the room he was firing from.

Then, a week after these purchases, he brought a cheap pair of diving goggles with a snorkel, a length of 1-inch-wide blue plastic hose, some waterproof tape, and a small battery powered electric fan. These items were to make the infamous breathing apparatus, later found lying across the floor and chairs in 32-135.

In the aftermath of the attack, a retired LVMPD officer claimed that they believed the shooter made this device to counter the effects of tear gas. However, the retired law enforcement officer was mistaken. Because as it has already been shown, had it been for that purpose, the gunman would have simply used a military gas mask. The breathing system was to counter the effects of the noxious gases expelled by the firing of so many rounds in a confined space.

In mid-August the gunman made a reservation at The Congress Plaza Hotel in Chicago. While making the reservation, the shooter specifically asked for a room that overlooked the Lollapalooza festival, taking place at Grant Park at the time his stay. Just two days before he was due to check in, though, the gunman cancelled his room and got a full refund. Again, this was a further attempt to steer any potential surveillance operation away from his true intensions.

On September 1, 2017, the gunman purchased two more rifles, which each were capable of firing 7.62 rounds. In the aftermath of the attack, these two rifles were later found in 32-134. Like other times he purchased firearms, the gunman also purchased more ammunition and extra magazines.

During the first and second weekends in September 2017, both Danley and the gunman stayed at the Mandalay Bay together, for the final times. After their first stay, once they arrived back at their home in Mesquite, Danley helped the gunman load countless magazines and place them into duffle bags. Then, on their final stay at the hotel together, the following weekend. She witnessed him standing in front of the windows, looking out towards the venue and the fuel tanks.

Since early September 2017, the gunman began to pressure Danley into taking a trip to see her family in the Philippines. At first, she was reluctant to go. However, after several days of being pestered by the gunman to take a trip to see her family, Danley relented and agreed to go and see them. The gunman booked her a direct flight from Las Vegas airport to depart on September 14, 2017.

On September 5, the gunman conducted several online searches relating to the Route 91 Concert and the Mandalay Bay Hotel. The searches relating to the concert seemed to be focusing on the size of the crowd and the schedule for the event. While the searches of the hotel were trying to determine how tall the Mandalay Bay was.

Around September 6, 2017, both Danley and the gunman visited the City of Mesquite landfill, which many locals used as an unofficial gun range. During this range practice, Danley assisted him with setting up targets at various distances, for him to shoot at.

It is believed that during this trip to the landfill, one of the targets was placed at around 600 yards from the firing point. The gunman then lay on the roof of his car and fired at the target, learning how to zero in on a long-range target.

This was not the first or the last time that Danley had been with the gunman to fire the weapons. It was later discovered she had been with him on countless other visits to the land fill.

On September 10, 2017, the shooter attended the Crossroads of the West gun show, in Phoenix Arizona. While at the event, he met a stall holder selling different types of ammunition, mainly hard to find illegal ammunition, such as tracer rounds.

The seller was a person by the name of Douglas Haig, who toured various gun shows on the west coast offering the illicit items, which he manufactured himself. This was not the first time Haig and the gunman had met though, as they the gunman had purchased 40 to 50 .308 incendiary rounds from Haig at a gun show in Las Vegas in late August 2017.

The purpose of the gunman's visit to the Crossroads of the West gun show was to order 600 rounds of .308/7.62 caliber tracer rounds along with 120 rounds of .223 caliber tracer rounds. Haig agreed to sell the gunman the tracer rounds, however, the gunman claimed he was going on a cruise, so the order would have to be picked up on September 19, 2017. Haig agreed, and they arranged for the gunman to visit Haig's house in Phoenix, to pay for and collect the illegal rounds.

In the aftermath of the attack, many of the tracer rounds were found close by the broken-out window in 32-134, in an Amazon Prime box with a label on the lid containing Haig's name and address. The remainder of the rounds were discovered either loaded into several magazines that were found on the dresser in the room or loaded into one of the rifles on one of the beds.

The tracer rounds were the only illegally purchased firearm related item the shooter would acquire, for use in the attack. LVMPD would later describe the tracer rounds in their final report as, "*Frangible Incendiary, Armor Piercing and Armor Piercing Incendiary ammunition.*" However, it was later determined that the rounds were not capable of punching through armor plate.

To add more of a smokescreen and further throw anyone off the scent of his actual plan, should someone be watching him. Between August 27 to September 14, the gunman booked rooms 2315, 1220, and 1703 at the Ogden Hotel in Las Vegas, with the dates spanning September 17 to September 28, 2017.

At the time of the reservations, the Life is Beautiful concert was taking place, which was being held adjacent to the Ogden. All the rooms that the gunman reserved were north facing, which overlooked the music event.

From September 12 to 14, 2017, the gunman and Danley stayed at the Tropicana Hotel on the Vegas Strip. They were given a two-floor suite along with food and beverage credit and some money for casino free play. During this visit, the gunman lost a total of $38,000.00.

After leaving the Tropicana on September 14, the gunman took Danley to the airport in Las Vegas and dropped her off, to catch her flight to see her family. This would be the last time that she ever saw the gunman. He then returned to their home in Mesquite for the next few days.

Sometime on September the 16, 2017, the gunman wired Danley $50,000.00 to her bank account in the Philippines. This would be the first of three transactions he would make to her.

At around this time, to prepare for his suicide at the end of his attack, the gunman also cleared all his credit card debts, which amounted to some $170,000.00. Along with this, he sent a final check for $13,000.00 to the IRS for his outstanding taxes. The only debts he left outstanding was $60,000.00 of his $100,000.00 at the Mandalay Bay casino, which he used in the days before the attack, and $270 for the court fees from his 2012 court case against the Cosmopolitan.

On the afternoon of September 17, the gunman checked into room 2315 at the Ogden. While staying at the Ogden, the shooter was captured on the security cameras moving countless bags to his rooms, just like he would at the Mandalay Bay. During his stay at the Ogden, he would either visit his home in Mesquite, or gambling at the El Cortez casino across the street from the hotel, which was similar with his routine while staying at the Mandalay Bay.

A strange event occurred on the night of September 17, 2017, shortly after he checked into his first room at the Ogden, which was very out of character for the gunman. While playing a video poker machine at the El Cortez casino, he became agitated and banged the machine he was playing. At first, the slot attendant simply asked him to calm down. However, when he did this a second time, the attendant had security remove the gunman from the casino.

The reason this was strange, was because in all the years that the gunman was known to gamble, this is believed to be the only time he was asked to leave a casino. After being asked to leave, the gunman then went back to his room at the Ogden.

At around 04:50 a.m. on September 18, he left the Ogden and headed to McCarren Airport to catch a flight to Reno, to stay the night at his Del Webb house. Then, on September 19, the gunman flew from Reno to Phoenix Arizona, where he went to pay for and collect 720 tracer rounds, he ordered from Douglas Haig.

While in Phoenix, the gunman rented a Kia Forte from Payless car rental, to drive to Haig's house then back to Las Vegas. During the transaction on September 19, Haig noted that after the gunman paid cash for the rounds, he took the time to put on gloves, prior to moving the box of ammunition he had just purchased to the trunk of his rental car.

The journey from Phoenix to Las Vegas, should have taken the gunman around five hours, but on that day, it took him over six hours. It later transpired that he made frequent and unexpected stops at several gas stations along the route and would stay at these areas for various amounts of time. It seems the shooter was stopping to make sure that he was not being followed back to Las Vegas.

At around 11:20 p.m., on the evening of September 19, the gunman arrived back at the Ogden. After arriving back at the complex, he parked the rental car on the 2nd floor of the parking garage. Shortly after 11:26 p.m., the gunman was seen entering the hotel and heading to his room, with a laptop bag and roller suitcase.

A short while later, at around 12:24 a.m., on the morning of September 20, the gunman moved his Chrysler Pacifica minivan from the 5th floor of the parking lot and went and parked next to the car he parked on the 2nd floor.

According to security camera footage the gunman transferred items from the rental car to his vehicle. Then, shortly after 12:50 a.m., the gunman returned the hire car to the Payless Car rental desk at McCarren Airport. He returned to the Ogden for around 1:16 a.m., via an Uber ride share.

Less than an hour later, the gunman left the Ogden and drove to his home in Mesquite, where he would remain until later that evening. While at his home in Mesquite, at around 3:00 p.m., a neighbor spotted the gunman in the drive of his house doing something in the rear of his minivan. Around five hours later, the gunman left his home and drove back to the Ogden, arriving a little after 9:10 p.m.

Once back at the Ogden, the gunman was seen taking a roller suitcase and trash bag to his room. Before going to his room, though, he stopped by reception in the main lobby, and informed the concierge that he needed to check into his second room, which was 1220. After completing the paperwork and given the room key, the gunman headed up to the guest levels of the hotel.

Just over an hour later, at around 10:40 p.m., the gunman headed back to the lobby and checked out of 2315. For unknown reasons, the gunman checked out of this room a day earlier than expected, as he had paid through September 22. After checking out of the first room he booked, the gunman then headed back to room 1220.

Between 11:54 p.m. on the late evening of September 21 until around 12:45 a.m. on the morning of September 22, the gunman was captured on the Ogden security cameras going back and forth from his vehicle to his room with a rolling suitcase. Then at 2:46 a.m., he was spotted again heading to his vehicle with the same rolling suitcase and a trash bag. Shortly after this, he left the Ogden and drove to his house in Mesquite, arriving for a little after 4:00 a.m.

On the morning of September 22, at around 8:00 a.m., while at his house in Mesquite the gunman searched online for the Life is Beautiful event schedule. The concert was due to start later that afternoon at around 3:00 p.m., however, the gunman was still at his home in Mesquite when the concert started. He would remain at his house until the afternoon of September 24.

During his time at in Mesquite on the 23 to 24 September, the gunman conducted countless online searches for various events and locations in Las Vegas. Such as the Gary Reese Freedom Park, and Arizona Charlie's Decatur mall and casino, along with searching for other hotels close by the Route 91 Concert and the other end of the Strip near Fremont Street. He also looked up various museums, like the Neon Museum and Discovery Children's Museum, along with the Mob Museum.

The gunman also conducted searches for events in and outside of Las Vegas for after October 1, 2017. It can be assumed that he did this as another effort to try and throw any potential surveillance operations off the scent of his true intensions. And show that he planned to be alive after October 1, 2017.

After nearly a full day at his house in Mesquite, the gunman headed back to the Ogden on September 24, at around 2:20 p.m. He was captured on security cameras in the parking garage at the Ogden for around 3:31 p.m. Shortly after this, at around 4:00 p.m., he was then seen on the lobby cameras speaking to the concierge, as he was checking into his third and final room at the complex, 1703. Later that night, at around 9:12 p.m., the gunman headed back to the El Cortez casino.

However, he left the casino for around 10:10 p.m., but did not arrive back at the Ogden until around 11:10 p.m. As to where the gunman was during this missing hour, no one is certain. But there were some possible sightings of him at the California Hotel and Casino, at around this time.

During the early hours of the morning on September 25, which was the morning that the Life is Beautiful ended at 1:00 a.m. The gunman was captured on the Ogden security camera system, several times, either in the main lobby of the complex or walking around the hallways. He was first spotted in the lobby at 1:37 a.m., with a plastic bag, then shortly after, he was captured just walking around random hallways in the Ogden, until 2:59 a.m.

No one is certain as to what the shooter was doing in the lobby or walking the hallways that night. However, considering how paranoid the gunman had become that he was being watched by law enforcement, due to the attack he was planning. It seems that he was walking around the public areas, to see if law enforcement were in the building getting ready to stop any possible attack.

On the afternoon of September 25, 2017, at 3:33 p.m., the gunman checked into his Vista Suite at the Mandalay Bay hotel. He parked his car in the self-parking garage.

He initially booked his room while staying at the hotel with Danley for the finial time on September 9, 2017. At the time he made the reservation, he gave a check in date of September 25 to then check out on October 2, 2017. He requested a room ending in 235, but he did not give a specific floor number.

After making his booking, the hotel reservation system automatically assigned him 33-235 on September 20. Then, less than twenty-four hours later the system changed his room to 32-235. By the time of his check-in, though, on the afternoon of September 25, he was given room 32-135.

Once the gunman was checked in, he left the Mlife VIP check in desk, and walked around the casino for close to an hour, seemingly just looking around. Then, shortly before 4:45 p.m., the gunman went to the self-parking garage and retrieved his car, then drove it around to the main entrance of the hotel, to use the hotel valet service. One of the hotel security cameras captured the gunman's vehicle driving into the main entrance valet line, at around 4:49 p.m.

At the valet, the gunman informed the hotel employee that he needed help with his bags, and a bellman and luggage cart was called for. Shortly before 4:52 p.m., a bellman arrived with the cart and loaded four large suitcases from the car and headed to the room, with the gunman following closely behind pulling a smaller roller suitcase.

While walking towards the main entrance of the hotel, the gunman asked not to be taken to his room via the main elevator, as he preferred using the service elevator. As this was not an unusual request, the bellman obliged. During the time that the Bellman and the shooter spent together, the shooter seemed at easy, and even made several funny jokes.

At 5:05 p.m., the gunman and the bellman arrived at room 32-135, on the 100-wing of the 32nd floor of the hotel. After entering the room, the bellman took the four large bags off the luggage cart and placed them in the main living room of the large Vista Suite. The gunman then gave the bellman a generous tip for helping with his bags, and the bellman left the shooter alone in his room.

After the attack, the bellman that helped the gunman to 32-135 on September 25, was asked about the weight of the bags. The bellman claimed, the bags were not overly heavy, nor did the bellman hear any metal clunking sounds coming from the luggage. It is certain that the first four large suitcases did contain at least four rifles, but the gunman used plastic wrapping, plastic shopping bags, along with other lightweight materials as a means to fill the bags out. As a security measure, the gunman secured the zips of each of the large suitcases with a padlock.

Shortly after being left in his room, the gunman engaged the deadbolt on the main door to 32-135, at 5:31 p.m. The shooter would remain in 32-135 until 9:33 p.m., when he would leave the room and head to the main valet to retrieve his vehicle, so that he could head back to his house in Mesquite. At 9:40 p.m., the hotel valet dropped the gunman's car to him, at the main entrance of the hotel. The gunman then drove back to his house arriving shortly before 11:00 p.m.

From the late evening of September 25 until the early evening of September 26, the gunman would remain at his house in Mesquite before heading back to Las Vegas. At around 3:30 p.m. on the afternoon of September 26, the gunman wired another $50,000 from his account to Danley's account in the Philippines. A few hours later, at around 7:50 p.m., the gunman left his home and headed to the Ogden hotel, arriving a little before 9:00 p.m.

After parking his car in the Ogden parking garage, the gunman then went to the El Cortez casino and gambled until around 10:16 p.m. Shortly after 10:23 p.m., the shooter returned to the Ogden and spent a brief time in one of the rooms he rented, before driving back to the Mandalay Bay. At around 10:45 p.m., the gunman arrived at the main lobby valet, and asked for a bellman to help him to his room with several bags.

Within a few moments, a bellman arrived at the gunman's car and removed six large suitcases from the vehicle and loaded them onto the luggage cart. Both the bellman and the gunman then headed to room 32-135 with the bags, again via the service elevator.

Just like the day before, the gunman pulled a small roller suitcase with him, as he walked to the room. The gunman and hotel bellman arrived at 32-135 for 10:52 p.m., the bellman then put the luggage in the main living room of the suite, and left after the gunman tipped him.

By the late evening of September 26, the gunman had a total of ten large bags in his room, and at least ten rifles he would use during his attack. Again, just like the first four bags, the shooter used lightweight filler materials to cushion the area around the weapons, to give the impression the bags contained nothing more than clothes, and the zips on the bag were also secured with a padlock.

A little after 11:04 p.m., the gunman left 32-135 and headed to the hotel casino, where he would gamble from the late evening until the early hours of the following morning. At around 7:18 a.m., on the morning of September 27, the gunman had finished gambling and was back inside 32-135.

Around mid-afternoon on September 27, the gunman called his MGMRI VIP casino host and stated that he did not like the view from his Vista Suite on the 100-wing of the hotel and, he requested to move to a suite on the 200-wing with an adjoining room.

The gunman was informed that this was not possible, as there were no suites available on the 200-wing, but if he liked, she could get him the adjoining room to 32-135 from September 29 until the end of his stay. Reluctantly the shooter agreed to this offer, but it was evident he was not happy about not getting a room change.

For the remainder of the afternoon on September 27, until the early evening, the gunman would spend his time in 32-135. While in the room, he ordered room service and had the room cleaned. Then from 5:32 p.m. until 7:54 p.m., the door to 32-135 was opened and closed by the gunman several times. It seems that during this time the shooter was starting to prepare items in his room for the attack, and he was constantly checking the hallway to see if anyone other than guests were in the hallway.

At 7:56 p.m., the shooter left 32-135 with two large rolling suitcases, and headed to the valet to collect his vehicle. Shortly after 8:03 p.m., the gunman had his car returned to him and he left the hotel, where he headed to the Ogden. The gunman arrived at the Ogden a little after 8:29 p.m., parked his car in the garage and headed to rooms he rented. A short while later, at around 8:35 p.m., the gunman went to the main lobby of the Odgen and checked out of his final two rooms.

After handing the keys into the main reception, the gunman then headed back to the parking garage. His vehicle was spotted on security camera, leaving the Ogden garage at 8:45 p.m., where he headed back to his home in Mesquite. At around 10:00 p.m., the gunman arrived back at his house, where he remained until 10:50 p.m. At a little after 10:52 p.m., the gunman left his house and headed to the local Walmart, which was about ten minutes away from he lived.

While at Walmart, the gunman purchased a pack of razor blades, fake flowers, a vase, a Styrofoam ball, and some luggage items. In the aftermath of the mass shooting the fake flowers, vase, and Styrofoam ball was found inside 32-135, on a shelf close to the main entrance door to the room. Many people have questioned as to why the gunman purchased these items, as they are out of place and seem to have no purpose.

After studying the attack, though, and looking at what purpose the items would serve, the reason as to why the gunman purchased them makes sense. The gunman was trying to find a way of hiding the webcam that he planned to place on top of the cart. This would ensure that if anyone come close to the cart during the attack, they would not see the camera. The camera he planned to place on the bottom of the cart, was easily hidden by arranging the tablecloth in a certain way.

Once the gunman had purchased the few items from Walmart in Mesquite, he then left the store and headed back to his house. For the remainder of the night of September 27 until early evening of September 28, the gunman remained in Mesquite.

At around 2:50 p.m., on the afternoon of September 28, the gunman made the third and final wire to Danley's account in the Philippines for another

$50,000.00. Shortly after this, he then went to a nearby gun store and purchased his final rifle for the attack, a .308 bolt action rifle. After buying the rifle, he then returned home.

The gunman left his house at around 5:20 p.m. and drove to the nearby landfill to test fire his new rifle. After a short while of test firing the weapon, he then drove back to his house in Mesquite, arriving a little after 6:05 p.m. Upon returning to his house on this occasion, a neighbor spotted him, but did not speak to the gunman.

A little after 8:40 p.m., the gunman left his house in Mesquite and returned to the Mandalay Bay, arriving at around 9:46 p.m. Again, the gunman dropped his vehicle off at the valet line close by the main entrance and headed to his room. This time, he was spotted on security cameras with two rolling suitcases and a laptop bag. On this occasion, the gunman used the main guest elevator bank to head to his room on the 32nd floor, entering 32-135 at 9:53 p.m.

The gunman stayed in the room for a few minutes, presumably checking the items of luggage he had left in the room, to make sure no one had tampered with them. Then, at 10:02 p.m., the shooter left 32-135 and headed to the casino to gamble. By 10:18 p.m., the gunman was sitting at one of his preferred video poker machines.

After two hours of playing video poker, the gunman returned to his room in the early hours of the morning on September 29, at a little after 12:43 a.m. The gunman remained in 32-135 until 2:35 a.m., when he left and headed back down to the casino to resume playing video poker. After playing for another three hours, the gunman then headed back up to 32-135 at 5:43 a.m., arriving at his room four minutes later at 5:47 p.m. The shooter would remain in his room until early afternoon.

Just after midday on September 29, the gunman left 32-135 at 12:20 p.m., and headed down into the casino level of the hotel, to get some food. Shortly after 12:28 p.m., the shooter was witnessed sat at a table in the Mizuya Sushi restaurant, eating one of his favorite meals, California Sushi Rolls.

After eating his food, he paid and headed back to 32-135, arriving back in the room for 1:20 p.m. Within ten minutes of being back in the room, the housekeeper knocked on his door to see if he wanted his room cleaned which he agreed to. At 2:00 p.m., housekeeping returned to 32-135 and started cleaning.

While housekeeping cleaned the room, the gunman sat at his laptop seemingly focusing on what was on the screen, and on occasion looking to see where the room cleaner was. Then, just as the cleaner was about to vacuum the room, the gunman told her not to bother. After this, she went to remove the room service cart that had been in the room since the afternoon of September 27, but the shooter told her to leave the cart as he was using it as a table.

After housekeeping finished cleaning 32-135, the gunman remained in the suite for a short while, before heading down to VIP desk, at 3:00 p.m. to check in to 32-134. While at the check in desk, the gunman used Danley's Mlife players card and gave her name as the occupant. By 3:07 p.m., the gunman was heading back up to his rooms.

Once back up on the 32nd floor 100-wing, the gunman first entered 32-134, at 3:09 p.m. It seems that the gunman went into the room to unlock the adjoining door to 32-135. After some four minutes the gunman then left the room via the main door, and entered 32-135 at 3:13 p.m.

For the remainder of the afternoon of September 29 until early hours of the following morning, the gunman remained inside either 32-134 or 32-135. This a deviation from his usual habits of gambling from the late evening until the early morning, however, it was the opening night of the Route 91 music festival. So, it can be assumed that he spent the night observing the festival, to finalize his attack along with conducting a 'dry' run of his plans.

Then, shortly after 11:11 p.m., the gunman placed an order for room service, totaling $102.99, which arrived at the room just after midnight. At 12:52 a.m., on the morning of September 30, 2017, the gunman left 32-135 and headed to collect his car from the hotel valet. By 1:00 a.m., the shooter was heading back to his house in Mesquite, arriving a little after 2:00 a.m. The gunman then loaded up his car with more suitcases and headed back the Mandalay Bay, arriving a little after 5:56 a.m. By 6:03 a.m., the gunman was back inside of 32-135.

Later the same day, at around 12:04 p.m., the mini bar in 32-134 was restocked and the gunman refused for both 32-134 and 32-135 to be cleaned. Sometime around 12:15 p.m., the gunman then placed the Do Not Disturb sign on both 32-134 and 32-135. A little after 2:52 p.m., the gunman retrieved his car from the hotel valet and parked it in the self-parking garage. He then took two suitcases from the car and headed back to rooms, entering 32-135 at around 3:23 p.m. Shortly after dropping the luggage off at his room, he then headed down the casino to gamble.

By 3:30 p.m., he was sat in the high limits area of the casino playing one of a video poker machine. This was the second day of the Route 91 concert, which started at 3:00 p.m. At around 6:48 p.m., the gunman stopped gambling and returned to 32-135, entering the room a little after 6:53 p.m.

After being back in his rooms for close to 35 minutes, he then left at 7:28 p.m., via the door to 32-134. However, he was not captured on camera again inside the hotel using the guest elevators or walking though the casino, heading to the self-parking garage. The next time the shooter was captured on camera was some 24 minutes later, at 7:52 p.m., when his vehicle was spotted leaving the self-parking garage.

It is not clear why the gunman chose to leave his rooms via the door to 32-134, as he usually left the rooms via the door to 32-135. Nor is it known which route he took in the casino to access the parking garage, due to never been seen on any of the cameras in the elevators or casino. There is a possible explanation, though, as to why he exited the rooms via the door to 32-134 and why he was not seen until he was driving out of the parking garage.

Based on the gunman's patten of behavior, he only entered the hallway from the door to 32-134, when he was heading to the foyer, opposite 32-134. He used this door specifically to cross to the foyer, as the door to the room was recessed, so he could hide behind the wall by the door and peer down the hallway to see if anyone was around. If the coast was clear, he would then walk across the hallway and through the foyer door.

However, if he used the door to 32-135, if there was anyone in the hallway, they would have seen him the moment he opened the door. Because the double entry doors to 32-135 were located in the center of the north wall at the end of the 100-wing wing. So, this meant he would not be able to enter the foyer unnoticed. But by using the door to 32-134, he could covertly watch the hallway before crossing to the foyer.

Once inside the foyer, he could access the stairwell and descend to the lower levels of the hotel unnoticed. Because at the Mandalay Bay, cameras are only deployed in the casino, main resort areas, and all the elevators. Whereas guest hallways, stairwells, and parking garages do not have cameras in them. However, there were cameras at the entrance and exit of the parking garages, simply to monitor vehicles coming and going.

The question now, though, is why would the shooter want to make it appear that he was still inside the hotel? Honestly, there is no reasonable answer to this, unless he was timing how long it would take to descend to the car park via the stairwell. As there is no other explanation.

On the evening of September 30, the gunman arrived back at his home in Mesquite for around 8:57 p.m. and remained at the house until the early hours of the morning of October 1, 2017. At around 2:06 a.m., on the morning of October 1, the gunman left his home in Mesquite for the final time and headed back to the Mandalay Bay. His sickening and heinous attack was just eighteen hours away.

According to his cell phone location data, it was on this journey back to the Mandalay Bay that he discarded the hard drive. He arrived back at the hotel a little after 3:05 a.m. and parked his car back in the self-parking garage. Instead of going straight to his rooms, he went to the casino and gambled for around four hours.

At 7:34 a.m., the gunman decided it was time cash out and head back his room. After pressing the cash out button, he collected the voucher for $29,900.00 and and returned to the 32nd floor 100-wing. He entered 32-134 at 7:37 a.m. Based on the two cash out vouchers found in the gunman's room after the attack, he had just over $30,126.50 remaining of his initial $60,000.00 line of casino credit.

Just ten hours before the attack, on October 1, at 12:12 p.m. the gunman left 32-135 to move his car from self-parking and returned it to valet parking. After dropping the car off at the hotel valet, he took two rolling suitcases and a laptop bag from the vehicle and headed back to the rooms, via the guest elevators. After arriving back at 32-135, for a little after 12:31 p.m., the gunman then placed a final room service order to be delivered to 32-134.

The gunman's room service order arrived at 32-134 for around 1:37 p.m., which was now just nine hours before the attack. The hotel employee who delivered the food addressed the gunman as Mr. Danely, as the order was placed under the name Marilou Danley. Despite being called the wrong name, the gunman never corrected the mistake. He simply invited the room service attendant into the room and told them to place the cart by the bathroom.

Once the cart was in place, the gunman tipped the food server, and the hotel employee left the room. In the aftermath of the attack, the room service attendant was questioned by law enforcement on October 3, 2017. During the interview they clarified that they called the shooter Mr. Danley, but they knew by the time of the interview that it was the gunman that answered the door. In addition, it seemed that the gunman did not want to talk or engage in conversation.

From 2:23 p.m. up until 9:46 p.m., the gunman opened and closed the doors to both 32-134 and 32-135, countless times. As to why the doors to 32-134 and 32-135 were opened and closed by the gunman during this period, it is not certain. Because other than securing the bracket on the fire door and the placing the room service cart in the hallway, the shooter did not have a need to open and the doors to the rooms. Unless he was keeping an eye on the hallway, to see if the sounds of his preparations was arousing suspicion.

Shortly after 3:00 p.m., the final day of the Route 91 Concert, got underway. Based on ticket sales it is estimated that by 4:00 p.m., there were some 22,000 people inside the venue enjoying the concert. None of these people, though, could ever imagine in their most horrific nightmares, what was set to happen to them that night.

While there is no evidence to say exactly what the gunman was doing in the rooms in the hours leading to the attack, or how he arranged his firearms. There are clues that can be used to determine the steps he took for his final preparations.

In 32-134 he laid out three 7.62 and .308 caliber semi-automatic rifles and one bolt action rifle, on the two beds in the room. The bed that was closest to the window, the shooter laid out three of the 7.62 and .308 semi-automatic rifles. All the rifles on this bed were fitted with optical sights and bipods. On the bed farthest away from the windows, he placed the .308 bolt action rifle, which only had a scope fitted to the weapon.

The dresser in 32-134, which was located on the north wall of the room under the TV, is where the gunman placed five fully loaded 30-round magazines, which held both normal 7.62 and .308 rounds and 7.62 and .308 tracer rounds. On the floor by the window in 32-134, the gunman placed the Amazon Prime box with the remaining tracer rounds inside, which had not been loaded into magazines.

During the attack, the gunman used 32-134 to fire specifically at the fuel tanks, and out of the four rifles the gunman laid out in the room, only two of them were used to fire tanks. The weapons fired by the gunman from 32-134 would later be marked as exhibits 21 and 24.

Based on the bullet drop calculations of the gunman, the distance was 700 yards, which he obtained by using google earth, because even though he had a laser range finder. The laser is not able to go through the glass windows, so it would have been useless until the window was broken out.

Room 32-135 was the primary room used by the gunman during the attack, to fire countless volleys into the concert venue. In the aftermath of the attack, most of the evidence recovered from both the hotel rooms was discovered in 32-135.

Just inside of the double entry doors of 32-135 and off to the right was an enclosed walkway that led behind the wet bar and into the secondary seating area of the room. In the entrance to the hallway, the gunman placed an unloaded .380 rifle fitted with a scope and propped up on a bipod. Also in this area, was a towel on the floor close by the weapon, with a drill bit under the towel.

During the search of the room, it was discovered that at some point before the attack, the gunman had attempted to drill through the wall from inside the room and into the hallway, where he intended to place the endoscope, so he could spot anyone crawling towards the doors to the rear of the cart. However, the hole, which was close to the floor and on the east side of the entry doors, was only partially drilled as the wall was thicker than the shooter anticipated.

A few feet away from the door, was a small shelf recessed into the wall on the west side of the entry way. On the shelf the gunman placed the vase, fake flowers, and Styrofoam ball. There was also a mini fridge on the shelf, with a foam cooler on top.

Opposite the recessed shelf, was the corner of the wet bar counter, where the gunman placed a laptop which was connected to a camera on the inside of the door to 32-135 over the peephole. Next to this, was the monitor for the wireless camera that the gunman placed on the bottom of the room service cart in the hallway, outside 32-134.

Also, in the aftermath of the attack, a single sock belonging to the gunman was found close by the laptop on the counter, which has always been baffling. However, the gunman used the sock to cover the smoke alarm in the main room in 32-135, to stop it activating from the gas expelled from the rifles that would collect in the room during the attack.

There was also a tall bar stool with a high back, close to the corner of the wet bar, where the gunman placed a 5.56 rifle pointing towards the door, with a 40 round magazine loaded on the weapon and an EOTech sight and bump-stock attached. At the foot of the stool, the gunman laid another rifle on the floor, which was a .308/7.62 caliber weapon fitted with a bipod and optical scope and loaded with a 30-round magazine.

On the main part of the counter of the wet bar, the gunman placed several room keys for both 32-134 and 32-135, along with his and Danley's Mlife players cards. There was also a notepad next to the room keys and players card, where the gunman had written a final reminder to unplug the phones in the room. Alongside of the notepad was a blue baseball cap the gunman had been seen wearing around the hotel, in the days leading up to the attack.

A bit further along the counter of the wet bar, the gunman placed a pair of Bushnell binoculars, which he was using to survey the venue. He also placed his wallet, cellphone, and valet ticket in this area of the counter. Between the wallet and binoculars, he also placed a roll of packing tape, that he would use for various means, such as sticking the webcam to the peephole of 32-135.

At the front of the wet bar and adjacent to the main seating area of the room, were two more high-backed bar stools. On each chair the gunman placed a 5.56 rifle loaded with an extended 100-round magazine and fitted with bump-stocks.

Directly in front of the wet bar, in the main sitting room of 32-135, the gunman pushed together two single seat chairs to create a gun bin, where he intended to discard the rifles after he fired them into the venue. Just in front and in the center of the gun bin, towards the windows, were two small roller suitcases. Each case was filled with 50-round 5.56 pre-loaded magazines.

Just in front of the chairs, in the narrow walkway the gunman placed a steel square rolling case, which he used to hold casino chips. However, it seems that he converted the use of this to hold extra ammunition. Then, a bit further along the front of the wet bar, close to the corner was a backpack lay on the floor.

Off to the side of the gun bin, closest to the doors to the master bedroom was a small circular table with a towel draped over the top of it. The gunman placed at least two rifles here, each fitted with a bump-stock and loaded with a 100-round magazine. Close by the west window of the main sitting area was a brown three-seater couch, where the gunman placed a further two 5.56 mm rifles fitted with a bump-stock and EOTech red dot sights, but one was loaded with a 50-round PMAG, while the other was loaded with a 100-round extended magazine.

On the east side of the pillar in the main sitting area of 32-135, close by the window he would break-out to fire from the room in the venue, the gunman placed fourteen pre-loaded 100-round 5.56 magazines. On the other side of the pillar, directly in front of the window he would fire from, was a single armchair and two tables.

The gunman intended to use the chair as a firing position, placing the back of the chair towards the window and kneeling on the seat. He placed a rifle across the chair, which was the first weapon he intended to fire. Unlike the other weapons he planned to fire into the venue this rifle was loaded with a 40-round PMAG, but it was fitted with a bump-stock and had an EOTech red dot sight attached.

The shorter of the two tables next to the chair, he placed a further 5.56 semi-automatic rifle fitted with bump-stocks and loaded with 100-round magazines. Again, this weapon also had a red dot sight attacked. Placed next to the rifle was a piece of paper, containing bullet drop calculations, for both the venue and fuel tanks.

Based on the bullet drop calculation sheet found in the room, the gunman estimated that from 32-135 to the center of the venue was 500 yards, and from 32-134 to the fuel tanks was 700 yards. However, despite having a laser range finder, he would have been unable to use the device, as the laser was not strong enough to penetrate the glass and hit the areas he was measuring to.

It appears that the gunman used the measuring tool on google earth to initially determine the ranges. The actual distance between the window in 32-134 the gunman fired from to the fuel tanks was 671 yards. Then, the distance between the window in 32-135 to the center of the concert venue was 369 yards.

On the floor in front of the small table close by the window he was going to fire from, the gunman placed two 7.62 rifles fitted with a bi-pod and scope, and only one of the rifles was loaded with a magazine. Next to the side of the small table and chair, was a much higher table, where the gunman placed another two rifles. Again, each of these rifles were fitted with EOTech sights, bump-stocks, and loaded with an extended 100 round magazine.

Directly under the tall table, was a small rolling suitcase, which contained more pre-loaded magazines. The gunman also placed a .308/7.62 caliber rifle fitted with an optical sight and loaded with a 25-round magazine, on the floor on the east side of the tall table.

There were four chairs that were normally around the tall table, however, they were moved by the gunman and pushed up against the back of one of the couches in the secondary sitting area of the room, which was close by the adjoining door to 32-134. The gunman placed a rifle on each of these chairs, which all had bump-stocks and 100 round extended magazines. Also, one of the rifles had an EOTech sight attached.

The gunman had now finishing laying out the 23 rifles that he had taken to his rooms, which he planned to use during his attack. In addition to this, he had also placed countless fully loaded 25 to 100 round magazines around 32-134 and 32-135, which he also planned to use. It would later emerge that the gunman took over 6,000 rounds of ammunition into the hotel rooms.

On the floor in the small seating area of 32-135, close by the adjoining door to 32-134, the gunman had placed several bags and a marksmen's spotting scope. Like the binoculars, the spotting scope was also used by the gunman to survey his target. Plugged into the outlets along the south wall of the room, and obscured by the bags, were multiple chargers.

The gunman also set up the blue snorkel breathing system, which was laid across the floor of the main living room, in 32-135. The fan on the breathing apparatus was placed close by the door to the master bedroom, which would allow clean air to be sucked into the tube by the fan.

On the bed in the master bedroom in 32-135, the gunman had placed a briefcase on the bed containing his passport, check book, several gift cards, and some personal papers. The laptop that contained the sickening indecent images of children, was switched off but was laying open on the bed. It appears that in the hours before the attack, the gunman had viewed these images, on several occasions.

To the right of the bed on the south wall of the master bedroom, was a chaise lounge, where the shooter placed a rolling suitcase that contained tools. In the outlets on the wall close by the foot of the chaise lounge, were more chargers plugged in.

The small office desk in the master bedroom, located close by the windows in the room, had a towel draped over a section of the top of the desk. On top of the towel, the gunman placed a screwdriver, pair of pliers, scissors. There were also several lose tracer rounds on the table. Next to the desk were several bags of trash, and empty boxes also filled with trash. Inside one of the trash bags, was the laptop missing the hard drive.

Another trash bags close by the desk also contained countless torn-up 5.56/.223 bullet cartons. Close by the foot of the bed were some nine empty 5.56/.223 magazines. It seems that along with the countless magazines he and Danley loaded some weeks before the attack, he also loaded even more magazines while in the room.

In the nightstand drawer next to the bed, the gunman placed several small hand tools, along with a glass cutter. On the rim of the bathtub in the on-suit master bathroom, the gunman placed a single and double handled set of glass suction cups.

Based on the door lock records for 32-134 and 32-135, at 9:36 p.m. the gunman engaged the deadbolt on the entrance doors to 32-135, locking the doors for the last time. At 9:40 p.m., the gunman opened the door to 32-134 and engaged the dead bolt, which prevented the door from fully closing. He then peered around the recessed wall to make sure the hallway was clear, and crossed the hallway to the foyer, to secure the brackets to the fire door.

After only securing a solitary bracket to the fire door with three screws, the gunman then left the foyer and re-entered 32-134 at 9:43 p.m. Once back inside the room, he put the cordless drill and remaining brackets on the dresser and set about setting up his camera system.

After making the final preparations to the cameras on the room service cart, he then opened the door to 32-134 at 9:44 p.m. and placed the cart in the hallway, outside of the room. The gunman then moved the second room service cart into position, in the entry way inside of 32-134. He then connected the wires to the laptop and plugged the wireless camera power cable into the outlet on the wall in the entry hallway.

Between 9:46 p.m. to 9:47 p.m., the gunman made several adjustments to the camera secured to the dinner plate on top of the cart, along with the wireless camera secured to the bottom of the cart. Once he was happy with the view the cameras gave him, he then closed the door to 32-134 for the final time, and deadbolted the door at 9:47 p.m.

In the moments leading up to the attack, the gunman accessed 32-135 via the adjoining door, carrying the cordless drill and remaining brackets, and headed to the master bedroom to finish getting ready. Once inside the master bedroom, he placed the cordless drill and brackets on the chaise lounge and entered the on-suit bathroom.

While in the bathroom, he removed two sheets of toilet paper from the toilet paper roll. He then tore the toilet paper into two smaller strips, rolled them up, and placed them into his ears. This was to help him maintain his hearing during the attack, however, it is almost certain that by the time he fired his third volley of the night, his hearing would have been greatly diminished.

After inserting the toilet paper into his ears, he dropped the excess on the floor of the bathroom and went back into the master bedroom and put on a shooters pad on his right shoulder, to protect his shoulder from the recoil of the rifles. Then, he slid the diving goggles over his head to help protect his eyes from the noxious gases that were about to fill the room.

The gunman walked over to the toolbox on the chaise lounge and picked up the small sledgehammer that he used to break out the windows. For unknown reasons, the gunman wrapped packing tape around the head of the hammer. The shooter then dimmed the lights in the master bedroom.

He was now ready for his attack, so he entered the main sitting area of 32-135. But there were still some last-minute things he had to do before he was ready to fire. The next item on his final to do list was to turn all his cellphones on silent. As an added step, he also disconnected the landline phones in 32-134 and 32-135. He then covered the smoke detector with a sock.

After this, the gunman then took one final look around the living room in 32-135, to make sure everything was in its place for his attack. Once he was happy, he dimmed the lights in the main living area, so it was just bright enough for him to see what he was doing, during the attack.

Unbeknown to the gunman, at around the time he was taking one final look around 32-135. An unarmed hotel security guard who was conducting several guest door checks and was in the 100-wing stairwell and had attempted to open the fire door the shooter had secured with a bracket, a short while ago.

Unable to open the door, to head to 32-129 and complete his final door check. The security guard proceeded to the 33rd floor to and used the guest elevators to access the 32nd floor.

Meanwhile the gunman in 32-135, walked across the living room and through adjoining door into 32-134. Once inside 32-134, he turned the lights off, and walked over to the windows facing the concert venue and fuel tanks. At around 9:59 p.m., he proceeded to use the sledgehammer to break out the window, closest to the south wall of 32-134. Once the window was broken out, the room was ready.

After completing his preparations in 32-134, the gunman returned to 32-135 via the adjoining door. Once back inside the room, he then walked over to the the pillar close by where he laid out his extended magazines, earlier in the night, and at around 10:01 p.m., he smashes the window on the east side of the pillar. After breaking enough of the window out, he then dropped the sledgehammer to the floor.

At around the time the gunman broke out the windows, hotel security dispatch received at least ten calls from nine guests on the 100-wings of the 15th through 31st floors, and from one hotel employee at the front of the building. Each call related to people either hearing or seeing glass smashing close by their location.

Once everything was ready in 32-135, the gunman then walked over to west bar and picked up the tablet monitor with the feed for the wireless camera outside of the room. He then returned to the area of the broken window and placed the monitor on the small table. By placing the tablet in this location, it allowed the gunman to view the camera feed from the camera on the bottom of the room service cart, as he was firing.

The gunman then picked up the rifle laying across the arms of the chair he planned to use as a firing position, and wrapped the curtain around him, to obscure the light in the room and to reduce the amount of gas filling the room from the rifle fire. He then knelt on the seating area of the chair, facing out of the window towards the venue. There was nothing left for him to do now, other than prepare his weapon to fire and unleash his senseless and horrific attack.

While the gunman was setting up his firing position, the unarmed security guard had arrived on the 32nd floor 100-wing and completed his door check at 32-129 and was heading to the foyer area on the hallway to inspect the fire door.

Somehow, the security guard slipped past the cameras outside of 32-134, without the gunman noticing. In addition, the security guard also failed to notice the black webcam in an upright position and secured to the top of the dinner plate on top of the cart.

A few seconds later, the security guard was in the foyer and noticed that there was a bracket securing the fire door. With this, he used the house phone in the foyer, to inform both security and maintenance dispatch of the issue. While talking to maintenance dispatch, the call was transferred to an on-duty maintenance manager. After a brief conversation, the call between the security guard and the manager ended.

After ending the call, the security guard left the foyer, and as he did, he thought he could hear drilling coming from inside 32-135. However, he never paid much attention to it, and headed back down the hallway towards 32-129, away from room 32-135.

Attack

Shortly after 10:05 p.m. and 30 seconds, the shooter raised the first rifle he was going to use in his attack, and looked through the EOTech optical sight and aimed the rifle into the southwestern area of the concert venue. He then squeezed the trigger of the weapon, and the sound of the first shot rang out. After the first single shot, he fired five more single shots into crowd of people standing in the southwest section of the venue.

Initially, the crowd of over 13,000 people did not react to the shots, as they mistook the sounds for someone recklessly setting off fireworks. Then, almost as quick as the shots rang out, they faded away and there was a lull of some thirty seconds, before the gunman would fire his second, but more intense volley.

During this short respite, countless concertgoers and the LVMPD officers working at the event, started to look around to try and locate the area where the fireworks may have been set off, but they were all unable to locate the area. At least one person had been hit by the shooter, during his initial volley, and a few short moments later, the number of casualties were about to increase dramatically.

Shortly after 10:06 p.m., the sound of the second and more intense deadly volley filled the night air. This prolonged burst of at around 100 rounds, sent countless people in the event scrambling for cover. But many people located on the west side of the stage area, quickly found they were penned in. On the one side they had the torrent of bullets, while on the other they had a security barrier separating the east and west side of the area directly in front of the stage.

With little to no options, people either lay flat on the ground, sought what cover they could find, hunkered together in groups, or tried to flee the area. Countless people close by the dividing fence tried to scale the waist high metal barrier, and people on the east side of the divide helped as best they could, by being pulling people over the fence. Almost as quick as the second deadly volley started, it was over.

By this stage of the attack, the LVMPD officers working the event were scrambling to make their way to the section of the venue where the first casualties occurred, to engage the shooter who they believed was somewhere in the crowd. The dead and wounded were now being treated by those that were stood around them when the shooter started his attack.

Security cameras from the roof of the Mandalay Bay and inside the venue, captured the chaos inside of the concert grounds. Within a split second of the second volley, there was a hole created in the center of the crowd of people in the southwest area of the venue, just off the west side of the stage.

What no one realized at the time, though, was what the shooter was trying to do. He was not only trying to kill and maim as many people as he could. But also, he was trying to herd them to the east of the festival grounds. This was towards the direction of the fuel tanks he would later fire at, in the hopes of getting them to explode.

Between the second and third volley, there was a lull of about thirty seconds, which allowed people to escape the gunman's deadly clutches. Many people, though, on the westside of the stage remained laying on the floor or grouped together in what little cover they could find. To try and help people, a member of the lighting crew turned on all the lights on the stage, illuminated the entire area. However, this futile act only helped the gunman, as now he was able to see inside the illuminated venue.

At around the time of the second break in the gunman's attack, the hotel security guard on the 32nd floor 100-wing was close by 32-129 and was oblivious to the sounds of gunfire. All that was about to change though, because while the gunman was changing out weapons, he spotted the security guard on the tablet showing the feed from the camera on the bottom of the room service cart.

Not wanting to have his location reported, the gunman went over to the corner of the wet bar area, picked up a rifle and fired through the doors and down the hallway, to try and kill the security guard. To gauge where his shots were hitting, he used the security camera on the bottom of the cart as an aiming device.

Within a split second, the security guard realized what was happening, and that shots were being fired in his direction. He quickly ran a short distance down the hallway and, sought cover in a guest doorway alcove. The security guard then noticed he had been hit in the left calf. To raise the alarm, he used his hotel radio to contact his dispatch to let them know there was shots coming from 32-135.

Immediately, security dispatch altered all the armed units in the hotel and sent them to the 32nd floor 100-wing. By chance, two LVMPD officers were also in the casino area, and they also headed to the guest levels.

A little after 10:06 p.m. and 50 seconds the sound of gunfire filled the night air once again, and muffled the sound of screams and moans coming from those who were lay on the ground wounded. The third volley was just as intense as the last one and was still focused on forcing people towards the east side of the concert grounds.

Many unlikely heroes emerged that night; as concertgoers assisted one another to escape the carnage or provided medical aid to people laying on the ground riddled with bullet holes, while rounds were flying right over their heads and splashing on the ground around them.

As the gunman was firing for a third time, he quickly came to the realization that it was taking too long to change out weapons and build up his firing position in the back facing chair. So, after firing this volley, he discarded the weapon in the makeshift gun bin, and he chose to change his method of attack. Now, he would just simply stand in front of the window he broke out, and fire.

Due to the gunman no longer building up a firing position in the chair, there was a shorter pause between the third and fourth volleys, then what there was between the first and third volleys. On this occasion, there was only a seventeen second respite from the gunman's deadly salvo. By this point of the attack, though, people had notice that there was prolonged pause between the volleys, in which to escape.

This meant that when the gunman opened fire with his fourth volley at around 10:07 p.m. and 18 seconds. Hundreds of people who were now trying to escape the slaughter, were caught out in the open. Just like the previous three volleys, the gunman fired around a 100-round burst, into the crowd of defenseless victims.

It was around this time that one of the LVMPD officers working at the event was able to locate where the shots were coming from. Once the gunman was spotted, the officer used his patrol radio to relay the gunman's location, high up on the 100-wing tower of the Mandalay Bay, firing out of a window.

The gunman now noticed that his overall plan seemed to be working, whereby he was effectively using his shots to herd people to the eastern side of the venue, and out onto Giles Street. However, once on Giles Street, they were dispersing in all directions, and not just heading towards the fuel tanks.

The gunman then adapted his shot pattern to push people in the direction that he wanted them to go. With this, he started to strafe from the southwest area of the venue, around towards Giles Street in a northeasterly arc, across the concert grounds. This change in tactic pushed more people towards the fuel tanks. Again, almost as quick as it started, the shooting stopped.

At around the time of the fourth volley, many of the local hospitals in Las Vegas and the surrounding areas had been informed of the attack on the Route 91 Concert, and they were told to prepare for thousands of casualties. With this, any medical staff that was not undertaking vital duties were ordered to the main entrance of the Emergency Department with beds and wheelchairs and wait for the mass of victims heading their way.

Due to a shortage of ambulances, any type of vehicle that could be used to ferry people to the hospitals was utilized. From Ubers and taxies to pick-up trucks and cars, a convoy of vehicles began to make their way to the hospitals with people who were in critical condition. To help speed up the transfer of the wounded, countless LVMPD officers were instructed to close any road they had to, to ensure the convey could rapidly get to hospitals.

One person that ferried people to the hospitals, was a concertgoer, who had parked his pick-up close by the venue. At some point during the attack, a bullet punched through the driver's door and hit the driver in the left leg. Un-phased, the person continued to ferry countless victims in the cab and the bed of his truck, on numerous occasions.

After his umpteen trip, he had lost a lot of blood, but was still willing to go back for more people. However, due to his blood loss, it was unsafe for him to drive, and several LVMPD officers and two nurses forcibly removed the driver from his vehicle and took him into the hospital for treatment.

The pause between the fourth and fifth volley lasted around eighteen seconds, before the shooter opened fire again. At around 10:07 p.m. and 45 seconds, the night air was filled once more with the sound of intense gunfire. On this occasion though, the gunman only fired some 93 rounds, instead of his usual 100 rounds. He also maintained his arc firing pattern, to continue to push people to where he wanted them.

Then there was another silence, and once again, the moans and screams of the wounded either in the venue or at one of the many hastily established casualty collection points outside the venue, filled the silence. There were also screams from those who were either scared to within an inch of their life, or crying for their loved ones who were either dead or wounded.

After thirty seconds no volleys had been fired, which seemed unusual, to the victims of the attack, as they had expected another torrent of bullets, which never seemed to come. With an extended lull, many people inside the venue broke cover and ran for their lives following the steady stream of people to the east side of the venue. However, some people were still leaving by the western side of the venue onto Las Vegas Blvd. and were being directed down the strip towards East Reno Ave. and away from the Mandalay Bay.

Some forty-five seconds passed before the sound of gunfire was heard again. The reason for such a long pause, was because the gunman was leaving 32-135 and entering 32-134, via the adjoining door. He now wanted to start his grand finale, by making the fuel tanks explode. After entering 32-134, he picked up a .308 semi-automatic rifle and lay across the bed closest to the window, to line up his shot.

At a little after 10:08 p.m. and 40 seconds, he commenced firing the sixth volley of shots. This time though, it was not a torrent of rounds. It was aimed single shots, but no one knew where they were going. Now, the gunman started to fire his volley at the fuel tanks, in the hopes he could get them to explode.

Over the course of the next forty seconds, the gunman would fire five more aimed shots at the tanks. Luckily, though, none of these rounds hit the tanks as he seemed to be firing high. By around 10:09 p.m. and 20 seconds the gunman had become frustrated with not being able to hit his target, so he gave up and went back to firing into the venue.

After the fifth shot at the tanks was fired, there was around a twenty-three second lull, before the gunman opened fire into the venue. However, his seventh volley was nothing like the previous bursts. Instead, it was broken down into three short busts, which totaled around twenty-three shots. The seventh volley fired by the gunman occurred at around 10:09 p.m. and 40 seconds.

The reason that the seventh volley was different from the other shots fired into the venue, was because something had caught the gunman's attention, on one of the cameras monitoring the hallway. The motion detected was the hotel maintenance technician, who had been sent to the floor to remove the bracket from the fire door. However, no one had told the second hotel employee about shots being fired on the floor.

As the maintenance technician drew closer to 32-135, the shooter watched and waited for him to get nearer the door. However, the wounded security guard popped his head out from the doorway alcove that he was hiding in and shouted at his fellow employee to take cover, because someone was firing a gun down the hallway. Initially, the maintenance technician was stunned, but within a split second he dived into a doorway alcove on the west side of the hallway.

Just as the second hotel employee took cover, the gunman fired two short bursts totaling 22 rounds, through the door and down the hallway. These shots occurred at around 10:10 p.m. and 36 seconds. Luckily, the second hotel employee was not injured.

After firing the second volley down the hallway, the gunman waited a few seconds, to see if either of the employees would come out from their hiding spots. However, neither hotel employee dared to re-enter the hallway, for fear of being killed.

Knowing that his location had been discovered, the shooter estimated that he would only have around six minutes before law enforcement would be at the rooms. So, he went back to firing into the venue.

With his focus back on the concert grounds, at a little after 10:10 p.m. and 56 seconds, the shooter fired his eighth volley into the venue, which was still being illuminated by the bright stage lights. On this occasion, he fired around 98 shots.

At around the time of this volley, the two hotel employees taking cover in the hallway, chose to break from cover and head to the guest elevator bank. Due to the wound that the security guard had received to his left calf, the maintenance technician helped him as best he could. Within seconds, they entered the core center of the floor close by the elevator bank, just as a hotel maintenance manager and an armed hotel security manager arrived on the floor.

By this point of the attack, the venue was nearly empty. The only people inside the concert grounds were either deceased, too wounded to move, people still taking cover, or concertgoers and law enforcement providing what medical care they could to those who were wounded.

After the eighth volley, there was a pause of around twenty seconds, before the gunman fired his ninth burst, at around 10:11 p.m. and 33 seconds. This time though, the gunman was not directing his shots into the venue, as he had spotted a group of LVMPD officers who were attempting to cross from the sidewalk on the west side of the concert grounds, to the other side of Las Vegas Blvd.

The officers were trying to enter the hotel, so they could stop the attack. But just as the first few officers were about to set off across the road, the gunman opened fire. Immediately, they stopped in their tracks and turned around, then ran back to a line of police cars parked along the intersection of Mandalay Rd. and Las Vegas Blvd.

The group of officers hunkered behind the patrol vehicles, as rounds impacted all around them. At least two of the officers were hit, one in the neck and the other in the arm. During this volley, the gunman fired some 96 rounds.

A twenty-three second pause followed the ninth volley, which allowed the police officers to move away from the patrol vehicles and take cover behind a wall just outside of the venue. Then, at around 10:12 p.m. and 05 seconds, another barrage of bullets was fired by the gunman into the venue.

Again, his shot pattern was in a strafing arc across the concert grounds, in a last ditched effort to push the last few people towards the fuel tanks. This volley consisted of around 100 rounds.

The attack had been going on for some seven minutes by this point, and scores of people were wounded, and there were at least thirty people dead. The gunman had fired at least 700 rounds, and there was still more to come.

At around 10:12 p.m. and 30 seconds, the gunman opened up with his eleventh volley of the night. This volley was just as unrelenting as previous ones, but now, the gunman was starting to lose his momentum. After firing some 100-rounds, the shooting stopped for around forty seconds, before he would fire again.

In the longer than usual respite between the eleventh and twelfth volleys, the LVMPD officers on the corner of Mandalay Bay Rd. and Las Vegas Blvd. made another attempt to cross the road. This time, they were successful.

But now, a new problem was starting to emerge, at the makeshift casualty collection points. Due to the volume of casualties, the critically wounded were not being moved to the hospitals fast enough, and medical supplies were running desperately short. Those assisting the wounded resorted to making tourniquets and bandages out of their t-shirts, and whatever other items they could use.

Inside the venue, the civilians and first responders were doing their best to deal with the casualties. For those that were too wounded to walk, people were tearing up the metal security fencing inside the venue, to use as makeshift stretchers. To give the dead some respect, they were covered with banners and items of clothing. By this point of the attack, all the traffic was being diverted away from the area of the concert grounds.

Then, the respite was over, at around 10:13 p.m. and 30 seconds, the sound of the thirteenth volley filled the night air. The gunman fired at least 99-rounds this time, but now, he had given up his arc configuration. Instead, he was firing all over the venue, or wherever he thought people may still be hiding in the concert grounds. At the end of the thirteenth volley, the gunman ceased fire for just over a minute.

The fourteenth volley fired by the shooter occurred at around 10:14 p.m. and 46 seconds. Just like the one before, he was firing wherever he thought people may be hiding. But now, though, he seems to have lost his momentum and lust for blood, because he only fired some 51 rounds this time.

After around fifteen seconds, the gunman opened-up with his fifteenth and finally volley, into the venue, which occurred at around 10:15 p.m. and 13 seconds. It seems that the gunman was now done, because this volley consisted of only 46 rounds, before the gunman ceased firing. While he may have been finished with firing into the venue, though. His attack was not fully over, as there was one last thing he wanted to do.

With a rifle in hand, the gunman left 32-135 and went through the adjoining door into 32-134, for one last attempt at the tanks. As he entered 32-134, he threw the 5.56 mm rifle he was carrying onto the bed furthest from the windows. On this occasion, though, he decided that it was time to use the tracer rounds, in hope they would be powerful enough to punch through the steel and ignite the fuel.

The gunman then grabbed a magazine loaded with tracer rounds and inserted it into one of the rifles, on the bed closest to the window. He then dropped to his knees, and just like before he lay across the bed in the room and lined up his shot. As the gunman adjusted his scope, he must have been able to see the masses of people still around the tanks and on Giles Street.

After some thirty-six seconds, the sixteenth and final volley commenced. This volley could have been the most deadly of them all. But thankfully, it was not. At around 10:15 p.m. and 56 seconds, the gunman fired a single shot at the fuel tanks, this time it hit. As it impacted the top rim of the tank, white phosphorous sparks flew in all directions. However, the tank failed to explode.

Undeterred, the gunman took another shot with a tracer round, at around 10:16 p.m. and 06 seconds. This time, though, the round hit nearly dead center of the tank, and it made another splash of sparks when it impacted. Despite puncturing the outer layer of the tank, the round never fully penetrated the inner layer of metal.

In a fit of anger, the gunman stormed out of 32-134 and back into 32-135, slamming the adjoining door behind him. He then walked through the main living area of the suite pulling the sock off the smoke alarm as he went and discarded it on the counter of the wet bar.

He then went into the master bedroom and took off his goggles and shooters pad and threw them on the desk. After this, he removed the laser range finder from one of his pants pockets and thew it on the desk, close by the towel. He then pulled his .38 snub-nosed revolver out of his other pants pocket and walked back into the main living area of 32-135.

Once back in the main sitting room, he walked over to the wet bar and removed the .38 snub-nose from its holster, and slung the holster onto the counter of the wet bar and, walked over to the window he had been firing from, in 32-135. For a few moments, he stood at the window looking in the direction of the concert grounds and the fuel tanks, surveying the carnage he had created. The gunman was now done, because in his mind he had very little time left before law enforcement arrived at his door.

Resigned to his fate, the gunman then stepped back from the window and lay on the ground. One of the rifles he had fired during the attack, lay under him. He then titled his head back and opened his mouth and with using his right hand, placed the barrel of his revolver to the roof of his mouth. Without hesitation, he used his right thumb to pull back the hammer and squeezed the trigger. His death was relatively pain and almost instantaneous.

The time was now around 10:16 p.m. and 16 seconds, and the shooter was dead. Some eleven minutes had elapsed since the start of the attack. In that time, the gunman fired over 1,000 rounds, killed 58 people, and wounded hundreds of others. In the years that followed the attack, two more people would succumb to their wounds from the attack, which increased the death toll to 60 people.

Chapter Three:
Police Response to the 32nd Floor

"A lie will get halfway around the world, before the truth has a chance to rear its ugly head."

-Author Unknown.

In the days and weeks that followed the Las Vegas Mass Shooting, LVMPD were heavily criticized for their overall response, to the 32nd floor. For many people, it was hard to understand why it took the first two officers over ten minutes to arrive on the floor, after the shooter fired his first shot. Then, it was even harder to understand why it would take the SWAT team over seventy-two minuets to assault the shooters' room, after the attack ended.

There were other issues, though, which became known in the aftermath of the attack, that seemed to reinforce the critics claims about the response by law enforcement to the 32nd floor. Because several weeks after the attack, it emerged that two LVMPD officers were already inside of the Mandalay Bay, when the attack started; and they also responded to the 32nd floor, within moments of the shooter firing his first shot.

However, the officers along with four hotel armed security managers only made it as far as the 31st floor 100-wing stairwell, and never attempted to close in on the shooters' location. Even though, while they advanced down the 31st floor 100-wing hallway they could hear the torrent of volleys still being fired by the gunman, and chose to retreat, rather than close on the shooter's location on the floor above.

Once this information became public, all the officers who responded to the 32nd floor on that fateful night, were given a black eye and marred with the same claims of cowardice, as the two officers who failed to close in on the gunman's location. However, when you remove the actions of the two LVMPD officers that failed to adequately respond to the 32nd floor. Along with understand how law enforcement are trained to deal with active shooters.

It becomes clear that all the officers who did make it to the floor that night, did so with the utmost courage and dedication to duty. All while facing great peril and unknown risks, should the gunman turn his attention to them, in an enclosed space, such as the hallway. Despite the risks faced by the officers, though, they still ran headlong into the fray.

Setting the Scene

The Mandalay Bay Hotel and Casino sits on 120 acres of prime real estate, at the south end of the famous Las Vegas strip, and close by the Welcome to Las Vegas sign. The main complex consists of several sub-levels that are a labyrinth of tunnels, which are off limits to guests and only used by staff to store various items, house kitchens, and ensure the effective operations of the hotel and casino.

Then there is the ground level, which boasts a 147,922 square foot casino, vast events center and theaters, and the beach at Mandalay Bay. Then the 3,209 guest rooms are contained with a 42 story triplex towers, with the top floor being a nightclub called the Foundation Room. To access the guest levels, you use one of the three guest elevator banks at the core center of the building or one of three stairwells at the end of each wing.

Once upon the guest levels, you arrive at the elevator bank, which is located just off the core center. The core center measures 21 feet at the widest point and has three wings jutting off it. The 100-wing that runs north, the 200-wing runs southeast, and the 300 wing runs southwest. Each of the wings are nearly identical in size and shape, which start long and narrow then they open out at the far end of the hallways by the suits.

The length of the hallway from the core center to the suite doors at the far end of the hallway is 333 feet. From wall to wall in the hallway, the narrowest point is 5 feet 8 inches wide, then the width increases from the guest doors recessed in the alcoves to 9 foot 3 inches.

Each wing has a total of eight doorway alcoves on each side of the hallway, which contains two guest doors per alcove. There are a total of thirty-five rooms on each hallway, with the final room being at the far end of the floor and is usually a suite, with the suite entry doors facing down the hallway.

To say that the Mandalay Bay Resort and Casino is an impressive and vast complex, is an understatement. And on the night of the attack, every inch of the hotel and wider complex had to be searched, which was an overwhelming and daunting task for countless members of law enforcement.

Police Tactical Training for Active Shooters

For normal everyday beat cops or detectives, the standard training for dealing with an active shooter falls into two categories: active and passive threats. An active threat is where the shooter is actively shooting people, and in this instance, officers are trained to close with and neutralize the threat. In a passive situation, which is where the shooter is no longer firing, officers are to contain the suspect and wait for a SWAT team.

LVMPD Officers in the Venue

On the night of October 1, there was a total of forty LVMPD officers of varying ranks and one civilian employee, working an overtime assignment at the concert. The forty-one LVMPD personnel were broken down into six sections.

Four of the sections had a total of thirty-eight officers and dealt with duties either inside the venue monitoring the crowd (9 officers), manning the entrance and exits (7 officers), or outside of the venue controlling both vehicle and foot traffic (22 officers). The final two sections, which comprised of two senior officers and the single civilian employee, were tasked with event coordinator and command post duties.

When the initial six single shots were fired by the gunman, the officers working at the event, like the concertgoers, assumed that someone was recklessly setting off fireworks in the crowd or close by the venue. Nearly all the officers started to look around, to see if they could pinpoint the location of where the sounds were coming from.

Within a split second of the intense volley being fired, all the officers inside and outside of the venue quickly responded to the incident. The officers inside the fenced area of the festival grounds, rapidly made their way towards the southwestern corner of the concert grounds, as this was the area where the first casualties occurred.

A group of officers, who were outside of the venue at the midsection of the west perimeter fence and just finishing up dealing with an intoxicated concertgoer; immediately ran down the sidewalk towards the intersection of Mandalay Bay Road and Las Vegas Boulevard, which would take them to a gate that gave them to access the southwestern zone of the venue.

By the time the gunman commenced with his second intense volley, at least one of the LVMPD officers was able to confirm that the shooters' location was somewhere high-up in the Mandalay Bay, and not within the grounds of the venue.

Once this information was relayed over the police radio network, the officers inside the venue continued to push to the southwest corner through the crowds, to get to people who had been wounded. While the group of officers outside of the concert, who had run down the sidewalk, were now in concealed positions behind a cinderblock wall at the intersection of Mandalay Bay Rd and Las Vegas Blvd, actively trying to spot the shooter in the hotel.

Within a few seconds of the third volley of shots being fired into the venue by the shooter, several of the officers who were observing the north facing section of the Mandalay Bay, had located the shooters position. However, none of the officers in this group were able to fire up at the gunman, because they only had pistols, and the shots would have been relatively ineffective.

LVMPD Sergeant (Sgt.) Stuart Richmond, who was amongst the group of officers on the southwest corner, was a former British soldier, and due to his experiences in the army, quickly devised an attack plan. His idea was to run across the road in small groups to the other side of the street, then make their way into the hotel. Once inside the hotel, they would determine what floor the shooter was firing from and neutralize the threat.

However, the plan was put on hold, as officers were attempting to evacuate as many people from the venue as possible. They were also dealing with people who were highly intoxicated and wanting to get in on the fight. One member of the public actively tried to take a weapon from one of the officers, then there were other people attempting to steal shotguns from police cars, to fire up at the gunman.

Once many concertgoers had been safely removed from the area, which was about five minutes into the attack, the first group of officers started to set off across the road. However, the shooter spotted them, and fired a prolonged burst of rounds in their direction. All the officers in the group immediately took cover behind police vehicles or concrete bollards and waited for the firing to stop.

As the rounds were splashing around them or punching through the trunk and roofs of the police vehicles, Sgt. Richmond forcibly push a female officer under one of the patrol cars to give her more cover, along with ensuring the rest of the officers stayed behind cover. After what must have seemed like an eternity for the officers, the shooter stopped firing upon their location. While the shooter was raining bullets down on the officers, two of them had been wounded.

With very few options open to Sgt. Richmond, gave the order to retreat behind a cinderblock wall, to afford them better cover. As the group of officers arrived at the wall, they intended to take cover behind, they discovered a group of concertgoers who were also sheltering from the gunman's unrelenting attack. Sgt. Richmond then checked his fellow officers to see if anyone had been wounded and found that one officer had been hit in the neck, and another was hit in the arm. He then sent the wounded officers to the medical tent at the rear area of the venue, to seek treatment.

Once the wounded officers had left the group, Sgt. Richmond then gave the order to cross the road again. This time, though, their efforts were successful. By the time that Sgt. Richmond's group entered the hotel, they were informed there were already several LVMPD strike teams upon the 32nd floor. With this, they began the long and daunting task of clearing the casino and surrounding areas for either anyone sheltering in place, wounded, or any other possibly shooters.

Det. S Balonek – Spotting the Shooter

LVMPD Detective (Det.) Balonek was part of the LVMPD overtime shift working at the concert, and was assigned the duty of directing vehicle and foot traffic on the southeast corner of the festival grounds, at the intersection of Mandalay Bay Rd. and Las Vegas Blvd.

Within a minute of the gunman unleashing his attack, Det. Balonek had retrieved a pair of binoculars from his patrol car, which was parked close by his location on the street directly behind the area of the main stage. While scanning the front of the hotel to see if he could spot where the shots were coming from, he saw what appeared to be plumes of smoke coming out of a window, high up on the north facing tower.

After observing the window for a few moments, Det. Balonek saw the shooter standing about three to four feet back from the window, aiming one of the rifles in the direction of the concert venue. At around 10:07 p.m., Det. Balonek attempted to use his police radio to relay the approximate location of the gunman. Due to the high volume of radio traffic, though, he was unable to broadcast his message.

Det. Balonek then changed his radio channel from the events channel to the one used by LVMPD's northeast division. He then spoke to the dispatcher and relayed the information that the shooter was firing from a window on the north tower of the Mandalay Bay hotel. Based on the evidence released by LVMPD in the aftermath of the attack, Det. Balonek was the first LVMPD officer to confirm the location of the gunman, on the night of the attack.

Hendrix, Varsin and Armed Hotel Security Managers

At around 10:06 p.m. LVMPD Officer Cordell Hendrix and his trainee Officer Elif Varsin, were sat in the casino security office over by the west valet, along with several armed hotel security officers, dealing with the trespass of two prostitutes who had been discovered in one of the casino bars. While the officers were writing up the trespass paperwork, the initial transmissions came over their police radios of a 415A (active shooter) in progress at the Route 91 concert.

After hearing the transmission, one of the hotel security officers told Hendrix that the concert was across the street from the hotel. Within a few seconds, at around 10:07 p.m., the officers and four-armed hotel security managers left the safety of the security office and headed across the casino floor, towards the main lobby.

Their intension was head to the lower level of the hotel and use a pedestrian walkway that led to the intersection of Mandalay Bay Rd. and Las Vegas Blvd., which would have positioned them directly opposite the southwest corner of the venue.

However, mid-way across the casino floor, at around 10:09 p.m., one of the armed hotel security officers in the group heard a distress call come over his hotel security radio, regarding the wounding of an unarmed security guard on the 32nd floor. Officer Hendrix was immediately made aware of the radio transmission, and he (Hendrix) asked to be taken to the 32nd floor.

The group of six armed individuals then changed direction and ran towards the guest elevator bank, which was located a short distance away, to the northeastern area of the hotel between the casino and main lobby.

By chance, as the armed group entered the guest elevator bank that serviced floors 31 through to the Foundation Room, there was an elevator with the doors already open. The occupant of that elevator was one of the hotel's Facility Managers, named Shannon Alsbury. As the armed group entered the elevator, Alsbury asked which floor the group was heading, and one of the hotel security managers quickly responded that they were heading to the 32nd floor, due to a possible active shooter.

Alsbury, who was slightly stunned by the statement then proceeds to tell the armed group that he was also heading up to the 32nd floor, as he had spoken with a security guard a short while ago, via the house phone regarding the 32nd floor 100-wing stairwell fire door being secured. Alsbury then went on to say that when he was talking with the security guard, Jesus Campos, the security guard never mentioned anything about shots being fired, let alone being wounded.

As the group ascended in the elevator up the guest towers to the 32nd floor, the conversation quickly turned to how the armed group was going to close in on the shooters room, which by this time was known to be 32-135. It was at this point, Hendrix made the unusual call, to exit the elevator on the 31st floor and use the 100-wing stairwell to try and access the 32nd floor, despite the fact he knew the fire door was secured on the 32nd floor.

Hendrix's decision to take this route has never been fully explained by himself or LVMPD, nor does it seem logical. Because he had been informed that the suite was at the very end of the floor, close by the foyer, where the fire door was located. And he was fully aware that the fire door was secured, so there would have been no feasible way access the foyer and get to 32-135, as they did not have any tools to even attempt to open the door.

When the elevator arrived at the 31st floor elevator bank, the time was around 10:11 p.m. Hendrix, Varsin, and three-armed hotel security managers exited on to the 31st floor. While Alsbury and the fourth armed hotel security manager remained on the elevator to continue onto the 32nd floor. After the armed group entered the 31st floor, there was a moment of confusion as to which hallway the 100-wing corridor was, but within a few seconds the group had spotted the right hallway and began to proceed down it.

Hendrix and one of the security managers took the lead, while Varsin and the two other security managers stayed behind them. The formation used by the armed group was that Hendrix walked up the eastern side of the hallway, while the lead security manager walked on the western side of the hallway. Hendrix was followed closely by one of the other security managers, while the remaining security manager and Varsin walked behind the lead manager on the western side of the hallway.

As the group walked slowly down the hallway, Hendrix asked the security manager to his left if he had 'racked' his weapon, which referred to having his weapon ready to fire. The security manager said something in response, then made his weapon ready to fire.

Shortly after this, a radio transmission from LVMPD Officer Beason, who was directly outside the hotel and looking up at the north tower, can be clearly heard over the police radio stating he can see shot's coming from ¾ of the way up the north tower of the hotel. Hendrix then states out loud to the group that it seems this must be relating to shots being fired into the venue.

After this radio transmission from Officer Beason, the armed group increase their pace down the 31st floor 100-wing hallway. At around 10:12 p.m. and 31 seconds, Varsins Body Worn Camera (BWC) picked up a sound, which appeared to be that of a heavy drilling or loud continuous thumping. The distant sound does not seem to detour the mixed group of LVMPD and armed hotel security managers.

As the group got closer to the end of the 31st floor 100-wing hallway, the thumping sound then become unmistakable, and the group could clearly hear the rapid rifle shots being fired by the shooter from his room above the 31st floor, into the venue. Initially the group does not respond to the sound, and they continue to push forward.

Then, Hendrix suddenly stops mid stride and pushes himself up against the east wall of the hallway and exclaimed, "holy shit, that is rapid fire." The rest of the group then stop alongside him. After a brief pause, they slowly edge up the hallway, before coming to a nervous stop at the end of the hallway outside room 31-135. The armed group are now directly under the shooters' location, and just stand there, listening to the relentless attack on the innocent concertgoers.

While the group are standing at the end of the 31st floor 100-wing hallway, a guest tries to enter the hallway, but a member of the armed group tells the guest to get back inside their room. A few seconds later, Hendrix uses his police radio to transmit "I'm inside the Mandalay Bay on the 31st floor, there is automatic rapid fire on the floor above us. We can hear it above us, one floor above us." Based on the LVMPD radio logs, Hendrix radio message occurred at 10:12 p.m. and 59 seconds.

Within a split second of Hendrix's radio message, an LVMPD dispatcher asks for confirmation that a group of officers are inside the hotel, close to the gunman's location. Before Hendrix can respond to the dispatcher, another message is then broadcast across the LVMPD radio network, stating the shooter is firing automatic fire from an elevated location and people should take cover. Once this broadcast is over, Hendrix then confirms to the dispatcher that there is a unit inside of the hotel.

For the next few moments, the mixed group of LVMPD and armed hotel security just stood around, seemingly shocked. While they are standing there, you can hear other LVMPD officers relaying messages across their radios, regarding the mass casualties inside of the event grounds. Then, for unknown reasons, the group begin to retreat, back down the hallway, towards the area they had just came from.

After covering around twenty feet, the armed group then move into the doorway alcoves on the east and west side of the 100-wing hallway. It was at this moment that Varsins BWC footage captured Hendrix looking shocked and bewildered, while taking cover in the door alcoves of 31-130 and 31-132, with one of the armed security managers alongside him. Varsin and the other security managers were across the hallway taking cover in the opposite alcoves. The armed group then held their position, for close to two minutes.

While the group are taking cover, at least two more volleys were fired by the gunman into the concert venue. Along with this, frantic messages from

LVMPD officers in the venue regarding the countless casualties can be heard.

Shortly after 10:15 pm, Hendrix then decides that it is time to move forward, once again. Cautiously, the group continued their journey and retraced their footsteps back to the end of the 31st floor 100-wing hallway, towards the door that led to the fire exit and into the stairwell.

At 10:16 p.m. and 02 seconds, the armed group of two LVMPD officers and three armed hotel security managers, finally entered the stairwell on the 31st floor. Hendrix is leading the group, and one of the hotel security managers holds open in the stairwell door, so the other members of the group can enter the area.

They all move along the enclosed landing cautiously, and head towards the stairwell that will take them to the 32nd floor 100-wing fire door. Varsin and the three security managers hold firm on the 31st floor stairwell landing, aiming their weapons up at the fire door on the 32nd floor, while Hendrix nervously edges up the flight of stairs to the 32nd floor.

At around 10:16 p.m. and 16 seconds, a faint bang can be heard on Varsins BWC, which sounded like a heavy door closing. No one in the group responded to the noise, however, it would later transpire that the sound was the gunman committing suicide in the living room area of 32-135, with a .38 snub-nose revolver. Shortly after the shooter kills himself, Varsin and the group of armed hotel security managers being their ascent up the flight of stairs to the 32nd floor fire door.

Just as Varsin nears the top step, two of the security managers pushed past her. One manager stays just in front of her, while the other pushes past Hendrix and turns left and onto the short landing on the 32nd floor, he then aimed his pistol at the fire door. Hendrix, meanwhile, stands close by the fire door, before he moves and repositions himself next to the security manager on the 32nd floor landing.

The armed group would hold their position in the stairwell until the breach team arrived at their location, at around 10:59 p.m. After the breach team cleared the gunman's room, at just after 11:21 pm, Varsin and another LVMPD officer from the stairwell were tasked with guarding the door to the shooters room, and Hendrix was assigned a duty in another area of the hotel.

Featherston and Beason – The First Officers on the 32nd Floor

On the night of the attack, both Officers Featherston and Beason were also working at the Route 91 concert on an overtime shift and were assigned the duty of directing the pedestrian and vehicle traffic at the intersection of Reno and Las Vegas Blvd., which is located some four-hundred-and-fifty feet north of the Mandalay Bay Hotel.

Like most other people that night, when the shooter fired his initial volley of single shots into the crowd, they both assumed it was someone recklessly setting off fireworks. Officer Featherston did also quickly scan the immediate area around him to see he could locate where the sounds were coming from, but he was unable to pinpoint the location.

When the gunman opened fire with his second volley, which was a prolonged burst. Featherstone began to quickly direct people who were crossing the road, to head west out of the area and to safety. Beason, who was standing in the middle of the road by this point, shouted at Featherston to come to his position. Featherstone immediately stopped directing people and closed in on his fellow officer.

After a very brief conversation, both officers decided to head up to the area of the concert to assist the LVMPD officers inside the venue, because they both had rifles, and the officers at the venue only had pistols. It was at this point that the police radio transmissions regarding the volume of casualties at the event, started to intensify. In order to get to the venue quicker, they used one of their patrol cars that was located nearby their location.

While driving at high speed towards the Mandalay Bay, they both heard countless radio transmissions from offices inside the venue, reporting mass casualties. Then, they heard Det. Balonek's transmission, regarding the shooter(s) firing from an elevated position somewhere in the hotel. Beason wasted no time in getting both he and Featherston to the area.

As they drew closer to the hotel, Beason chose to stop his police vehicle on the northeast corner, at the intersection of Mandalay Bay Rd. and Las Vegas Blvd. Within seconds of the vehicle coming to a halt, both Beason and Featherston were out of the patrol car and had set off running down a pathway, leading into the beach level of the Mandalay Bay.

While the officers were moving rapidly down the pathway, they were trying to look up and observe the front of the building to see if they were able to pinpoint where the shots were coming from. However, despite their best efforts, neither of them was able to see exactly where the shooter was located, as by this point, he had ceased firing and was in the process of changing weapons.

Unwilling to run into the hotel blind, with no clear direction of where to go, they decided that they would take cover behind a small wall, close by the entrance to the pedestrian subway to get a better look at the north tower of the hotel.

After a few tense moments, the shooter opened fire again and Beason was quick to spot the smoke coming from the shooters' rifle barrel, which was protruding from one of the windows near the upper section of the hotel. Beason pointed out the shooters' location to Featherston, then he raised his rifle to try and fire at the shooter. Sadly, Beason was unable to get a clear shot, so he lowered his weapon.

After lowering his weapon, Beason then transmitted over his police radio, "159, its coming from the 50th or 60th floor, ¾ up the Mandalay Bay tower. NORTH TOWER, OF, THE, MANDALAY BAY! It's coming out a window." Beason then turned to Featherston and ominously said, 'we gotta advance on there dude." Both officers, then set off again, towards the beach level entrance.

As the officers entered the subway leading to the hotel, they ordered people who were in the subway to get back against the wall and stay under cover. As they closed in on the end of the subway, one of the people in front of them attempted to exit the tunnel and hide around the side of the wall. Beason grabbed the person and shoved them back into the subway and told them to stay in the tunnel. The gunman then fired another relentless deadly volley into the concert venue.

Undaunted, both officers pressed on towards the beach entrance of the hotel, as shots rang out above their heads. As the officers crossed the road and were directly in front of the hotel, they were right under the shooters' location, and the sound of rifle fire was intense.

The shooter ceased firing for a moment, and both officers looked up at the building. Then another burst of fire from the shooters' location breaks the sound of silence, and Featherston says, "right there" and points out the location of the shooter. The officers make it to the lower entrance of the hotel, at just after 10:12 p.m. Several curious onlookers are standing around looking up towards the shooters room, so the officers tell them to get back inside the hotel.

As the officers entered the beach level foyer, Beason approached a member of hotel staff to ask where the security guards were. The hotel employee responded by saying that they do not know. The officers then continued towards the beach level guest elevator bank, and encountered another hotel employee, and asked them where they could find security. This employee just looked blankly at the officers and shrugged.

Beason was annoyed that they cannot find a security guard to get them to the guest levels of the hotel, as he was anxious to stop the shooter. So, as they draw closer to the lower guest elevator banks he yelled, "WHERE THE FUCK IS SECURITY! SECURITY!" Beason then turned to

Featherston and said, "fuck, we need security bro. Go back and get security."

Featherston immediately turned around, and ran back to the valet desk, where they passed by a few moments before. Once at the valet desk, he asks the hotel employee working at the counter, where are the security officers? The hotel employee responds that no one in the security office is answering the phone, but she will try again and see if she can get through.

Meanwhile, Beason continued to yell out loudly for security to try and get their attention, but no security officers were around. He then starts to walk away from the guest elevator banks and shouts, "I need to get on that floor, where that guy is shooting from." Seconds later, Featherstone and Beason meet back up by the valet desk, then start to head towards a set of escalators, which will take them to the main lobby. Both officers are now highly frustrated that they cannot get access to the floor and, due to the distance they had covered in heavy kit, exhaustion was starting to set in.

While crossing the expansive beach level lobby, the officers pass by a group of tourists who are intent on heading outside. Beason, who was highly frustrated and annoyed by this point, shouted at the group, 'hey, there is a guy out there firing an automatic weapon, you need to stay inside." A man in the group then starts to argue back, claiming that he needs to go outside. Beason looks directly at him and states, "you gotta to stay inside, because if you go out there, you could end up as a casualty." The officers then walk away from the group and head up the escalators to access the main lobby area of the hotel.

Once at the escalators, they enter the first escalator and as the steps move, they walk up the steps to the short landing at the top. As Beason and Featherston walk onto the second set of escalators, someone behind them shouts to get their attention. Featherston turns around and looks down to see who it is, and it happens to be a member of the hotel security team. Featherston calls out to Beason that security is behind them.

In unison, both officers start to turn around and walk back down the escalator, however, the security guard shouts for them to continue up the escalator, and once at the top to turn left and enter the main lobby of the hotel. The security guard quickens his pace to caught up with the officers, and within a few seconds he has passed Beason and Featherstone on the escalators, to lead the way.

Beason informs the security guard that they need to get into that room where the shooter is firing from, to which the hotel security guard responds that he will get the officers up there, but they need to follow him.

Once in the main lobby of the hotel, the security guard leads the officers across the lobby, towards an area that will get them to the service elevators. As the officers and the security guard get closer to the door that leads to the service elevator bank, the security guard stops and turns to the officers and tells them that once they come off the elevator on the 32nd floor, they need to go left and the room they are looking for is room 32-135, at the end of the 100-wing hallway.

The officers and security guard then enter the hotel service elevator bank, just off the main lobby area. As they walk through the door, one of the elevators has its doors already open with someone standing inside the elevator. Without hesitation, the hotel security guard yells out to the occupant of the elevator to hold the door, but the person inside looks at the security guard blankly and allows the doors to close. Immediately, the security guard went over and pressed the elevator call button, and frustratedly remarked, "come on, come on."

In no time at all, another hotel security guard appears from the third elevator down and says he can take the officers up. Just as the officers enter the elevator, they turn to the first security guard that got them to the service elevators and say they need access to that room. The security guard tells them his managers are already on the floor. Beason then asks again; "can we get access to that room?" To which the guard responded, "its 32-135." Beason asked the guard if that was confirmed, and the security guard said that it was.

After the service elevator doors close, they start to ascend to the 32nd floor, and they instinctively check that they have a round loaded in the chamber of their rifles. The security guard who is in the elevator with them, tells the officers he will get them halfway, then he will leave them alone with his manager. Beason asks the guard if they are going to have access to that room, and the guard responds, "apparently my managers are on scene, so as soon as you guys get there, they will let you know."

Beason then turns to look at Featherston and says, "what you wanna do? We have to make entry to that room. Or do you want to wait for two more." Featherston responds that they will have to make entry. Beason then replies, "if he is still shooting, we are going to have to." Featherston acknowledges by saying, "we're going to have to, as I don't know if anybody is even close. I think everyone else is pinned outside."

In less than two minutes, the elevator comes to a stop and the doors open, as it arrives on the 32nd floor 200-wing service elevator bank. The security guard then leads the officers out into the service elevator bank foyer and on to the 200-wing 32nd floor hallway. As the security guard opened the door, to enter the hallway, he steps into the hallway and points down the corridor towards the center of the floor and tells them to go that way. Despite being exhausted, Beason and Featherston advance down the 200-wing as fast as they can.

While moving down the hallway, Beason uses his police radio to tell LVMPD dispatch that they are now on the 32nd floor with hotel security and the shooter is in room 32-135. Based on LVMPD radio logs, this message was transmitted at 10:16 pm and 54 seconds. As the officers headed down the 200-wing corridor towards the core center of the floor, they can just make out an outline of a person in the distance at the end of the hallway, who appears to be leaning up against a wall.

The officers move as fast as they can because they are determined to get to the shooters' location and stop him from murdering more innocent concertgoers. Both Beason and Featherston are now within twenty feet of the person standing at the entrance of the 200-wing hallway and core center, when they notice that the person seems to have their left pant leg raised.

Beason draws level with the person at the entrance of the 200-wing hallway, and finds that it is Jesus Campos, the unarmed security guard wounded by the shooter during the attack. Beason then enquires why his pant leg is pulled up to his knee, to which Campos then turns his back to the officer and points out the small wound on his left calf.

Beason asks if it's a GSW (gunshot wound), to which Campos responds, "I don't know if it is a pellet or a twenty-two." Beason looks slightly confused at Campos' statement, then walks away from him. Based on Beason's BWC footage, he and Featherston arrived at the core center of the 32nd floor at 10:17 p.m. and 12 seconds. Considering the size of the hotel and the distance the officers covered on foot, they responded to the floor in rapid time.

Beason then walks over to Shannon Alsbury, whose been on the floor since at least 10:12 p.m., and speaks to him to establish if they (LVMPD) have access to the room. Alsbury then starts to tell them that the room is at the end of the hallway and goes on to state that from what he (pointing at Campos) was saying, they put a bracket on the stairwell fire doors. So, there is no access to the shooters' room from that area, so they will have to walk up the 100-wing hallway.

Alsbury also states that there are armed hotel security managers on the floor above and below the 32nd floor in the 100-wing north stairwell. He then points to the entrance of the 100-wing hallway and tells Beason if he looks down the hallway, the shooter is in the room all the way to the end with the double doors.

Both Featherston and Beason then walk over towards the entrance of the 100-wing hallway, and Beason uses the wall as cover and proceeds to look down the 100-wing to observe the shooters room. Featherstone stands close behind his fellow officers and also peers down towards the shooters room.

After taking a quick look, Beason steps back and then turns to face his right and asks what direction the shooter was firing. Campos walks over and leans against the wall next to Beason and says, "it's probably the peephole. Look out for that." Beason turns to look back down the hallway, then turns to Campos and asks if he was firing down this way, referring the hallway. Campos responds by saying he was, and that is how he got hit.

Beason looks down the hallway for a few more moments, then he tries to use his radio to contract LVMPD dispatch, but it seems the radio traffic is too heavy for him broadcast. He then steps away from the entrance of the 100-wing hallway and walks to the right of the core center. After waiting a moment, he is finally able to transmit a message to LVMPD dispatch.

He informs the dispatcher that a hotel security officer has been wounded by the shooter on the 32nd floor, after the gunman fired down the hallway. However, the injuries are not life threatening, and the security guard is being tended to by other hotel employees. The LVMPD radio logs states this transmission occurred at 10:17 p.m. and 49 seconds.

Suddenly, a Mandalay Bay armed bike patrol security officer emerges from the 100-wing hallway and enters the core center, walking right down the middle of the floor and passed Beason and Featherstone. Just as the bike officer is walking out of the 100-wing hallway, Featherston asks what number the room is, and the bike officer stops, then turns around and points back down the hallway and responds, "32-135. The double doors at the very end"

Featherston now walks forward a little bit, then leans over to look down the 100-wing, to look up the long hallway and get a visual of the doors to 32-135. As Featherston leans forward, not only is he able to see the room doors at the far end of the hallway, but also, he notices that there are armed hotel security offices just a few feet inside the hallway, seemingly securing the entrance to the 100-wing.

Beason meanwhile is trying to relay another message to LVMPD dispatch but is unbale to update anyone with more information. After a few seconds, Beason remarks, "fucking radio". Alsbury tells him he needs to step away from the elevators, because they cause issues with communications and create 'dead spots.' Beason follows the advice and walks to another part of the core center, which appears to resolve the issue.

Featherston then asks Alsbury if there is another route to the shooters' room, and the manager confirms there is, but the shooter seems to have bracketed the fire door. Featherston then seeks to determine what kind of bracket is securing the door, but no one answers his question.

The relative silence at the core center of the 32nd floor suddenly gives way to muffled sounds of screaming and shouting. Alsbury then realizes that people are trapped in the elevator, as he gave orders to his staff to shut the elevators down. He uses his hotel radio to get one of his maintenance staff to override the controls and get the guest off the elevator as fast as possible.

At 10:22 p.m., two more LVMPD officers arrive at the core center of the 32nd floor. As the officers walk from the 200-wing hallway into the core center, Beason tells them that it is now a barricade situation, as the shooter is holed up in his room. One of the newly arrived officers responds by telling Beason, they must assault the room. Beason then firmly tells the officer that there have not been any shots fired for several minutes.

The newly arrived officers then started to tell people standing around the core center that he believes there are two shooters in the room. Also, he was at the event when the shooting started. Campos then walked over to the officer and states that he was hit in the leg. The officer then asks if the gunman had been firing down the hallway, to which Campos half turns his back to the officer and points out the small hole in the center of his calf with dried blood around it.

Based on the LVMPD radio log, Beason relayed a message at 10:23 p.m. and 52 seconds stating, "Threat contained, stop vehicles coming down the Blvd. towards Mandalay Bay. We need SWAT at Mandalay Bay; shooter is on the 32nd floor in room 135."

Around two minutes after Beason used his radio, one of the officers that arrived on the floor at around 10:22 p.m., also uses his radio to transmit a message, regarding Campos being wounded. The officer stated that a security guard has been shot on the 32nd floor of the building, the time of this message was 10:25 p.m. and 56 seconds.

By 10:26 p.m. the four LVMPD officers on the 32nd floor, were starting to take up positions to cover the entrance to the 100-wing hallway, in preparation for the assault down to the shooters room.

Clearing the 32nd Floor 100-Wing

As the four officers are preparing to make their way down the 100-wing hallway, towards the shooters room at the far end, six more LVMPD officers arrive on the floor. There are now a total of ten members of the strike team.

Beason and another officer take the lead and stand on either side of the hallway and aim their rifles in the direction of the shooters room. The remaining officers form up behind them, for the charge down the fatal funnel. The third officer to arrive on the floor, seems to have taken charge of the assault team, and he starts to delegate tasks to his fellow officers.

While the officers are forming up, one of them asks hotel security for a master key to the guest doors, as they want to clear the rooms as they move down the hallway. It seems that hotel staff are reluctant to hand one to the officers, so the lead officer begins to raise his voice and demand a key from hotel staff. This tactic seems to have worked, as within a few seconds, a master key card is handed to the officer.

Suddenly, a guest from one of the rooms on the 100-wing hallway emerges and he is pulled to one side by two officers, who then try and search the guest. However, the person resists as they are a foreign tourist and do not speak English, so they are unable to understand what is going on. The officers gave up on trying to wrestle the person to the ground, so they searched him standing up. It is quickly determined that the person is just an innocent tourist, so they place him in a contained area of the floor, until he can be taken down to the lower levels of the hotel.

At 10:28 p.m. and 05 seconds, the LVMPD assault team enters the 100-wing hallway to close in on the shooters room. Beason and another officer are still at the head of the column, aiming their weapons at the shooters' room doors. Directly behind the point-men, in the middle of the column were five officers who would rotate between either searching the guest rooms or opening the doors with the master pass key. At the rear of the column were two officers that would act as rear protection, and if needed they would act as casualty evacuation.

Once inside the hallway, the first area the officers had to clear was several storage closets to the left-hand side of the corridor, and then a recessed area on the right-hand side where several vending machines were located. After clearing these areas, the officers move forward. As they advance up the hallway, they stay as close as they can to the walls to present a smaller target as possible.

Between the officers' and the shooters room at the end of the hallway, there was a total of eight room alcoves on each side of the hallway, that had two doors in each alcove, which made a total of thirty-two rooms. Then, there were two further rooms between the officers and the shooter, which accounted for a total of thirty-four rooms. At this stage, the officers were unaware that the shooter had rooms 32-134 and 32-135.

A little after 10:29 p.m., the first set of room alcoves on the 32nd floor 100-wing were reached, which was rooms 32-101 through 32-104. The point officers pushed to the far side of the alcove and partially obscured their bodies behind the alcove wall, with their weapons trained towards the shooters room.

Then the five officers in the team tasked with searching the rooms, pushed into the west side of the alcove and opened doors 32-101 and 32-103 and commenced their search. Meanwhile the two rear officers were located on either side of the hallway and looked back down the corridor to the core center.

In less than a minute, the first two rooms were cleared, and the master access key was passed across the hallway so the doors to 32-102 and 32-104 could be opened. After each of these doors were opened, the search officers then crossed from one alcove to the other and searched these rooms. During the search of the even numbered rooms, two guests were found and directed down to the core center of the floor.

While the search team were undertaking their work, the officers that stood guard in the hallway started to talk about the type of weapon the shooter was firing. Due to the high rate of fire, many of the officers wrongly believed that the shooter was using a belt fed machinegun. One of the officers remarked that if the shooter was to turn his attention to them and fire down the hallway, nearly all the officers would be killed, as the sheetrock walls offered little to no protection.

By 10:31 p.m., all four rooms in this section were cleared, and the officers then move onto the next section of rooms. However, by now, more officers have arrived on the floor and head up the hallway to help with searching the 100-wing hallway. Due to the increased number of officers and lack of space, some officers have no choice but to stand directly in the middle of the hallway.

On the next set of rooms 32-105 through 32-108, the officer's change tactics. Instead of searching two rooms on the same side of the hallway, then moving onto the next two rooms on the other side of the hallway. They now opt to search the rooms opposite one another at the same time. Rooms 32-105 and 32-106 were searched first, then rooms 32-107 and 32-108.

A total of four guests were found during this section of searches, with room 32-108 containing a family of three. The occupant of room 32-107 was highly intoxicated, which caused the officers searching the room minor issues when they evacuated the person down to the core center. To show what rooms had been cleared, the officers propped each door open.

At a little after 10:34 p.m., the strike team had searched rooms 32-101 through 32-108, which meant ¼ of the total hallway had been cleared. On the next section of rooms 32-109 through 32-112, the officers evacuated a total of 4 guests. Just like in room 32-107, a highly intoxicated guest was discovered in room 32-112. This time, though, the officers were a lot swifter in getting the drunken guest out of bed, clothed, and to the safety of the elevator bank by the core center.

Since the start of the incident at right around 10:05 pm, many of the officers in the strike team had covered over a mile, getting from their locations outside of the hotel and up to the 32nd floor, in heavy gear and braving the relentless volleys fired by the gunman. Now the officers were showing signs of exhaustion. With this, after clearing rooms 32-109 through 32-112, it was decided that the strike team would rest for a few minutes and drink some water, before moving onto the next section of the rooms.

Another issue that was causing problems for the officers was the intense level of radio traffic on the police radios, so it was hard for them to relay messages of their movements. With this, many of the officers had taken to using their own cellphones to communicate their movements and progress on the 32nd floor to LVMPD dispatch.

Just after 10:41 p.m., the strike team moved from the alcoves of rooms 32-109 through 32-112 onto the alcoves of 32-113 through 32-116. By now, the officers had settled into a grove and were able to clear the rooms quickly and efficiently. From this point on, when guests were discovered inside any of the rooms on the 100-wing hallway, officers would ask them if they heard gunshots.

Some of the guests claimed to not have heard anything, while others said they did. Considering the high rate of rifle fire into the concert venue, and the volley down the corridor, it is surprising not many of the guests heard gunshots.

In rooms 32-113 through 32-116, another four guests were found, who were swiftly evacuated down to the core center of the floor. Once at rooms 32-113 to 32-116, the officers were within one-hundred-and sixty-feet of the shooters' location.

Just as the strike team was preparing to move from rooms 32-113 to 32-116 onto the next section of rooms, a guest suddenly appeared in the hallway from a room ahead of them, which was closer to the gunman's location. The officers beckoned for the person to run towards them and keep going until they reached the core center of the floor. After the person had run past the point officers, the strike team then progressed onto the next set of room alcoves, for rooms 32-117 through 32-120.

By 10:46 p.m., the officers were now within one-hundred-and-thirty-five feet of the gunman's location and had cleared over half the rooms on the hallway. It was at this point that the officers in the strike team noticed that the air in the corridor began to become thick with smoke and dust, from where the gunman had fired so many rounds. Some of the officers also started to point out the bullet strikes on the walls in the hallway, from where the shooter had fired down the hallway, earlier in the night.

Prior to moving onto the next set of rooms on the corridor, the two-point officers observed a large object directly outside of the doors to shooters' room, which appeared to be a room service cart. One of the officers used his optical sight on his rifle to look at the object in more detail. As the officer looked through his scope, he confirmed to the officers around him that it was a room service cart.

Then for a moment, he paused, and stated that it looked like there was a black object sitting on top of the cart. Despite the officers' best efforts, he was unable to make out exactly what the object was. After surveying the object for a few moments longer, the officers in the strike team then moved onto the next set of room alcoves for rooms 32-117 through 32-120.

After searching rooms 32-117 to 32-120, the strike team decided that they would remain here, and wait for SWAT to arrive to breach the gunman's door. The officers in the strike team now formed a line between the door alcoves, to act as a base of fire, should the shooter open fire down the hallway again.

As the initial team of officers were holding firm at their location, outside rooms 32-119 and 32-120, LVMPD Sgt. William Matchko, arrived on the 32nd floor. Within seconds of arriving, Alsbury gave Sgt. Matchko an overview of the events on the floor during the attack and the progress of the officers who had cleared the rooms.

Matchko then went over and looked down the hallway and noticed several officers from the search team lying on the floor in the middle of the hallway, which was exposing their position. Matchko decided that he would go up to where the officers were located and start to organize them into better positions so that if the shooter did fire down the hallway again, very few officers would be hit.

Shortly after 11:08 p.m., two SWAT snipers arrived on the 32nd floor 100-wing hallway and took over the position of watching over the doors to the shooters room. The large crowd of LVMPD officers which had assembled around the area of rooms 32-117 through 32-120, were either directed to rooms close by the SWAT snipers or sent back down to the core center of the 32nd floor to await further orders. The two SWAT snipers would remain covering the doors to the shooter's rooms until after the breach team entered room 32-135.

LVMPD Assault Team

The six-man LVMPD Assault Team who would enter rooms 32-134 and 32-135, a little after 11:21 p.m., were not a co-ordinate strike force from LVMPD SWAT. The team was comprised of two SWAT officers, along with four other officers from different departments, who, happened to bump into each other on the 31st floor 100-wing stairwell.

LVMPD Officers Levi Hancock, Joshua Bitsko, Dave Newton, Sean O'Donnell, Matthew Donaldson, Stephen Trzpis, and Blake Walford were the six members of Assault Team. Levi Hancock would act as the overall team commander, as he was the most senior SWAT officer on the floor, with Joshua Bitsko acting as his second in command as he was the most senior officer by rank.

Initially, Hancock and O'Donnell would arrive at the hotel shortly after the attack ended and entered via the main lobby. However, once at the main elevator banks, Hancock and O'Donnell were having issues accessing the 32nd floor, as hotel security were unable to activate the elevators and were unable to contact maintenance. So, O'Donnell suggested that they should ascend to the 30th floor as that set of elevators was still operational and then use the stairwells between the 30th and 32nd floors.

Hancock and O'Donnell arrived at the core center on the 32nd floor at around 10:50 p.m. and entered the floor via the 200-wing stairwell. Once at the core center of the floor, Hancock looked down the 100-wing hallway towards the double entrance doors of room 32-135. He then questioned Alsbury and the LVMPD officers at the core center, regarding the direction the shooter had been firing. To which he was told, he had fired down the hallway, as well as, into the venue.

Hancock then asked Alsbury how easy it would be to turn off the lights in the shooters room? Alsbury told him that was not possible, because it would shut down several floors. So, there was no way to isolate just 32-135.

Having determined that the power to the rooms could not be isolated and that the gunman had also fired down the hallway, this left Hancock with two options:

One, move down the 100-wing hallway directly at the shooters room, and possibly get killed in the process, as by this point no one knew the shooter was already dead.

Two, access the 32nd floor 100-wing stairwell and as silently as he could, break open the fire door, which would place him to within six feet of the shooters room.

Based on Hancock's assessment, he felt the fire door option offered the best tactical advantage. After arriving at his conclusion, both he and O'Donnell headed down the 300-wing hallway of the 32nd floor and enter the stairwell to drop down to the 31st floor, then walk down the 300-wing hallway, then go down the 100-wing hallway and come back up the 100-wing stairwell.

Shortly after arriving on the 31st floor 300-wing stairwell, Hancock and O'Donnell bumped into Bitsko, Donaldson, Newton, and Trzpis. The six-man Assault Team was now formed, and they headed to the 100-wing stairwell on the 31st floor, to gain access to the 32nd floor fire door.

As the team moved down the 100-wing hallway, that lead to the stairwell, Bitsko reminded the other members of the group to be careful. Because there were already officers in the stairwell covering the door. Bitsko also used his police radio to inform the other LVMPD officers in the 100-wing stairwell between the 31st and 32nd floors, that they were entering the area.

Once the Assault Team entered the stairwell, they then pushed passed the crowd of LVMPD officers and armed hotel security guards, that had amassed in the stairwell. The Team then arrived at the 32nd floor fire door at a little after 10:58 p.m. With seconds of Hancock arriving at the location, he initially pulled on the door to see how much force he would need to open it. He quickly determined that he would need to use his small pry-bar in his breachers kit to pull the door open.

As he inserted the pry-bar between the door and door frame, another member of the ad hoc Assault Team, Officer Newton, pulled on the door handle to provide extra force. The screws securing the 'L' shaped bracket to the door and doorframe gave way within a few seconds, and the door popped open with little noise.

Before opening the door fully, Hancock instructed several of the officers stood around the stairwell to remove the lightbulbs from the light-fittings, as he did not want bright lights filtering into the hallway when they opened the foyer door to the hallway. As the lightbulbs were being removed, Hancock told Bitsko to slightly open the fire door, so they could peak inside the small area. But despite the best efforts of Hancock, he was unable to fully see into the foyer area.

Once the area close to the fire door was in partial darkness, Hancock fully opened the fire door, while Bitsko and the other officers covered the doorway. Once it was fully open, the officers found that the foyer was clear. Hancock and Bitsko then moved in and closed on the foyer door that led to the hallway. Two other officers followed behind them, to remove the foyer light. After the light was removed, Bitsko and the other officers backed out of the foyer.

Donaldson then moved into the small foyer, to join Hancock. Slowly, Donladson opened the foyer door. To give them both a bit more protection, Donaldson placed a ballistic shield just in front of them. At just after 11:04 p.m., The door was opened, and Hancock surveyed the area outside the shooters room. Immediately, he spotted a room service cart outside of room 32-134, and the wires running from the cart and under door into 32-134. Hancock closed the door, and turned to Bitsko, who was in the fire door entrance to the foyer, to tell him about the wires on the cart.

Bitsko then moved closer to the foyer door that led into the guest hallway, and Hancock slowly opened the foyer door, so that Bitsko could look at the cart. Bitsko took a quick look at the cart with the wires running under the door into room 32-134 and edged back from the door. He told Hancock that it appeared the wires were connected to what looked like a camera on top and bottom of the cart. Hancock, then fully opened the door and Donaldson pushed in front of Bitsko to place the shield in the open doorway.

The three members of the Assault Team, then stood in the foyer with door to the hallway wide open, to see if they could get a response from the shooter. After a few seconds, Donaldson relayed to Hancock and Bitsko that he could see bullet holes in the entrance doors to 32-135, from where the shooter had fired down the hallway, earlier in the night. The three officers then stood there for a few moments longer, before Bitsko moved between Hancock and Donaldson, so he could get a better look at the room service cart.

After a few more seconds, Bitsko then used his radio to transmit that there were three LVMPD officers at the end of the 100-wing hallway, by the fire door. The three members of the breach team then closed the door and moved back into the stairwell area. Once back in the stairwell, Hancock then instructed McDonald to request that people stay off the radio channel they were on, as they may need to relay time sensitive information to dispatch.

Just after 11:07 p.m., Hancock and the other two members of the Assault team then began to discuss the best way for them to breach the shooters room. After formulating a plan of attack, Bitsko informed one of the officers in the stairwell that they had to contact Sgt. Matchko, who was still in the 100-wing hallway of the 32nd floor. Bitsko wanted to relay a message to him that Hancock and himself were going to enter the hallway right by the shooters' door to get a better look, and they did not want the officers at the other end of the hallway firing on them.

It seems that the officers in the stairwell were having issues with their radios and cell phones, which prevented them from communicating with the other officers in the 100-wing hallway. So, Hancock used his police radio at just after 11:09 p.m. to tell dispatch that they needed to contact the officers in the hallway and get them acknowledge that they knew officers were going to peek out into the hallway from the foyer, to get a better look at the shooters' door. Within seconds, an officer in the hallway responded to Hancock's message, and affirmed they understood not to fire as it was LVMPD officers in the area of the foyer and not the shooter.

At 11:09 p.m. and 11 seconds, Hancock slowly emerged from the foyer door and edged into the 100-wing hallway, and slowly peered around the doorway to look at the shooters' door. After looking at the door for a few seconds, Hancock stepped back into the foyer and told his fellow officers that he was going to use a breaching charge to blow the door open. Hancock then left the foyer area and went back into the stairwell to prepare the charge. Bitsko and McDonald stayed at the foyer door and took a closer look at the room service cart.

After looking at the room service cart for a few moments, both Bitsko and Donaldson agreed that before the breach occurred, the camera on the cart would have to be obscured. The only option they could see to obscure the camera, was that as Hancock placed the charge on the doors to 32-135, someone would have to run across the hallway and cover the camera. Bitsko agreed that he would run across the hallway and cover the camera, and Donaldson would remain at the foyer door covering Hancock.

By 11:15 p.m., Hancock had prepared the breaching charge and informed the other members of the Assault Team of the plan to storm the shooters' room. A few seconds after 11:16 p.m., Hancock exited the foyer door and entered the 100-wing hallway and slowly walked the six feet towards the door of 32-135. He then stuck the breaching charge on the shooters' door, while Bitsko covered the door to 32-134 and Donaldson covered the door to 32-135.

Within 30 seconds, Hancock had set the charge and started to move back towards the foyer, while sticking the detonation cord to the floor as he went. Once he was out of the hallway, Bitsko and Donaldson tactically moved back into the foyer and closed the door.

At a little after 11:18 p.m., the charge was finally set and Hancock arranged the six-man Team into formation, ready for the assault on room 32-135. At 11:19 p.m. and 27 seconds, Hancock radioed LVMPD dispatch to inform them that the explosive breach was ready, and they needed to tell the officers in the 100-wing hallway to take cover. He also told the dispatcher to inform the officers in the hallway not to rush the room, as once the charge was detonated, they were going to wait to see if the shooter responded to the door being blown open.

Once Hancock had it confirmed that the officers in the 100-wing hallway were in cover, he stated "breach, breach, breach", then blew the door to 32-135 open with the breaching charge, at 11:19 p.m. and 55 seconds. Within a few moments of the charge exploding, the fire alarm activated, and the Assault Team slowly moved into position. While they waited at the foyer door, Hancock constantly watched the shooters' room to see if there was any movement.

At exactly 11:21 p.m. and 10 seconds, Hancock stepped closer to the shooters' room, and a few seconds later, Bitsko crossed the hallway to the room service cart and flipped over the plate that the camera was sitting on.

As Hancock waited right outside of the shooters' door, the remaining members of the team rushed forward to join him. At 11:21 p.m. and 59 seconds the LVMPD officers finally entered the shooters' room for the first time. Hancock and one other officer immediately turned left once inside the room, and walked down a small hallway at the back of the wet bar and then entered the main living area. Two other members of the breach team headed straight into the room and into the main living area. Bitsko and Newton remained in the hallway and covered the door to 32-134.

After the main search team entered 32-135, they found the shooter lying on the floor of the main living area of the suite, dead from a self-inflicted small caliber gunshot wound to the roof of the mouth. After the first five officers cleared the main area, Bitsko entered the room at 11:22 p.m. and 24 seconds, and headed to clear the bedroom. Within one minute and nineteen seconds of the breach team entering 32-135, the main living area and bedroom were cleared.

The officers then found that the adjoining door to 32-134 was locked, so Hancock conducted a second explosive breach.

While Hancock prepared the second charge, the remaining members of the breach team were either taking a closer look at several wires that were on the floor of the room that disappeared into a pile of bags, or they were confirming over the police radio that the room had been cleared.

Shortly after 11:25 p.m. and 43 seconds Hancock detonated the second charge of the night and blew open the adjoining door between 32-134 and 32-135. Just as Hancock detonated the charge, LVMPD officer O'Donnell accidentally discharged his weapon into the wall of 32-135.

For a few seconds after the breach, there was confusion as to who fired the shots, which caused officers from the hallway to run towards 32-135. However, it was quickly confirmed that the shots fired were from one of the LVMPD officers, by mistake. At 11:28 p.m., rooms 32-134 and 32-135 were declared safe and two officers were placed on the doors to secure the area.

Shortly after the rooms had been cleared, the remaining rooms on the 32nd floor 100-wing hallway were evacuated. Due to the high volume of calls for other potential active shooters on the Las Vegas Strip that night, the officers that formed the breach team were quickly reassigned to other calls.

Chapter Four:
The Tale of Two Police Reports

"The police are the public and the public are the police; the police being only members of the public who are paid to give full time attention to duties which are incumbent on every citizen in the interests of community welfare and existence."

-Sir Robert Peel, Father of Modern Policing, 1829.

The LVMPD investigation into the Las Vegas Mass Shooting, lasted around three months. During that time, some 2,000 leads were investigated, 22,000 hours of video and 252,000 images were viewed and analyzed, over 3,000 witness statements were collected, and some 500 sightings of the gunman were reviewed.

On top of this, the LVMPD detectives investigating the case encountered countless internal and external roadblocks, jurisdictional disagreements, along with contending with untold levels of misdirection from various agencies and organizations. All the while, still trying to do the best job they could to get answers for the victims of the deadliest mass shooting in modern American history.

Then, due to what many saw as missteps on the part of the detectives, it was claimed that they were incompetent and not fit for the task. But again, despite this, the core group of LVMPD investigators pressed on with their duty, with unwavering commitment and dedication to the task before them.

Now, for the first time, the lid can be lifted on the investigation to expose what really befell the LVMPD detectives on their quest to find answers. And how it was that the two case reports released by LVMPD in the months that followed the attack, were really produced.

Investigation

After the Assault Team found the suspect dead on the floor in the main living area in 32-135 and cleared room 32-134, the focus of LVMPD then shifted from a defensive posture, to investigating the who and why of the incident.

One of the first steps in the investigative process was determining the name of the shooter, because by this point, they already knew that Stephen Paddock was the registered occupant. However, they were not aware if he was a victim of the attack, because someone could have forced entry into his room and killed him; and then fired into the venue. Or if in fact he was the shooter. So, up until they could positively identify the shooter, Paddock was viewed more as a possible victim rather than a suspect.

The duty to discover if Paddock was the gunman or not, was assigned to name of the lone gunman Sgt. Matchko, who had responded to the 32nd floor of the hotel, during the attack. At just after 11:35 p.m., Matchko entered 32-135, and set about trying to find anything that may lead him to confirm the shooters name.

By 11:40 p.m., just over ten minutes after the Assault Team had officially called an end the incident. Sgt. Matchko used Paddock's Nevada State driving license to positively confirm he was the person responsible for the attack. It was also determined that no one had left 32-134 or 32-135 since around 10:05 p.m., which was confirmed by Campos, as he was on the floor since around that time. Although LVMPD were able to quickly confirm who the shooter was, an issue soon arose.

Amongst the trove of documents found in 32-135, which is what led to such a fast identification, there was an Mlife players card belonging to a Marilou Danley. Then, when the hotel checked their records, they found that 32-134 was listed under Danley's name. The hotel also discovered that Danley's Mlife card had been used in the hotel on the morning of October 1. Furthermore, the hotel also claimed there was a third person on the booking for 32-135, who was not Danley or the gunman.

As neither Danley or the third person could be found, LVMPD asked the hotel to check the door records for both 32-134 and 32-135, so they could see when the doors to the room were locked. It was confirmed that the doors were locked for the final times between 9:36 p.m. to 9:47 p.m. This mean that if Danley and third person had assisted the gunman to prepare the rooms for the attack, they left would have left the area by no later than 9:47 p.m.

LVMPD then checked the vehicle registration database and discovered that the gunman owned two vehicles. The Chrysler Pacifica parked in the hotel valet, and a 2017 Hyundai Tucson that was missing. There was now a distinct possibility that there may be a second or even third attack coming. Or the possible co-conspirators had left the area altogether and could be anywhere by now.

To ensure that they were nowhere in the hotel or casino, photos of Danley and the third person were quickly circulated around LVMPD officers in the complex, to start checking people to see if either of the missing suspects could be found, but they were not located.

There was an issue, though, as LVMPD were prevented from searching the hotel rooms for any vital clues, which may have helped locate the two missing suspects. Because under United States law, prior to any evidence gathering, law enforcement must obtain search warrants to obtain evidence from any locations associated with a suspect or the incident.

Shortly after 11:50 p.m., senior commanders in LVMPD assigned the investigation to the Homicide Section (HS). To assist the Homicide Section with their investigation, several other departments within LVMPD were tasked with helping the HS. One of the many departments was the Homeland Security Section (HSS).

From the moment HSS were assigned to help, they hit the ground running. Firstly, they submitted a mass of warrants to search the areas in the hotel associated with the incident, along with the warrants for the festival grounds and the properties owned by the gunman.

HSS also traced several family members of the shooter, and called the gunman's mother Irene Hudson, his younger brother Eric Paddock, and one of the gunman's ex-wives. Along with chasing up any other leads that were time critical. Such as trying to trace Danley and the third person.

There were two breakthroughs, which occurred around 12:30 a.m., on the morning of October 2. The first involved Danley, as a member of the HSS team was able to find a Facebook profile for her, however, it appeared that as they were viewing the profile, she changed the settings to private. However, there were still no clues to where she was.

The second breakthrough involved the third person, as it was discovered that they were at their home in another state. LVMPD contacted the local police department and asked them to go and interview the possible suspect. It was found that this person was the occupant of 32-135 prior to the gunman. Also, they did not have any connection with Danley or the shooter. This excluded them from the investigation.

With this, LVMPD then spoke to the hotel again, to see what they had to say, because it did not make sense as to how the third person and Danley were connected to the gunman's booking. It transpired that when the room records for 32-135 were reviewed, an overzealous staff member somehow included the name of the guest who stayed in 32-135, prior to the gunman.

Then the reservation for 32-134 was checked, again, and it was found that Danley did not check into the room in person. It appeared that the gunman paid for the room, and simply used Danley's Mlife players card to reserve the room.

This was unusual, though, as normally anyone who checks into a room at a hotel in Las Vegas, must show a valid form of ID at the time of check in. Not only is this state law, but also, it is a strict policy enforced by MGMRI. So, how the gunman was able to use just a player's card, it is unknown. It was also odd that the check in agent never questioned as to why it was a male checking into the room, but it was listed under a female's name.

Yet, this would not be the only time that MGMRI caused issues for investigators. Because over the course of the entire investigation, there would be countless occasions where MGMRI were seemingly misleading detectives or were seen to try and control the narrative surrounding the events that occurred inside the hotel around the time of the attack.

In one sense, this new breakthrough, was a sigh of relief for investigators, as now they could eliminate one person form their investigation. Also, Danley was downgraded from a possible suspect to a person of interest. But it still did not answer where she was, as she had still not been located.

At around 12.20 a.m., on the morning of October 2, the first of the search warrants was granted, which allowed the Homicide Detectives (HD) along with Crime Scene Investigators (CSI) to search 32-134 and 32-135 along with the 100-wing 32nd floor. By 12:35 a.m., both the HD's and CSI officers, commenced their search for clues of the 32nd floor 100-wing. The hallway and the rooms were both searched simultaneously, to speed up the evidence gathering process.

As expected, the hallway yielded very little information. Other than the location of where the rounds impacted when the shooter fired down the hallway and that blood drops outside of 32-122, 32-124, and 32-135 came from Campos' wound to his left calf. Other than this information, there was nothing of substance seemingly gained from the hallway.

An issue also arose though, with the hallway evidence, in relation to the room service cart. Because when the CSI officer photographed the camera under the dinner plate, on the top of the cart. They realized that the camera lens was obscured, by the rim of the plate, so they push the plate backwards, to make the lens was visible.

However, they noticed that the camera was upside down, which meant the image would have been upside down. Also, because the camera was secured to the plate with packing tape, it was hard to keep the lens visible, as the plate was hard to balance.

To remedy this, they cut away the packing tape securing the webcam to the plate and turned the camera the right way, then they placed the plate back on top of the camera without obscuring the lens. Then the CIS officer retook the photo, which depicted the plate on top of the camera. However, a few days later, it emerged that Sgt. Bitsko flipped the plate on top of the camera, just as the assault team entered 32-135. Before that, the camera was sat on top of the plate, fully visible.

The evidence gathering from the room, proved to be a little more fruitful. Because LVMPD officers found evidence that suggested how the gunman truly planned to unleash his attack. Such as, he never intended to smash the windows in 32-134 or 32-135, he seems to have preferred to cut the glass to create firing holes. This was confirmed by the glass cutter in the nightstand and window suction cups in the bathroom.

There were also some odd items found in the room, which made no sense, such as the fake flowers, vase, and Styrofoam ball. And the fact that the gunman only secured one bracket to the door, when he had another fifteen in the room. These items were out of place, as it was seen that the gunman took exactly what he needed to the room. So, why take these extra items, which seemed to have served no purpose.

One thing that did shock investigators, though, was the number of weapons in the room. Because excluding the .38 snub nosed revolver, the gunman took twenty-three rifles into the room, and of these, he fired fourteen of them. They were also shocked at the volume of ammunition in the room because they found 1,057 empty shell casings and over 5,000 rounds of unfired ammunition. This information sent chills down the spine of many of the detectives, as they were starting to understand how deadly the attack could have been.

At around 1:50 a.m., the search and cataloging of evidence on the 32nd floor 100-wing, was abruptly stopped. The reason for this was because one of the CSI officers found four bullet holes in room 32-135, which was not consistent with the shooter firing them. One round passed through an arm of a chair, two rounds went into a TV cabinet, and one round went through the wall of 32-135 and into 32-134.

When LVMPD commanders were informed of this information, the Force Investigation Team (FIT) were brought in, to determine who fired the shots. In less than an hour, the FIT team found that the shots came from SWAT officer O'Donnell who had accidently fired his weapon, just as the adjoining door to 32-134 was blown open. Another issue also came to the forefront, at around this time.

There had been talk amongst several LVMPD officers, that one of their own did not adequately respond to the incident. It seemed that this officer was in the hotel at the time of the shots being fired and responded to the wrong floor, even though he knew exactly where the shooter was located. The name that came up the most was Cordell Hendrix.

At around 2:30 a.m., on October 2, 2017, senior commanders in LVMPD made the decision to remove the HS from gathering any more evidence inside of the hotel, due to the incidents involving the two officers. With this, they passed this portion of the investigation to the FIT team, as they were the department who normally handled investigations involving officer negligence.

Alongside the evidence recovery efforts at the Mandalay Bay hotel and the concert venue, by around 1:00 a.m. on the morning of October 2, countless LVMPD officers were sent to the local hospitals to start interviewing the thousands of victims from the event. One officer stated in their report that while at Valley Hospital, they estimated that there were some 1,500 victims at that hospital alone.

Due to the media interest in the event, several reporters had tried to enter the festival grounds at around 2:00 a.m., on the morning of October 2. To prevent this, several officers were ordered to close off Giles Street, to preserve the scene and prevent journalists photographing the deceased victims in and around the venue.

At a little after 3:15 a.m., another search warrant had been granted, which allowed LVMPD to search the gunman's vehicle. The vehicle was a 2017 blue Chrysler Pacifica registered in Nevada with plate number 79D401, which was in space 317 on the second floor of the hotel's east valet parking. The search of the vehicle started at around 3:25 a.m.

Prior to the vehicle being searched, an explosives detection dog was walked around the outside of the vehicle, to ensure the shooter had not wired a bomb to the car. When the dog did not give any indications that the gunman had boobytrapped the outside of the vehicle, LVMPD officers then went and looked inside the Pacifica to see if they could spot any possible IED's.

As the officers peered inside the rear of the vehicle, they noted that there was at least one small rolling suitcase visible, along with a case of Tannerite and several bags. Due to this, the drives side rear window was smashed, and the explosive detection dog was put inside the vehicle to see if there were any IED's inside the vehicle.

Within five minutes, the dog indicated that there was evidence of explosive substances, but no actual device. The officers then used a key they obtained from the valet station to open the side sliding door, on the driver's side of the vehicle. As one officer slid the door open, another kept a close eye to see if they could spot any wires that may trigger a device. However, nothing was seen.

When the car was searched, it was found that the small rolling suitcase contained a mixture of pre-loaded AR10 and AR15 magazines, which the shooter had wrapped in towels to stop them from moving around and making noise.

A total of fifty pounds of Tannerite was found in either one- or two-pound containers, and twenty pounds of various chemicals were found, which were able to be mixed together to make a bomb. The search of the car lasted around an hour before it was towed away to an LVMPD vehicle compound.

An interesting development occurred in the case at around 3:30 a.m., as the HSS had found out that by this time, Danley had deleted her Facebook account. Investigators found this strange, because by this point, the gunman's name had not been released officially. Neither was Danley's name anywhere in the public domain. So, LVMPD were curious as to why she would take this step how she would be aware that she was a person of interest.

By 3:45 a.m., the warrant to search the festival grounds for any evidence relating to the incident had been granted. As the concert venue covered some fifteen acres, any officers that were not assigned to vital duties were tasked with assisting the search efforts. The Homicide Section was given overall control of overseeing the search of the venue.

The first step in the search of the venue was for CSI officers to record the location of the twenty deceased victims, who were laying either close by the patch of grass or on the grass area, directly in front of the main stage. Eighteen deceased victims were found on the west side of the grass, while the remaining two victims were on the east side of the stage.

There were also four deceased victims found on the sidewalk on the east side of the venue, on Giles Street, which was one of many casualty collection points. Then there were two deceased victims located on in the Catholic Church carpark. Three final victims were found on East Reno Ave. at the Desert Rose Resort in the courtyard, which was also a casualty collection area.

Some months after the incident, it emerged that one of the victims that was listed as being found in the Desert Rose Resort courtyard, Melissa Ramirez, was moved to that spot by LVMPD officers searching the area around the venue, an hour or so after the attack. Initially, Melissa's body was discovered in a carpark in a small industrial complex at the south end of Haven St., which was very close to the venue.

The first press conference held by the then head of LVMPD, Sheriff Joe Lombardo occurred at around 2:45 a.m., on the morning of October 2, 2017. During this first media briefing, Lombardo named Danley as a person of interest who they wished to trace.

Shortly after 4:30 a.m., it came to the attention of HSS that in the days leading up to the gunman's stay at the Mandalay Bay, he had also rented several rooms at the Ogden Condominiums in Las Vegas. Several detectives from the Downtown Patrol Division and two LVMPD civilian employees who were computer forensic staff, were sent to the Ogden to search the rooms and recover any security footage from the hotel that may be helpful to the investigation.

The officers and civilian employees arrived at the Ogden a little after 5:10 a.m., and they were able to determine that the shooter had rented apartments 1220, 1703 and 2315. It was found that the bookings for the three units at the complex coincided with another concert, Life is Beautiful, and all the apartments rented by the gunman overlooked the event.

Due to the type of camera system employed at the Ogden, the computer forensic officers realized that they would have to remove the DVR system to download any footage they may need. With this, arrangements were made with the security company for replacement DVR's to be delivered to the Ogden, later in the day on October 2.

While the computer forensic officers waited for the security company to deliver the replacement DVR unit, they were ordered to view the footage in the Ogden security office and make notes of the sections they would need to download.

By 5:30 a.m., it was confirmed by LVMPD that Danley may have been located, but they were waiting for clarification on this matter. Despite this, she was still being considered a person of interest. It transpired that an attorney representing Danley, called the FBI field office and told them she was in Manila. However, he exact location was not confirmed, until the FBI could verify the information.

At around 6:30 a.m., LVMPD commanders were handed two notices from the FBI. The first notice informed the senior commanders that the FBI were taking over evidence collection at the Mandalay Bay hotel, the gunman's vehicle, and the houses owned by the gunman in Mesquite and Reno. In addition, both LVMPD and a Henderson Police Department who were a neighboring police force assisting LVMPD, were ordered by a judge to hand over to the FBI any evidence they had collected to that point.

In effect, the FBI were taking over the investigation with regards to the physical and digital evidence gathering and analysis, and there was not one thing LVMPD could do to stop it. However, the FIT team were allowed to observe the evidence recovery efforts at the hotel and Mesquite residence, but were not allowed to touch anything, as they were only there as observers.

Just after 7:00 a.m., the warrant to search the gunman's home in Mesquite was finally granted. Once the warrant was issued, LVMPD and the FBI liaised with the Mesquite Police Department, to arrange the search of the property at 1372 Babbling Brook Court.

Although no IED's had been found up to this point, law enforcement decided that they would require bomb disposal on scene to search the house in Mesquite for any possible devices before the main search of the property was conducted. This step led to a delay in the searching the property, which did not occur until after 8:00 a.m. on the morning of October 2.

To assist with the search, the LVMPD computer forensic officers at the Ogden were ordered to leave the complex and head to the shooters' property in Mesquite, to assist with any digital evidence recovery. However, shortly after leaving Las Vegas and heading towards Mesquite, the LVMPD computer forensic officers were told to turn around and head back to LVMPD Headquarters, as the FBI had stepped in and stated they would secure any digital evidence found at the house on Babbling Brook Court.

Just after 8:00 a.m., on the morning of October 2, the search of the Babbling Brook Court property, finally got underway. Inside the residence seven shotguns, five pistols, six rifles, and more exploding targets were found. Along with this, there were also hundreds of rounds of ammunition found for the rifles, and more Tannerite. Around fourteen removable hard drives and thumb drives were also found at the property. All the evidence discovered at the house was secured by the FBI.

At around 8:30 a.m., the Transportation Security Administration (TSA), to confirm to the FBI when Danley had departed the United States and when was she scheduled to return. Based on the TSA database, she took a direct flight from Las Vegas to Manila, on September 14, 2017. In addition, she had a return flight scheduled for October 3, 2017, landing at Los Angeles airport, which had been booked at the same time as her outbound flight from the U.S. The person that paid for the ticket, was Stephen Paddock.

The next development was the search of the gunman's second property in Nevada, located at 1735 Del Webb Parkway in Reno. Due to the distance between Las Vegas and Reno, the FBI took over liaising with the Reno

Police Department and their satellite office in reno, to exercise the search warrant at the property.

While the FBI were searching the property in Reno, they found two shotguns, five pistols, and even more rifle magazines and ammunition. There were also several more external hard drives and thumb drives discovered, which were all retained by the FBI for examination. More crucially, the missing Hyundai Tucson was found at the Reno address.

One thing that struck law enforcement during the searches of the two personal residences of the shooter was the lack of furniture at both the Babbling Brook and Del Webb houses. Other than a few items of furniture, there really was not much in them. It appeared that they were more comparable to temporary accommodation, more than anything else.

At around 10:10 a.m., on October 2, the FBI took over the search of the concert venue. This was because the FBI claimed that due to the size of the venue and the limited resources of LVMPD, they were struggling to cope. So, the FBI called in their specialist Evidence Recovery Teams to take over the collection of evidence from the concert grounds.

At around the time that the FBI assumed control of the venue, an unusual step was taken by senior commanders in LVMPD. For reasons unknown, they removed the Homicide Section from the investigation and handed it over to the FIT team. Now, LVMPD's internal investigators who usually worked alongside other investigative departments, and investigated officer negligence, were handed the biggest case LVMPD history, with no explanation as to why.

The trouble was, while the FIT team were exceptionally good at their job as detectives, they were not accustomed to dealing with the public. So, when they interviewed key witnesses, they fell short on asking hard hitting questions, and really did not push anyone. Then there was the fact, the FIT was accustomed to most of the evidence they use in their investigations, had already been collected for them. Now, though, they had to collect their own evidence. In effect, it appeared senior commanders in LVMPD handicap the investigation.

On the morning of October 2, at around 11:00 a.m. officers from LVMPD interviewed the owner of the units that the gunman rented in the Ogden. During this interview, the owner stated that when they went to check on the rooms after the gunman checked out, they had never seen them so clean. However, the shooter never left anything within the rooms, and it did not appear that the beds had been slept in.

Shortly after 11:15 a.m., several members of the Bureau of Alcohol, Tabacco, Firearms, and Explosives (ATF) arrived at the Mandalay Bay hotel to examine the weapons and ammunition, used by the gunman during the attack. However, when the ATF agents arrived at 32-135, they were informed by the FBI that as evidence was still being collected and cataloged, they were not to physically touch anything in the room. This prevented the ATF officers making any conclusive findings about the weapons and ammunition used in the attack.

At around 11:30 a.m., LVMPD put a requested into MGMRI to get access to the security camera footage relating to the gunman's movements around the hotel, in the days leading to the attack. They were informed that this was not possible, because the internal hotel investigators were still reviewing the footage and would be released to law enforcement once they were finished.

It later was claimed that when hotel security input the gunman's name into their guest tracking system, which was integrated into their security cameras, and used along with facial recognition. They obtained little to no hits, and any footage of the gunman that was retrieved, did not appear cover the time of his stay in the days before the attack. It covered the period of when the gunman stayed with Danley, in early September 2017.

When MGMRI initially received these results, though, they believed that this proved Danley or another female was with the shooter, in the days before the incident. Because there were countless times he was seen on camera with a large number of bags, and a female in tow. However, the date and time did not match, which made the operators believe that their internal systems were malfunctioning.

MGMRI went back and told law enforcement about their discovery, and the fact that their systems seemed to be a month behind. At this stage, though, LVMPD nor the wider world was aware that the FBI knew exactly where Danley was, as they were still verifying her flight information before they told LVMPD of the development.

A short while later, at around noon, the FBI officially informed LVMPD that they had now located Danley, and she was in the Philippines and had been since September 14, 2017. Once this fact was known to LVMPD, they then went back and told the hotel to check again, as it could not possibly have been Danley, because she had been out of the United States, for at least two weeks.

By this point though, several hotel security staff had told their work colleagues about the fact the gunman was seen with an oriental looking female in the days leading up to the attack. This had an adverse effect on the investigation, as various staff members made false claims about seeing the gunman.

Once LVMPD spoke to MGMRI, the system was rechecked, but again there was very little footage of the gunman in the days before the attack. However, a hotel employee had an idea. They input the gunman's Mlife players card number, to see what results that would return. This time, countless sections of footage was found of the shooter.

Now, a more accurate picture of the gunman's movements could be drawn up. However, when the footage was downloaded from the hotel camera system, it was not given directly to LVMPD. Instead, it was handed to the FBI, on or around October 5, 2017.

At around 1:00 p.m. on October 2, an LVMPD digital forensic officer went to the Ogden to recover the DVR system from the hotel, as the replacement system had been delivered. After arriving at the complex, they were informed by the Ogen security that the FBI had already retrieved the DVR system, earlier in the day.

After leaving the Ogden, the digital forensic officer went back to their office and wrote a statement highlighting the fact that the FBI had taken the DVR, without informing LVMPD. From reading the document, the level of frustration felt by the civilian employee, is evident.

From around 1:25 p.m., several FIT detectives started to pour over the countless hours of the BWC footage captured by LVMPD officers who responded to the incident. The primary focus was on determining when the shooter opened fire and when he ceased his attack. But several sections of footage from after the incident, also proved fruitful for detectives.

One such piece of footage, came from a BWC worn by an officer who was sent to monitor the hotel security cameras, in the aftermath of the attack. The video captured a conversation between the officer and a hotel security employee, which suggested that Campos was wounded at around 9:59 p.m. The officer then enquired further about this fact, and the hotel security employee looked at the hotel security log from the night of October 1, and confirmed that Campos contacted them at 9:59 p.m., saying he had been wounded.

The FIT team now had their first solid lead regarding Campos' wounding, however, it conflicted with the first statement given by Sheriff Joe Lombardo in the early hours of October 2. As Lombardo placed Campos' wounding at around 10:15 p.m., which was towards the end of the attack. Although now, there seemed to be evidence that suggested Campos was wounded six minutes before the attack even commenced.

After reviewing this footage, the FIT team detectives reviewed the footage from Varsins BWC, as they knew she had captured the moment that the armed group of LVMPD and hotel security managers were made aware of

Campos' wounding. However, this footage showed that Campos did not raise the alarm until around 10:10 p.m., which baffled the detectives. Irrespective, though, they now had two critical timeframes.

By this stage of the investigation, it appeared that LVMPD were solely tasked with establishing the timelines regarding the attack and interviewing witnesses. While the FBI took over the task of collecting and recovering the physical and digital evidence relating to the incident.

Another interesting development emerged in the case, during the early hours of the morning on October 2, when the terrorist group known as the Islamic State of Iraq and Syria (ISIS), claimed responsibility for the attack. According to the statement released by ISIS's quasi-official news agency Amaq, the gunman was a soldier of the Islamic State who had recently converted to Islam, some months prior to the attack.

Once this statement came to the attention of both LVMPD and the FBI, both of their counter-terrorist sections sprang into action, to check the validity of ISIS's claims. However, law enforcement were skeptical of the claims, because during the early stages of the investigation neither of them had found any evidence to back-up what ISIS was saying.

Around four hours after the claims were made by ISIS, it was conclusively proven that the gunman did not have any known association with ISIS, any other terrorist faction, or extreme political cause. To a point, around eight intelligence agencies in the United States, Europe, and the Middel East had confirmed that the suspect was not on any watch lists regarding any terrorist organization or extreme political group.

Furthermore, during the in-depth searches of the properties owned by the shooter, the hotel rooms, and his vehicle. There was no paraphernalia or digital evidence directly linking the gunman with ISIS. In fact, family members of the gunman had already confirmed that he was never known to be politically minded or showed any signs of being interested in religion.

Once it was conclusively proven that the gunman had no connection to ISIS or any other terrorist organization, LVMPD released a statement on the afternoon of October 2, 2017, that the claims by ISIS proved to be unfounded and false. But despite this, for several more days, ISIS still tried to claim that the gunman was a soldier of Islam and launched the attack in the name of ISIS.

By the late evening of October 2, 2017, law enforcement had amassed over 8,000 witness statements from people inside the venue, guests from inside the hotel, or people that were close by the venue at the time of the attack. Along with this, they had collected and cataloged over 6,000 items of physical evidence, mainly from rooms 32-134 and 32-135. And some 3,000 digital artifacts, mainly from the four laptops owned by the shooter that were found in either 32-134 or 32-135, along with photos and videos from various victims.

On October 3, the FIT team spent much of their time reviewing the mass of witness statements collected from people who went to local hospitals. Meanwhile, the FBI team, which was led by Senior Agent in Charge (SAC) Aaron Rouse from the FBI Las Vegas field office, was spent cataloging the last few items of physical evidence in rooms 32-134 and 32-135.

However, the evidence collection from the venue was still in its early stages, due to the mass of bullet impacts that had to be logged, along with personal property scattered around the venue from concertgoers. It would take nearly twelve days to fully process both scenes.

Also, the ATF were still being prevented from physically examining the weapons and ammunition used by the gunman in the attack. But they were able to determine that all the weapons owned by the shooter were obtained legally. In addition, they were also able to confirm that over ninety percent of the ammunition used in the attack was also legally obtained.

The only illegal firearms related items that were found to have been obtained by the gunman were some 720 tracer rounds found in 32-134 and manufactured by Haig. The ATF were quickly able to trace Haig, as the Amazon box containing the rounds, still had an address label on under Haig's name. Just over three years after the attack, Douglas Haig, was sentenced to thirteen months in federal prison for the illegal production of ammunition.

By mid-afternoon on October 3, law enforcement was able to confirm that the gunman acted alone while planning, preparing, and undertaking his attack. However, there was still a question mark over how much Marilou Danley really knew about the gunman's plans. The answers to those questions were soon to be forthcoming, as she landed at Los Angeles airport on the evening of October 3, and she was set to be interviewed on the morning of October 4.

In preparation for Danley's return to the United States and questioning by law enforcement, two detectives from the FIT team flew to LA to interview Danley, along with the FBI at the FBI field office in the city.

By this stage of the investigation most of the gunman's family members had been interviewed at length. If LVMPD spoke to them, this was usually done over the phone, whereas the FBI sent agents from the closest field office to conduct interviewers. However, due to how private the shooter was in the latter stages of his life, the information obtained from the family members was of little use. So, investigators hoped that Danley would be able to provide a better insight to the gunman, and his day-to-day life.

Overall, though, according to the family members spoken to, the gunman was non-political, was not known to be violent, nor did he seem to have an interest in religion. But there was one consistent theme that did emerge and was stated by some of the gunman's close family. Whatever drove the shooter to commit such a heinous and sickening act, was something substantial. Also, he would have spent months methodically planning the mass shooting.

October 4, 2017, was a milestone in terms of the information gained during the investigation. Because not only would law enforcement have the chance to interview Danley, but also, they would interview the two hotel employees who were shot at by the gunman, on the 32nd floor.

Danley was the first interview to occur on that day, which took place at the FBI field office in L.A. Present in the interview were several FBI agents, two LVMPD detectives from the FIT team, Danley, her attorney, and Danley's daughter. Overall, it was claimed that the interview with Danley, produced nothing of substance with respect to a motive. However, she was able to give some insights that law enforcement was not aware of, such as the true state of his health and some strange events she witnessed.

According to Danley, the gunman seemed to be encountering issues with his memory, as it appeared he was becoming more forgetful. She also stated that he was starting to suffer from frequent nightmares, and he was becoming more easily exhausted. Danley also claimed that the gunman was still able to have sexual intercourse, but due to how fatigued he would become afterwards, their sex life was virtually non-existent.

Investigators also asked Danley about the wire transfers from the gunman to her account in the Philippines, between September 16 to 28, totaling $150,000.00. She claimed that initially she believed the gunman was trying to break-up with her, but he assured her the money was so she could buy her family a house in Manila. So, after he reassured her, she never thought nothing more of it.

Towards the end of the interview, she did give some reveling information, regarding the planning of the attack. Because not only did she admit to helping the gunman load countless magazines and place them into either suitcases or duffle bags. She also stated that while staying with the gunman in early September 2017 at the Mandalay Bay in room 60-325, she observed him looking out of the windows in the direction of the concert venue.

After Danley's first interview on October 4, she was questioned on several other occasions, about information that had come to light after her first interview. However, seemingly, she was not able to offer any more insights into the gunman or the attack.

Latr, on the early afternoon of October 4, just after 1:00 p.m., both hotel employees who were fired at by the gunman on the 32nd floor, were interviewed by law enforcement. The interviews took place on the 32nd floor 100-wing of the hotel in separate guest rooms.

Jesus Campos, who was the unarmed security guard wounded by the gunman, only gave a vague account of his movements leading up to the attack, and what happened on the 32nd floor before, during, and after the incident. He also claimed that he accessed the 32nd floor from the 31st floor via the guest elevators, after leaving the fire door. Then, when he was asked if he saw the room service cart in the hallway wired with cameras, he said he did not. His interview was over in around fifteen minutes.

The second hotel employee, named Steven Shuck, was a little more forthcoming with information when he was questioned. But other than confirming the time he entered the 32nd floor and at roughly what time he was shot at, he was not of much use to law enforcement. However, Schuck did clear up the matter of what his role was in the aftermath of the attack, which again, caused more holes to appear in Lombardo's initial statement about Campos' wounding.

Because Lombardo claimed in his first press conference that even after being wounded, Campos remained on the floor assisting law enforcement with guest evacuations. However, not only did Schuck confirm it was him who helped with guest evacuations. Campos confirmed in his statement that on the night of the attack by 10:40 p.m., he was in the lower levels of the hotel getting medical treatment for his leg.

Once these three interviews were completed, law enforcement now had a more accurate picture of the gunman, and certain events that occurred upon the 32nd floor 100-wing, during the attack. This enabled the FIT team to draw up a more accurate timeline and sequence of events, relating to the whole attack and, a more in-depth suspectology was produced.

Around the late afternoon of October 4, the FIT team asked the FBI to supply copies of all the footage from the hotel, along with the footage from the Ogden, and any other digital evidence that may assist them in their investigation. But the FBI refused to give any copies of the footage or digital media to the FIT team.

However, the FBI did tell the FIT team that they could visit the FBI field officer in Las Vegas to review the evidence, which the FIT team accepted. But when the detectives from the FIT team arrived at the field office, they were shown short clips of the footage and copies of the evidence summaries, and nothing more. So, very little information was gained from the evidence review.

During the review, the FIT team detectives asked the FBI if they could have copies of the footage and evidence summaries, to take with them. But the FBI refused to hand them over, but they did agree that the detectives could take notes for future refence.

Thinking that this was an isolated incident, and since all the evidence may not have been fully processed at that time. The detectives did not protest too much and hoped that going forward, the FBI would be more agreeable to share the evidence they collected. However, this would later prove to be a false hope, as the FBI gave very few copies of their findings to LVMPD.

By the morning of October 5, a new and very apparent issue started to emerge for the FIT team. This issue really had no way of being resolved, neither did they have the power to stop it. Because by this stage of the investigation, Sheriff Joe Lombardo had made it a habit of interjecting his own theories into the mix, during the countless media briefings. In addition, he was also making claims that certain items of evidence were being discovered, when they were not.

As to why Lombardo felt the need to do this, it is not very clear. But irrespective of what anyone said, even from federal agencies, Lombardo just kept on going with his half-baked ideas and lies about evidence being discovered. And there was no end it, because even when he was publicly called out on this, he still did not stop.

So now, the FIT team were contending with Lombardo, the discount with countless items of evidence, along with being prevented from accessing nearly all the physical and digital evidence collected by the FBI. In effect, they were fighting an uphill battle, which had no end in sight. To the outside world, though, they were seeming even more incompetent by the day. But despite this, they still pressed on.

Another blow was about to hit the FIT team, which occurred on the afternoon of October 6, as they were told that the vast resources at their disposal was slowly being drawn down. When the detectives asked why this was, considering the scale of the investigation, they were informed that it was an open and shut case. They no longer needed the might of the LVMPD behind them. But to the FIT team, there were still countless questions, with no clear answers.

By this stage of the investigation, many of the VIP casino hosts assigned to the gunman, during his time gambling in Las Vegas had been questioned. And the information they were giving to detectives, was priceless. Because many of them gave an insight to the shooters' gambling habits, and his losses. Crucial information was also gained, which showed some casinos, such as those owned by MGMRI and Caesars Entertainment, were actively changing out the video poker machines on the gunman.

Another issue faced by the FIT team was devising an accurate timeline as to when the unarmed security guard was wounded. Because now, there was another version of events and timings, which suggested his wounding occurred around the middle of the attack. Also, by this stage of the investigation, the FIT team had not been allowed to interview many of the hotel employees who had information about the incident, despite repeated requests.

There was hope in sight, though, because on the late afternoon of October 7, the FIT team were told that they would have access to several key hotel employees, on October 10. The key employees were mainly hotel managers and hotel security employees. However, most of the room service attendants, luggage handlers, housekeeping, and food severs had encountered the gunman in the days leading up to the attack, had already interviewed by this point.

This now gave the detectives just over 48 hours to review all the evidence they had relating to the timelines and the incident and produce a list of questions, for the key hotel employees who may have vital information the detectives were missing.

Just hours before the staff interviews were due to commence, the FIT team learned that a hotel staff member who did not work on the night of the attack but recovered security footage from the hotel camera system the day after the attack, may have inadvertently altered the time and date on the hotel security cameras. So, this person was also added to the interview list.

On the morning of October 10, 2017, the staff interviews commenced around 9:00 a.m. In each interview, there was an LVMPD detective, an FBI agent, and the hotel staff member. In addition, when MGMRI believed that a hotel staff member was a critical witness, one of their inhouse attorneys was also present in the interview.

Out of the thirty or so staff members to be interviewed by law enforcement, on October 10. It was found that some of the hotel employees seemed to either be confused or may have not been entirely honest, when questioned. However, there were several snippets of information gained, which answered countless key questions. Mainly relating to the timeline of Campos wounding, and other key events. LVMPD were also finally given full access to hotel security logs and door lock records from 32-134 and 32-135.

The biggest take away from all the hotel staff interviews, on October 10, related to timings of Campos' movement, and certain events that occurred on the night of the attack. Such as how many times Campos contacted security dispatch, or how certain security process worked. This allowed the FIT team to get a better understanding of what Campos should have been doing on the night of the attack.

What was interesting though, during the staff interviews conducted in the first few days that followed the attack, which took place mainly with housekeeping staff, baggage handlers, or food servers. It was found that the gunman used the hotel inner workings to his own advantage, and also allowed him to obtain certain items, without arousing suspicion.

One example of this, was the large number of towels the gunman acquired, which he was using as padding in some of the bags containing weapons. In the aftermath of the attack, the countless extra towels the gunman had obtained from the hotel, were found in 32-135 in many of the bags he used to ferry his arsenal into the hotel. It seems that he was asking different housekeeping staff for the towels, so as not to arouse curiosity.

Also, it was noticed that when the gunman placed at least two room service orders, he would order enough for two guests. This led many people to believe there was an extra person with him, during his stay. However, the gunman knew that by placing an order for two people, the food would come on a room service cart, and not in a bag. And as he needed at least two carts, he placed at least two room service orders for two people.

Based on interviews with some of the bellman, who helped the gunman to his room with his luggage. It was found the weight of the some of his bags, were heavier than what some guests usually are. However, while the bags were practically heavy, they were not excessively heavy. What this was meant to mean, the detectives could not really understand.

Mainly because, it was found that each rifle taken into the hotel was placed inside bags with padding, and typically each bag only contained one rifle. And the gunman ferried most of the ammunition and tools into the hotel, without the assistance of the bellman and after the weapons were already in 32-135. Yet, when the rooms were searched, there really wasn't any heavy items found. Neither was there any evidence to suggest the gunman had taken anything heavy back out of the hotel with him.

This led detectives to believe that maybe, some of the bellmen were trying to overstate what they truly witnessed. And surprisingly, most of the false leads, or inaccurate statements mainly originated from the luggage handlers. One of the most prominent fabricated statements from a bellman, related to the claim the gunman had been to the Route 91 Concert and been in the company of a female.

The tempo of the investigation began to slow to a crawl by October 15, because no new information was coming in. The main role of the FIT team now was to review the evidence that had been collected by LVMPD and see if anything more could be gained. Along with this, the usual requests were sent to the FBI to review evidence they had collected, because much of the analysis had now been completed by their labs.

As usual, when the FIT team put in the requests, they were told that they could attend the field office and review the information and make notes. However, in a turn of events, the FBI did give the FIT team some copies of their reports, such as the ballistics analysis. Other than that, though, not much information was passed from the FBI to the FIT team.

The FIT team were now also focusing on the gunman's financial records, to determine where most of his money had gone in the years leading up to the attack. They were also trying to determine how much money he had spent acquiring his arsenal and supplies, for the attack. Another area they looked at was his gambling records for various casinos up and down the strip.

It seemed that at one point, his wins were off the charts, and he was losing very little. However, towards the latter end of 2014, he appeared to have run out of luck, because his losses started to outweigh his wins. Then, by 2016 his fortune was dwindling due to his losses, and he was not able to quickly recoup the money he was losing at video poker.

Senior commanders in LVMPD renewed their efforts to close the case, as to them it was open and shut. They had the suspect, they had a fair overview of his finances, all they were lacking was a motive. At around this time, Danley was still being viewed by the FBI and the FIT team as a possible accomplice in the planning and preparation of the attack. To a point, they were both still issuing warrants to get access to various online accounts she owned, such as her emails and Facebook account.

Around the end of October 2017, a new lead came in though, from a detention officer at the Clark County Detention Center (CCDC), who contacted the FIT team. They claimed that an inmate had approached them and told them about an interaction they had had with the gunman, some weeks before the attack. This was news to the FIT team, as they had a good idea of the shooters' movements, but they still wanted to speak to the inmate, to see what they had to say.

Just over a week later, on November 7, 2017, a FIT team detective along with an FBI agent went to CCDC to meet with the inmate. The interview lasted just short of thirty minutes, and it was clear that the inmate had never met the gunman. Mainly because he could hardly describe him, nor could the inmate describe the vehicle the shooter was known to have been driving on that day and time.

According to the prisoner, some weeks prior to the attack the gunman reached out to him in response to an ad the inmate had placed in a local magazine, regarding selling plans to modify an AR from semi-automatic fire to fully automatic. While it is not illegal to sell this information, it is illegal to convert civilian weapons. Based on the witness statement, the inmate claimed that the gunman asked him to convert his weapons and the shooter would pay him $500 per weapon. However, the inmate declined and only offered to sell the instructions.

The inmate went further, by claiming that while he was meeting with the gunman and discussing the conversion of the weapons from semi to fully automatic. The shooter burst into anti-government rhetoric and claimed that the response to Hurricane Katrina was just a dry run for the government to start taking more control. It was also claimed that the shooter appeared to be fanatical about gun rights.

Towards the end of this section of the statement, the inmate said that shortly after the gunman started to make his feelings known about the government, the shooter stated that "Somebody has to wake up the American public and get them to arm themselves." The inmate then claimed that after the gunman allegedly made this remark, the inmate told the shooter he was sorry, but he could not do business with him.

For the remainder of the interview the LVMPD detective and FBI agent asked the inmate various questions, regarding the alleged meeting with the gunman along with questions about the inmate's background. However, there were times when the questions asked by law enforcement did move back to the claimed meeting between the inmate and gunman, along with what vehicle the gunman was driving.

Several times during the interview with the inmate, both the detective and federal agent asked how the inmate communicated with the gunman to arrange the meeting. To which, the inmate replied that it was via email. After the meeting concluded, the FBI agent contacted the FBI lab that had access to all of the gunman's email accounts to see if there truly was any communication between the shooter and the inmate. However, it was found that no such communication took place.

Some months after the mass shooting, several media outlets sued LVMPD to release any evidence they held regarding the incident. After a lengthy court battle, the media outlets won and LVMPD were ordered by a judge to release the information. When several journalists found this statement in the evidence release, several stories were published that gave the impression this meeting did take place. However, law enforcement had uniquely ruled out the possibility of any such meeting transpiring.

By the end of November 2017, even more pressure was applied by senior commanders in LVMPD for the FIT team to wrap up their investigation into the mass shooting. In addition to this, the FIT team were told that they had until the middle of January 2018 to publish their preliminary findings into the incident. This signaled to the detectives investigating the mass shooting that they were being forced to close the case file and move on, even though there were still countless lose ends to chase up.

There was an issue, though, for the FIT team as the FBI had still not shared much of their official findings with the LVMPD detectives. So, the question arose, how would the FIT team get access to all the information held by the FBI, because after all, the Bureau held nearly all the physical and digital evidence relating to the incident.

After several internal discussions between the FIT team detectives, a plan was devised which would help them get access to as much evidence as they possibly could. The plan was simple, undertake a mass evidence review and obtain any information that the FIT team deemed to be vital to their investigation. To facilitate this, a formal request was made to the FBI for a mass review, which was granted.

Several days later, seven members of the FIT team spent an entire day at the FBI field officer in Las Vegas, pouring over whatever information the federal agency would allow them to access. Along with this, there were specific items of evidence that the FIT team wanted access to, but they never let the FBI know exactly what information they were looking for. But overall, it was mainly digital evidence and some security camera footage of the gunman from various times and places.

After ten hours, the seven members of the FIT team left the FBI field officer with countless notebooks filled with information, pertaining to the Las Vegas Mass Shooting. However, they were not able to get all the answers they wanted, but they now had a far better understanding of the shooter and the incident than they had before.

The Preliminary Case Report

Prior to the initial case report being written, a discussion took place between the FIT team, as there were several points that had to be finalized before anyone could start writing the document.

The first issue was what information to put into the report, as there was still a disconnect between what the FIT team could prove and what they suspected, due to how the FBI seemed to control much of the evidence they had collected. Then there was still an issue relating to the timelines, and what time certain events occurred. Finally, whose name was going to be assigned as the case officers, as the investigation was assigned to the entire team and not a single detective.

After a lengthy discussion, it was decided that the only information that would go into the report was what could be proven beyond a reasonable doubt. This way, if someone scrutinized the report, the facts would check out, and no one could be blamed for interjecting even more speculation and hearsay.

When it came to the timings, it was agreed that the word approximately would be used to show that the timings were not entirely accurate, but the events occurred around the time stated. Then, the case officer assigned from the FIT team, was Detective Trevor Alsup.

In addition, to reflect the fact that the FIT team were not the only division of LVMPD to investigate the case, credit would be given to the Homicide Section also, and a section of the report would also show what each supporting department did during the first few weeks of the investigation.

Now came the task of writing the actual report, and it was felt the best way to do this was to assign each section of the document to various officers within the FIT team, so it was more a collaborative effort rather than a sole venture. But the introduction and preliminary findings would be written based on input from both the FIT team and the Homicide Section.

Within a week of the report being started, a new problem arose, which related to the total number of pages the document contained. Because other than the bulk of the witness statements and some crime scene photos, LVMPD knew very little. Even with the mass of information obtained from the FBI in the mass evidence review, the report only contained some thirty pages. To get around this issue, an ingenious solution was devised.

Firstly, the line spacing in the report was increased so that the space between the paragraphs was greater than they usually would be. Then, any reference diagrams used in the main sections of the report were enlarged, so they took up more space on the page. Once these touches were applied to the document, the report contained some fifty-three pages.

To further add to the total number of pages, the FIT team decided that they would also add an appendix section into the report, which would contain twenty-nine crime scene photos. The photos used were a mix of pictures taken by the CSI officers in the early hours of October 2, along with two photos supplied by the FBI, and several photos taken by the FIT team while they were in the hotel rooms when the FBI were conducting their search.

Once all this information was compiled and the photos added into the report, the document now contained some eighty-one pages. All the FIT team had to do was get the senior commanders in LVMPD to sign off on the report, which they did with relative ease and a few minor edits. But unbeknown to the FIT team at the time, several days later, senior commanders in LVMPD published the report on the LVMPD website and gave copies to several media outlets.

The result of the report being released into the public domain, was that the FIT team's investigation into the mass shooting would be placed under a microscope by the media and public alike. The fallout was not good for anyone, because several issues arose once the report was published.

Mainly, it seemed that the overview of the incident itself seemed to name the security guard, more than it did the suspect. To a point, between pages 5 to 7, which specifically looks at the incident, Campos is mentioned twelve times, whereas the shooter was only named three times. In fact, the security guard was named before the shooter even was, so this raised questions.

When LVMPD was asked to comment on this fact, they gave a somewhat plausible explanation. By claiming that they took the stance that the shooter should not be the focus of the report, and the victims should take center stage.

But this argument quickly lost credibility when several journalists drew attention to the fact that of the fifty-eight victims killed on the night of the attack, and the countless others wounded, were only given a brief mention. Whereas Campos took center stage. This seemed to reinforce the theory stated by several news outlets after the attack, that MGMRI were somehow manipulating the investigation in their favor.

The interesting aspect is, though, is how some of the information was written. Because there are several areas of the document which show how the evidence was collected, and, highlighted the fact that the FIT team were prevented from doing their job. Either by hinderance of senior commanders in LVMPD or by the FBI.

Due to how the preliminary report was received by the media and the public, along with the controversy that it caused. Senior commanders in LVMPD decided that a second report was to be published, which would document the entire investigation and highlight certain areas.

The Final Case Report

Within days of the concerns being raised in the public domain about the contents of the preliminary report, senior commanders told the FIT team that by no later than July 27, 2018, they wanted a second more comprehensive case report completed, which would be published by no later than August 3, 2018.

The task was one that the FIT team did not particularly relish, but they set to work on producing a document that they hoped would exonerate their role in the investigation.

The first draft of the report was ready by the end of January 2018, as the document expanded upon the first case report. However, when the FIT team submitted the document to the senior commanders, it was sent back due to various concerns. The concerns noted how honest the report was, and this did not impress the upper echelons in LVMPD. So, the FIT team edited the document as best they could.

By the middle of February 2018, the second draft of the report was submitted to the commanders. Again, though, they sent it back for various reasons and told the FIT team that it still needed more work. And again, the issue that the commanders had was with the openness of the report, which did not please certain senior officers.

This process of the FIT team submitting the report for approval and senior commanders sending it back for editing continued for five months. In total, the document underwent some sixty revisions, until senior commanders were agreeable with the contents. However, despite the jostle between the FIT team and senior commanders, there were sections of the report that were not edited. And if edits did occur in these sections, the information being published still reflected the true findings of the FIT team.

One of the main points that the FIT team tried to instill in the report was the conflicting information obtained from interviews with hotel staff members. Along with how the timeline was not accurate, and how evasive Campos seemed, during his interview. To show these issues, the FIT team made several references to draw attention to the problem.

An example of this is the footnotes and other notes contained in the final report. Because in various pages of the document, the FIT team draw attention to conflicting or unfounded information. For example, on pages 34, 49, 59, and 60 the FIT team added notes implying that hotel employees had made false statements while being questioned.

Then there are sections of the final report where the FIT team left clues that there was more to their investigation than they were allowed to publish. Because again, there are notes and open-ended statements that give this impression. And it would later transpire, when senior commanders in LVMPD wanted these sections of the report removed before final publication. The FIT team stood their ground and insisted that those areas would not be altered. And if they were altered, they still gave an insight into the issues the team faced.

By late July 2018, the final case report was completed and signed off by senior commanders in LVMPD. The report contained 187 pages, with 127 pages detailing the FIT team's findings, while the other 50 pages contained the gunman's autopsy report, and specific medial testing and lab results of samples taken during the autopsy. Also, the guest door locking system records from 32-134 and 32-135 were also contained in the final section of the report.

Again, though, despite the best efforts of the FIT team, they were never truly able to tell the public how problematic the investigation was, and how they were hindered at various times of their work, by both the FBI and senior commanders. Due to this, the public believe the detectives were incompetent and being led astray by the hotel at every twist and turn. When in fact, the FIT team did the best job they could, irrespective of the roadblocks, misdirection, and anything else that was privately thrown at them.

Chapter Five:
The Campos Conspiracy

"It seems from our perspective in the press that they [MGM] are managing a lot of the storyline."

-Tucker Carlson, Former Fox News Presenter, Oct. 25, 2017.

During the early press conferences given by the former head of LVMPD, Sheriff Joe Lombardo, on October 2, 2017, regarding the Las Vegas Mass Shooting. The world first learned of the heroic actions of an unarmed hotel security guard, wounded by the gunman close by 32-135. In the days that followed these statements, the hero security guard was named as Jesus Campos.

Within days of these statements being made and Campos being declared a hero, concerns were raised by the media, as he was nowhere to be found. Then, on October 5, 2017, a dramatic change was made to the time he was wounded. Now, it was claimed that he was wounded at 9:59 p.m., six minutes before the gunman fired into the venue, not at the end of the attack, like it was initially stated.

By October 17, 2017, the timeline of Campos' wounding changed again. With this revision, it was now claimed he was wounded by the gunman, between 10:06 p.m. to 10:07 p.m. So, the time of his wounding, went from the end of the attack, to before the attack even started, to just as the first shots were fired. Curiously, this version would not only become the official and final timeline, for when Campos was wounded. It was also co-authored by MGMRI.

Due to the three-timeline revisions, along with the fact that when Campos was due to speak to the mainstream news networks, he canceled at the last minute. Combined with the way in which he was first portrayed as a hero, then appeared more as a victim of circumstance. There has been increasing speculation as to what really occurred, upon the 32nd floor 100-wing, on that fateful night. This has given rise to something I have come to call, the Campos Conspiracy.

The main question is, though, was the conspiracy born out of media hype and speculation. Or is there truly something being covered up by either MGMRI or LVMPD? Because while countless theories have been put forward, there has never been a conclusive answer arrived at. So, for the first time, ever, the Campos Conspiracy will be reviewed in-depth. This will finally determine if something is being cover-up, or if the FIT team detectives were as incompetent, as it was claimed.

To finally answer the long-standing question of incompetence or a cover-up. The review of the Campos Conspiracy will examine the three timelines published, and then test it against the official evidence. This will not only show how each timeline was devised but will also highlight any flaws in them.

The initial reports stated that Campos was sent to the 32nd floor 100-wing to check on a guest open door, close by the shooters' location. Once on the hallway, Campos heard suspicious sounds coming from the gunman's rooms, at the end of the hallway, so he went to investigate. However, as he drew close to the door of 32-135, the gunman became aware of his presence and fired some 200 rounds at him, through the double entry doors to 32-135, and down the hallway.

One of the rounds was claimed to have struck Campos in the left thigh, but despite being wounded, he was able to take cover in a nearby doorway alcove. Shortly after this, he used his hotel radio, and raised the alarm. Moments later, a group of LVMPD and armed hotel security managers, who were on the guest levels, looking for the gunman's location. Responded to the radio call for help, and evacuated Campos from the hallway.

It was then claimed that even though he was wounded, Campos remained on the guest floors for the remainder of the night, helping with evacuations. LVMPD also credited his presence on the floor as being the catalyst for the gunman ceasing his attack, as by wounding Campos, it exposed the gunman's location.

The first thing that is Surprising, no one questioned this version of events, not even the fact that despite being fired at by some 200 rounds in an enclosed area. The only wound Campos sustained, was to his left leg. As to why no one questioned this, it is not clear.

What was never publicly known, though, was that by the afternoon of October 2, the FIT team had a different version of events. Because based on their preliminary investigation of Campos' wounding, the evidence they discovered, did not fit the official story. Yet, despite this, senior commanders in LVMPD were not interested in the truth. They were only interested in pushing the story that Campos was a hero.

It was not just LVMPD that knew, as both the FBI and MGMRI became aware very early on that the initial version, was nowhere close to being accurate. However, as to why neither the FBI or MGMRI objected to the version being endorsed by LVMPD, it is not readily clear. With this, Sheriff Lombardo was allowed to continually proclaim that Campos was a hero.

This was not the only issues, though, as several former hotel security employees spoke to the media and claimed, there was no systems in the hotel that monitored guest doors. So, there was no conceivable way that Campos could have been on the floor for this reason. However, this was not true, as the hotel did have a system that monitored guest door.

The system in question is called the Hotel Service Optimization System, or HotSOS for short, which was first rolled out at the Mandalay Bay in mid-2007. At the time of the initial rollout, the only departments that utilized the HotSOS system, was maintenance and housekeeping. The way the system first worked, was if a guest had a maintenance issue or wanted extra towels, then the front desk would input the information into the HotSOS, and the relevant department would respond.

In 2014, the system underwent an upgrade at the hotel, which added a security logging feature into the HotSOS. This meant, all guest door lock actions were monitored, such as, when a guest used their key card to open the door or when the deadbolt was engaged. In addition to this, if a door remained open for anywhere from twenty minutes to an hour, a notification would be automatically sent to hotel security dispatch, for a security guard to check on the door.

To confirm the system was utilized at the hotel around the time of the attack, there are two references online, which shows that it was operational. The first was a paper written by a former student studying hotel management at the University of Las Vegas, which examined the rollout of the HotSOS in 2007 at the Mandalay Bay. The second reference is from the company that makes the system, who has actively used the Mandalay Bay as a case study to market the HotSOS system, since 2015.

Another aspect that is interesting, is the claim that the gunman fired 200 rounds, at Campos. The gunman only fired a total of 33 rounds, at both Campos and the second hotel employee that was on the floor that night. Also, by the time the statement was released, senior commanders in LVMPD would have been aware that the gunman fired no more than 33 rounds, down the hallway. As to why an extra 167 rounds was included in the total, it is not clear.

The latter part of the claim that Campos was wounded at the very end of the attack and was evacuated from the hallway by LVMPD. Stems from two separate LVMPD radio transmissions, which were broadcast by some of the first LVMPD officers, who arrived on the 32nd floor after the gunman stopped firing. These two radio messages were from Beason and unit 182SE, which occurred between 10:23 p.m. to 10:25 p.m. Very little context was given in the radio messages, other than the shooter fired down the hallway and, wounded a hotel security guard.

It appears that the first version of events was based on several incidents that occurred that night, and someone mashed them into a logical sequence, then added a little more to it to make it sound dramatic. As to who the culprit is, it is hard to say for certain. But the only person that seems to be responsible for this story was Sheriff Joe Lombardo. Because no other officer appears to have been the cause of this false narrative.

On October 9, 2017, LVMPD made dramatic changes to the story, surrounding Campos' wounding. It appears that the FIT team were sick and tired of seeing the lies pushed by LVMPD. So, they threatened to mutiny, if senior commanders did not revise the timeline. However, this new version of events, caused a stir within the media.

In the new version, it was stated that Campos was assigned four door checks on the 30th floor and one door check on the 32nd floor, at around 9:30 p.m. Shortly after 9:40 p.m., Campos arrived on the 200-wing 30th floor service elevator bank, to start his door checks, on both the 30th and 32nd floors.

After he completed the first set of door checks on the 30th floor, he used the 100-wing stairwell to go between the 30th and 32nd floors. However, after he arrived at the 32nd floor 100-wing stairwell fire door, he found that he was unable to open it. So, he decided to head down to the 31st floor, and use the guest elevators to access the 32nd floor.

Once Campos had accessed the main area of the 32nd floor, he headed down the 100-wing and checked on 32-129, which was his final door check of the night. Then, he continued on to the foyer area at the far end of the floor close by 32-135, to see what was preventing the fire door from being opened. When Campos arrived at the foyer, he spotted an 'L' shaped bracket, screwed to the fire door and door frame.

After discovering the bracket, he then used the house phone in the foyer, to contact hotel security dispatch to ask if they knew what the bracket was doing on the fire door, but they did not know anything about it. Security dispatch then transferred his call to hotel maintenance, so he could inform them about the issue.

The hotel maintenance dispatcher who answered the phone to Campos, was also unaware of any work crews on the floor, or what the bracket was doing there. The dispatcher then transferred his call to the on-duty maintenance manager, Shannon Alsbury. The call between Alsbury and

Campos lasted around two minutes, before the maintenance manager told him that he would send someone up to the floor, to remove the bracket.

After the call ended, Campos then left the foyer, and started to head to the core center of the floor, to head to the lower levels of the hotel. However, just as he was leaving the foyer, Campos claimed to hear a loud drilling sound, coming from deep inside 32-135. But he never investigated what was going on, and simply chose to leave the floor.

As Campos was walking down the hallway and drew close to 32-129, he suddenly realized that someone was firing down the hallway at him. He then ran down the corridor a short distance before he dove for cover, in the doorway alcove of 32-122 and 32-124. As he entered the alcove, he realized that he had been hit on the back of the left calf.

Campos then used his hotel radio at around 9:59 p.m. to inform security dispatch about shots being fired from 32-135 and he had been hit in the leg. After relaying this message, he then used his cell phone to call dispatch as he did not think his message went through. He spoke to the dispatcher for a few minutes, then ended the call.

At around 10:10 p.m. a second hotel employee, Steven Schuck, who had been sent to remove the bracket entered the 100-wing 32nd floor hallway. As Schuck walked towards the foyer area, he saw Campos hiding in the doorway alcoves. Once Campos spotted Schuck, he told him to take cover as someone was shooting down the hallway. Schuck immediately dove for cover, into the doorway alcove he was close to him, just as the gunman then fired a second volley down the hallway.

Both Schuck and Campos remained in cover, until around 10:13 p.m., when they felt it was safe to leave the area. After entering the core center of the 32nd floor, two hotel managers arrived on the floor via the guest elevator. Campos was sent to the lower levels of the hotel at around 10:35 p.m., while Schuck would spend the rest of the night assisting with guest evacuations.

This new timeline was created using both physical evidence and witness statements. Overall, though, it appears that it was primarily based on Campos own version of events, contained in his October 4 statement. Below is an extract from his witness statement, where he describes his movements on the night of the attack, and how he was wounded.

"Um, approximately 2200 hours I received a call from dispatch, uh, told me to go check the doors that – we have a hot SOS system which indicates which door is propped open for a long period of time. Um, on my patrol I was on the last room which was 30 – I was on my way to 32129. As I was approaching the stairwell from the 31st floor to the 32nd floor the – the door – the – the door that leads to the stairwell to the hallway was, uh, locked or secured – locked. And I thought it was

out of the ordinary because those doors are always open. Uh, so I dropped down the 31st floor. I went down the hallway into the elevators – I believe it was the center core elevators – and then from there I walked all the way down to the last room on the left which is the door that leads into the stairwell. As I – as I observed a metal bracket that was keeping the door shut, I called our security dispatch. They stated they weren't aware and to contact engineering. I contacted engineering. They stated they weren't aware of the situation either. At that moment in time I heard noises which I assumed were drills or a, like, very loud drill. So I started walkin' away from the room. As I got in front of 32129 that's when I heard gunfire. As I got hit I – I was pinned in front of 32121 and 32123. I noticed I was bleeding. And at that moment in time I got over the radio and, uh, my mobile, uh, phone to contact dispatch that shots were fired and that I was hit. I gave 'em the location of the 32135 because that's where the shotes were being, uh, coming from. Uh, later at that time when he dispersed a full – full magazine, uh, I don't know if he started shooting back outside. At that moment in time my shift manager [REDACTED] my two outside units [REDACTED] they arrived to the center core. At that moment in time he wasn't shooting out towards the hallway. That's when I breached and made my way down to the center core. After the center core, uh, four metro officers showed up. At that moment in time I was given the green light to go downstair – the 200 wing elevators – down to the baggage area."

Extract of LVMPD Witness Statement, Jesus Campos, October 4, 2017, at 1310 Hours.

From reading Campos' own version, the first thing that stands out, is the fact that he only mentioned one specific timeframe. This was 22:00 hrs or 10:00 p.m., when he believes, he was dispatched to the guest floors. However, the hotel security log places him heading to the 30th floor, some fifteen minutes before this time, at around 9:35 p.m.

It seems, though, what Campos was trying to imply was that he only arrived on the guest levels around five minutes before he was wounded, if indeed, he was shot at around 9:59 p.m. This means that his door checks on the 30th floor, must have been relatively close to one another, and not spread out. Also, the time he spent at each door, was relatively short.

Another intriguing aspect of Campos' statement is his remarks about the fire door being secured. Because he stated that it was out of the ordinary that he could not open the door, as those doors are always open. However, despite this, he would not report the issue with the fire door immediately, he left it until sometime later.

It is possible, though, Campos chose to delay reporting the issue with the fire door, as he was heading directly to the 32nd floor. So, there is a chance that as was heading to the 32nd floor, there would not be much time between him discovering the door and then accessing the floor. So, he felt that would be ok.

What is also interesting, is how he described accessing the 32nd floor, after leaving the area of the fire door in the stairwell. Because he even though he sates he dropped down to the 31st floor, he only implies that he may have used the guest elevators, to access the 32nd floor. There are two other sets of evaluators he could have used on the 31st floor, but he would have had to walk right by the guest elevators, to get to the other sets of elevators.

So, it seems more logical for him to use the first set of elevators he came to, due to the issue with the door. However, with how he phrased the comment, it can be speculated that he could have used one of the other set of elevators on the 31st floor, to access the 32nd floor.

Campos' claim regarding his actions after he accessed the 32nd floor, is also noteworthy. This is because, he gives the impression that he headed right to the foyer area of the 100-wing, to check on the fire door. However, the guest in 32-129, confirmed that Campos arrived at her door for around 9:55 p.m. Then, after leaving her door, he headed in the direction of the foyer, at the end of the hallway.

The hotel security log from the night of the attack, confirms that Campos must have checked 32-129, prior to heading to the foyer. Because the notes on the log relate to a nanny in 32-129, who was watching a child asleep across the hallway, in 32-130. She had propped her door open, to watch the door to the room the child was sleeping in. However, the log notes do not mention anything about a bracket.

When LVMPD conducted the hotel security staff interviews on October 10. It was confirmed by several security employees who were working in the security dispatch office, on the night of the attack. Campos initially cleared his guest door checks via his radio. Then, a few minutes later, he called down to the dispatch office via the house phone in the foyer on the 32nd floor 100-wing hallway, to report the bracket on the fire door.

This shows that even though Campos claimed that he found it odd that the fire door was secured. It seems based on the fact he never reported it when he cleared his door checks, he was not overly concerned about it. Why this is, it is not clear. But it certainly is strange how he found it out of the ordinary for the door to be secured, yet he never reported it, at the earliest opportunity. It appears he waited until he physically saw the bracket.

Out of everything Campos said, during his witness statement, the most striking comment, is his remark about hearing a drilling sound coming from 32-135. Because by this point of the night, he knew the fire door should not have been secured, and there were no work crews in the area. Yet, within six feet of the fire door, he hears someone using a drill, and chose not to investigate and walks away from the room.

It honestly does not make sense, as to why he would do that. After all, he was fully aware that it was not a hotel maintenance crew, and he was already aware the bracket should not have been there. But instead of doing his job, as he was a security officer and was meant to check on suspicious activity. He chose to walk away and leave the area, without a single thought for what may be going on.

The time of Campos' wounding used in this version of events, was obtained from a section of footage captured on a BWC worn by an LVMPD officer. In the aftermath of the attack, several officers were assigned to the hotel security dispatch office, to monitor the hotel security cameras and relay any time sensitive information to the officers searching the hotel and casino complex.

While in the security dispatch office, one of the LVMPD officers was talking to a hotel security dispatcher, about what time it was when the shooter opened fire on the venue. The security dispatcher then tells the officer, they were contacted by one of their security guards, stating they had been shot, on the 32nd floor. The LVMPD officer then asked what time this call came in, and the security dispatcher responded by saying, 9:59 p.m.

The security dispatcher then goes on to state that there was a supplementary note on the log, entered by another member of the hotel security team at around 11:15 p.m. However, it is not clear as to what is on the additional notes, but it sounded like she said that it was stating Campos reported being shot between 10:10 p.m. to 10:20 p.m.

It was later determined by the FIT team, once they got access to the hotel security log, on October 10. The 9:59 p.m. entry that the security dispatcher was referring to, related to Campos clearing his door checks. However, interestingly, the FIT team were never given the information about the supplementary notes, so they were unable to confirm what it even said, or if indeed, it related to Campos being wounded.

The next part of Campos' statement that is interesting, is where he indicates his location in the hallway, when the shooter first fired at him. According to Campos, he was close to 32-129, and evidently his back was turned away from the doors to 32-135. Later in his statement, he claimed that had he not been shot, he would not have known where the gunman was located. This is interesting, for several reasons.

Firstly, Campos was facing away from 32-135, when the gunman opened fire on him. This means, between Campos and 32-135, there were at least three other doors, where the shooter could have fired from. So how did he know the exact location, while his back was turned? Because there was the possibility that a shooter could have ran into the hallway, fired at

Campos, then returned to the room. Evidently, this was not the case, and the shots did come from 32-135.

Secondly, on the night of the attack, he told the first two LVMPD officers that arrived on the 32nd floor, on the night of the attack. To watch out for the peephole on the door to 32-135, as that is where the shots came from that were fired at him. The FIT team detective conducting the interview, was aware of this information, as he asked Campos about it.

Campos confirmed that he did initially say this, to the officers. But between the night of the attack and October 4, he had been told by multiple people about the gunman placing a table in the hallway, which had cameras attached to it. However, on the night of the attack, Campos claims to have not seen the room service cart, or as he put it, the table.

It is not clear as to what Campos was trying to imply here, and the detective interviewing Campos never pushed this matter. However, the FIT time officer did try and get an answer if Campos saw the cart in the hallway. Because the FIT team never believed he did not see it, due to the fact of the highly visible camera, and that it was jutting out into the hallway. Either way, Campos never outrightly said he say the cart, but he did imply he may have done, and he was not going to admit to it.

When you combine what Campos initially claimed where the shots came from, along with the fact that in his October 4 statement, Campos stated he know exactly where the shots came from, even though his back was turned. It shows that he must have been a lot closer to 32-135, when he was wounded. Because there is no way that Campos would be able to determine a possible location where the shots came from, or the exact door the shooter was stood behind if, he was not stood close to the door.

Something else that people have struggled with, is what Campos initially reported he had been shot by. Because in his original radio message to hotel security dispatch, he stated shots had been fired from 32-135 and that he had been hit in the leg with either a pellet gun or .22. Now, the sound of a pellet gun, .22 caliber weapon, and a rifle are all very different. So, it makes no sense that someone would be firing a rifle, but he gets hit with a pellet or .22.

Evidently, Campos was confused about what he was shot with. Because the wound to his left calf was small and did not produce a lot of blood. This was due to the fact, he was hit with bullet fragments, not an intact bullet. So, the wound was only small, which could have led him to believe it was a pellet or a small caliber weapon. Either way, though, it would not make any sense that someone was firing a rifle down the hallway, but he gets hit with a much smaller projectile.

The location Campos gives in his version of events, of where in the hallway he was when he was wounded, is also interesting. Because he claims that he was taking cover in the doorway alcove of rooms 32-121 and 32-123, when he was hit in the calf. Not only was it discovered that Campos was not wounded while in this location, but it was also determined, he never took cover in this alcove.

During the forensic examination of the 32nd floor 100-wing hallway, there was no droplets of blood, found in the alcove that Campos claimed to have taken cover. However, his blood was found in the alcove opposite, for rooms 32-122 and 32-124. Also, droplets of Campos blood were found outside of 32-135 and in several locations down the 100-wing hallway, heading towards the door alcove of 32-122 and 32-124.

Interestingly, the blood droplets on the floor in the hallway that came from Campos' wound, were not contact blood stains, they were passive droplets. In other words, the blood was not transferred there on the bottom of someone's shoe, after the fact. Campos must have been physically in that spot, for the blood droplets to be on the carpet.

To further confirm which alcove Campos took cover in, while Schuck was being questioned on October 4. He was asked where Campos was in the hallway, in relation to the alcoves that he took cover in. Schuck stated that Campos was in the alcoves on the east side of the corridor, diagonally from his location, and he was standing against the north wall of the alcove. This means Campos was in the alcove for rooms 32-122 and 32-124.

The detective conducting the interview, also ruled out the possibility that Campos may have crossed the hallway, after being wounded. Because on page 8 of Campos' statement, he was asked if he looked back up the hallway, after the shooter opened fire on him. Campos stated that he did not, as he was too afraid to pop his head out of cover. This means, if he was too scared to look, he was hardly going to run across the hallway to change locations.

What is also interesting about Campos' statement, though, is what he does not mention. Because he fails to mention that Schuck was in the hallway with him. Which is odd; considering the recording of Schuck's radio message to maintenance dispatch, about shots being fired down the hallway, the sounds of gunshots could clearly be heard in the background. Also, the hotel managers that arrived on the 32nd floor, just as Schuck and Campos exited the 100-wing hallway, at around 10:13 p.m. both confirmed Schuck was helping Campos out of the hallway.

Another thing that is intriguing, is the fact that Campos vehemently denies seeing the room service cart in the hallway, outside of 32-134, with the highly visible camera on the top. The officer who conducted the interview on October 4, did push him several times, in relation to the cart. But each time Campos was asked about the cart, he not only claimed that he did not notice it. But also, he made some odd remarks when claiming not to see it.

For instance, on page 10 of his statement, when Campos stated he had been told about the cart, or as he described it, a table outside of 32-134. The detective then asked, "Okay. But at the time you didn't notice that?" Campos' response was, "Yes, I didn't notice that." Then the detective said, "Okay. Um, do you remember the cart being in the hallway?" Campos responded by saying, "Nope. I don't remember recalling any carts in the hallway."

Campos' responses to these questions are unusual, to say the least. Mainly because his vernacular and he also, his mis-phrased his responses. Typically, when someone is saying they didn't notice something, they don't usually start by saying yes. Normally, they respond by saying no, they did not see it. Then he used the words remembering and recalling, one after the other. Not only do they mean the same thing, but also, why say them in the same together in the same sentence.

Although, interestingly, there is a piece of evidence, which may solve the argument of where Campos was wounded. Along with, if he did or did not see the room service cart outside of 32-134, on the night of the attack. The piece of evidence in question, is the crime scene sketch from the 32nd floor 100-wing, completed by LVMPD CSI officer Herring during the early hours of October 2, 2017.

The trouble is, though, on the sketch, the bullet impact zones in the hallway are numbered in reverse. This is because; when CSI Herring began to catalog the evidence in the hallway, they started at the far end of the 32nd floor 100-wing corridor, right by the entrance to the core center. They then walked up the hallway towards the gunman's rooms at the end of the hallway. In effect, impact 1 becomes impact 17, while impact 17 becomes impact 1.

By reviewing the sketch and keeping in mind that the impact areas are in reverse. It shows that bullet impact 17, is around 5 feet in front of the double entry doors to 32-135, and directly in line with the peephole on the eastern side entry door to 32-135. Also, the person who the gunman was firing at, was stood just off to the side of the room service cart, and out of view of the front camera secured to the top of the room service cart.

Along with this, around 2 inches in front of impact 17, is where the first droplets of Campos' blood, were found. This means, not only was Campos standing outside of 32-135 when the gunman fired his first shots. But also, this is the area where he was wounded, and it explains the remark about the shots coming from the peephole.

What is even more interesting, though, is that by looking at the crime scene sketch, you can trace Campos' route down the hallway to the area where he took cover, in the door alcove of rooms 32-122 and 32-124.

According to this information, after the first shot was fired, he then ran around and in front of the room service cart and stayed close by the wall in front of the door to 32-134, on the east side of the hallway. This is denoted by impact zone 16. Then, impact zones 15, 14, 13, 12 and 11 shows that he zig-zagged down hallway, until he got to the door doorway alcove of 32-122 and 32-124, at which point he took cover.

The physical evidence gathered in relation to the bullet impacts in the 100-wing hallway, also answer another question, relating to Campos. Around October 14, 2017, a photo of Campos emerged in the media, which showed him at an awards dinner held in his honor. The photo was believed to have been taken, sometime around October 8, 2017. In the photo, there is a band aid just above his left eyebrow.

When he appeared on the Ellen DeGeneres show, a few days after the photo was published, on October 18. There was no band aid, neither was there any visible injury above his left eyebrow. Despite there being a ten-day difference in the time the photo was taken and Campos' appearance on the Ellen show. There would have still been some type of indication that Campos had sustained a wound above his left eyebrow, but there wasn't.

Based on this evidence combined with the photo, it seems that someone was trying to imply that as Campos ran around and in front of the room service cart. When the bullet struck the wall and caused impact 16, a piece of sheet rock, or even another bullet fragment, hit Campos just above his left eyebrow. As to why someone would want to suggest this, it is not clear. But evidently, it seems someone was trying to make him out to be more of a hero.

Overall, it seems that Campos' October 4 statement, is not only the main basis for the second timeline. But also, it is mixed in with a little bit of facts, and a lot of lies, combined with a lot of opened suggestions. All of which, seem to play into the first story about Campos, being a hero. But also, his account in his October 4 statement could relate to countless other possible variations. Furthermore, when it is compared to other aspects of evidence, Campos October 4 statement, does not stand up to scrutiny.

All was set to change, though, shortly after this version of events was released. Because, by October 11, MGMRI went on the offensive against

LVMPD, mainly due to the 9:59 p.m. timeframe. According to the public statement released by MGMRI, the time stated for Campos' wounding, could not be relied. Mainly because, the time inserted into the logs, was manually added, after the fact.

Also, it was stated that MGMRI's own internal investigation found several more issues with the second LVMPD timeline. Firstly, they had proof that Campos did not enter the 32nd floor, until after 10:00 p.m. This was confirmed by the footage from the 33rd floor guest elevator, which he used to access the 32nd floor, after leaving the fire door.

Secondly, MGMRI stated that based on the time of Campos' radio call for help, his wounding occurred within 40 seconds of the attack starting. This was further backed up, by the fact that after he reported being shot. Both LVMPD officers and an armed hotel security detail, responded to the 32nd floor, from inside the hotel.

Along with this, MGMRI had been trying to enforce the belief that their internal security systems, had been having issues with maintaining an accurate time, for several months. And due to this, it was another reason LVMPD were having issues with confirming the time of critical events.

In this third sequence of events, Campos was now officially stated as going up to the 33rd floor, after leaving the fire door to access the main area of the 32nd floor, and arrived via the guest elevator to the 32nd floor, at around 10:01 p.m. Then his wounding was placed as happening when he left the foyer area, at around 10:06 p.m. to 10:07 p.m.

It was abundantly clear by this point in time that, either MGMRI were trying to cover something up, or the FIT team were highly incompetent. So, the main questions at this point are: Were MGMRI having issues with their security systems maintaining an accurate time, and if they were, to what extent. How long was Campos on the guest levels, before being wounded. And what time roughly was Campos wounded and, how quickly did he report the situation.

The first area to examine, is the claim by MGMRI that their systems were having issues maintaining an accurate time. Because if they were, then the 9:59 p.m. timestamp on the log, must be wrong. However, there was a system used by hotel security that was having issues, maintaining an accurate time. And funnily, enough, it was the one used to record hotel security radio transmissions, not the HotSOS security system.

On October 10, LVMPD interviewed the hotel security employee, who retrieved both the audio and video recordings, from the night of the attack. This person was identified in their statement as TB. According to TB, the hotel DVR system used for recoding security radio messages, had been having issues for over a year. To compensate for this, there was a policy in place that the system was checked on a regular basis.

Although, when TB went to download the audio files of Campos' radio call, they noticed the timestamp was wrong. To help investigators, they tried to fix these issues, even going as far as calling the manufacture to get their help to change the time on the audio recording. However, TB quickly discovered that any recordings prior to the system time change would still contain the digitally encoded timestamp, from before the change.

With this, TB wrote a statement to accompany the disc, not only explaining the issue. But also, how they were able to determine an approximate time the radio message occurred. This was based on the last known check on the system time and the timestamp on the recording. Based on their estimate, Campos contacted security dispatch at around 10:09 p.m. to 10:10 p.m., to inform them he had been wounded.

Having determined that one system was having issues, which was the one used to determine when Campos was wounded. The next question is, was the HotSOS system and hotel security cameras having the same issue. And as they were both linked to the same network time server, if one was having a time issue, so would the other.

To confirm this, by reviewing the BWC footage from one of the LVMPD officers, who was assigned to monitor the hotel security cameras, in the security dispatch office after the attack. It will be relatively simple to see if there was a timestamp issue, as their footage captured nearly all the security camera monitors in the office. The officers BWC used to determine this fact, had the serial number X83027377.

The trouble, is though, LVMPD had only just rolled out the BWC system, so nearly all the BWC's were set to Coordinated Time (UTC) and not Pacific Standard Time (PST). This is denoted by the Z at the end of the timestamp on the BWC footage. Basically, if the time and date stamp on the footage reads 05:10 20017-10-02, when this is converted to PST, the time on the night is 10:10 p.m. 10/01/2017.

After adjusted the time and date on the BWC footage to PST, it is then necessary to determine if there was any difference between the time shown on the footage to the time on the LVMPD Computer Aided Dispatch log. This is because, the FIT team used the CAD log as their master time clock, to synchronize all times to.

The easiest method to confirm if there was any difference in time between the BWC and CAD log, is to use the message broadcast across the LVMPD radio network, telling officers to stop entering the area from the north. This message was transmitted at 10:13 p.m. and 54 seconds. When this message occurred, the time displayed on the BWC footage was 10:13 p.m. and 37 seconds. This shows that the BWC footage was 17 seconds, behind the CAD log. The reason for this, is because the CAD log used internet time as a master clock, whereas BWC used satellite time. Overall, though, this is not a great difference in time.

After watching the BWC footage from X83027377, at the 48 minutes and 41 seconds timeframe, the footage clearly captures a hotel security monitor showing the overlayed timestamp. The time on the BWC was reading 10:59 p.m. and 29 seconds (converted to PST), while the time shown on the camera overlay was 10:59 p.m. and 39 seconds.

This shows that the hotel security system and HotSOS log time was 10 seconds ahead of the BWC footage time. That means, with the 10 seconds difference, the time lag between the hotel security cameras and HotSOS system, compared to the CAD log, was only 7 seconds. Again, this is an acceptable time difference.

A point to note here, is that both the hotel systems and the CAD log used internet time, as a mater clock. However, the reason that the CAD log was 7 seconds ahead, was because the internet signal to the Mandalay Bay system, had to travel a little further. This is what is called time latency.

This conclusively proves that, on the night of the Las Vegas Mass Shooting, the HotSOS log and hotel security cameras, were not having issued maintaining an accurate time. However, the hotel DVR system was, but there was a way to generate an approximate time Campos' transmission occurred.

It seems, though, that MGMRI were trying to stay one step ahead of any potential issues. Because they informed LVMPD, on or around October 10 that when the hotel security camera footage was being downloaded. The staff member who recovered the footage, had altered the main system time, to try and synchronize all the timestamps.

Not only does this claim sound bizarre. But again, this is another false claim made by MGMRI, for two reasons:

Firstly, the hotel employee who was claimed to have altered the time, was TB, who was the same person that downloaded the radio messages. During their interview with LVMPD on October 10, TB was asked if they touched the time settings on the camera system, which they denied.

Secondly, as the footage and HotSOS system contained digital timestamps, even if TB had altered the main system time. It would not change the time shown on HotSOS logs and camera footage, generated prior to the time change taking place.

Having determined that the only hotel system to have issues with timestamps, was the DVR audio recorder. It was time to review how long Campos would have spent on the guest levels, prior to being wounded. The first area to examine, is the time he would have arrived on the 30th floor 200-wing service elevator bank.

According to the HotSOS log entry, at 9:35 p.m., Campos informed security dispatch that he was heading up to the 30th floor to start his door checks. Then, the camera footage from inside service elevator 5410, which he used to take to the 30th floor 200-wing service elevator bank, shows him entering at 9:46 p.m. and 27 seconds. He is then seen exiting the elevator on the 30th floor 200-wing service elevator bank, 54 seconds later, at 9:47 p.m. and 21 seconds.

The footage showing Campos using the using guest elevator P18, to go from the 33rd floor to the 32nd floor, after discovering the fire door was secured. Shows that he entered the elevator at 10:00 p.m. and 18 seconds. However, for reasons unknown, the footage does not show Campos exiting the elevator on the 32nd floor. But it should have taken no longer than 15 seconds, for the elevator doors to close and descend to the 32nd floor. This places campos exiting at around 10:00 p.m. and 36 seconds.

This shows that Campos spent around 13 minutes and 15 seconds completing his door checks on the 30th floor, then accessing the 32nd floor, after leaving the fire door in the stairwell. There is a problem, though, as both pieces of footage from the service and guest elevators have the original timestamps masked, with superimposed times added to the footage. Also, the color has been removed from both sections of footage. This is odd, because the cameras used by the Mandalay Bay are color, and not black and white.

Along with this, there is another problem, with the footage showing Campos using guest elevator P18, as seems to be two pieces of footage spliced together. Because at around the 10:00 p.m. and 20 seconds mark, Campos seems to move so fast, that the camera does not catch his movement. This is evident, due to the location of this arm change positions, and the camera does not show a flowing motion, it is in one location at one point then another location a split second later.

Although, unlike the footage relating to the gunman, this footage was never released by MGMRI, in the aftermath of the attack. The first time it was seen, was when it aired on the ABC Nightline program, A Killer on Floor 32. So, there is a chance, the producers could have edited the timestamps, for the show. However, considering that there is footage of the gunman using elevator P18 on September 29, 2017, which shows the full timestamp. Had the producers of the show used an overlaid time for

Campos, it would be reasonable to assume that they would have done the same for the footage of the gunman. But they never did.

Then there is the fact that, the timestamp from the guest elevator footage, contradicts the HotSOS security log entry. Because the log states that Campos cleared his room checks by 9:59 p.m., but the elevator footage shows him using elevator P18 over a minute later. Considering both systems share the same time sever, the log entry should be timestamped after the footage, not before. And campos must have checked 32-129, because the notes on the log, reflect the information from the nanny.

There is no clear explanation, as to why the timestamps were masked on any of the footage. Because there was no reason for the ABC producers to hide them. And, it has been proven the times on the hotel security cameras and HotSOS log, were only 7 second behind the CAD log. So, it shows they were not malfunctioning. This is just another another anomaly, in the Campos Conspiracy.

To confirm the accuracy of these times, though, during the research phase of this book, I stayed at the Mandalay Bay on several occasions. On one of my trips, I specifically looked at the routes Campos was claimed to have taken that night, and how long it should have taken him. However, no one, other than the hotel and Campos knows what doors he checked on the 30th floor, and what he did at each door. All that is known for certain, about his time on the 30th floor, was that one of the door checks was on the 100-wing, close by the foyer. This is why he used the 100-wing stairwell to access the 32nd floor.

Along with this, there is no way to determine how long campos waited at the fire door on the 32nd floor 100-wing stairwell, after discovering he could not open the door. Then there is the fact, it is unknown how long he would have waited for the guest elevators on either the 33rd or 31st floors, because at different times of the day and night, the wait time varies.

Even though theses variables are unknown, a simple set of control measures was employed in the tests, which would overcompensate for his time on the guest levels. This would ensure a more accurate set of average results.

On the 30th floor, the route started at the 200-wing service elevator bank entry door. From here, I walked to the end of the 200-wing, then turned around and walked to the core center of the floor. Once at the core center, I then walked down and back up the 300-wing. For the 100-wing, I only walked from the core center to the foyer door, as Campos used the foyer to enter the stairwell. So, there would have been no need for him to walk back to the core center. In addition, a total of 2 minutes was added to the total time spent on the 30th floor, to account for the four door checks.

To account for any unknown actions, he may have undertaken at the 32nd floor 100-wing stairwell fire door. A thirty second pause was observed, before accessing the main part of the 32nd floor, via one of the two routes stated. Then, to account for the wait time at the elevators, each route was walked a total of 150 times, at various times of the day and night. Finally, to account for his door check at 32-129, I walked the length of the 100-wing hallway to the foyer, then added one minute to the time obtained for each route.

Here are the findings:

Average Time Trial Results

Route	Total Time	Distance
Version Two- Dropping Down a Floor	10 mins 10 secs	2,095 feet
Final Version – Going up a Floor	11 mins 11 secs	2,160 feet

The results were then applied to the timings stated in both the second version of events and the official narrative, as to when Campos entered the 30th floor on the night of the attack.

Results Route One – Campos Dropping Down a Floor:

Estimated Time Entering 30th floor 200-wing = 9: 40 p.m.
Total Route Time = 10 minutes and 10 seconds.
Estimated Arrival at 32nd Floor 100-Wing Foyer = 9:50 p.m.

Route Two – Campos Going-up a Floor:

Estimated Time Entering 30th floor 200-wing = 9: 47 p.m.
Total Route Time = 11 minutes and 11 seconds.
Estimated Arrival at 32nd Floor 100-Wing Foyer = 9:58 p.m.

Based on the results, had Campos truly entered the 30th floor 200-wing between 9:40 p.m. to 9:47 p.m., like it has been claimed in the latter two narratives. Campos would have been at the foyer area of the 32nd floor 100-wing between 9:50 p.m. to 9:58 p.m.

After looking at these results, it seems that the only feasible time he could have started his door checks, without having any large amounts of time unaccounted for, would be after 9:47 p.m. This would even allow him to sign off on his room checks by 9:59 p.m. Whereas, if he entered the floor at 9:40 p.m., he should have completed his door checks by no later than 9:50 p.m. This means if he did enter the floor at this time, he would have over ten minutes unaccounted for.

Another aspect that is interesting, is that Camps has always maintained he dropped down to the 31st floor, to access the 32nd floor. But the only footage of Campos using a guest elevator, comes from the on the 33rd floor. However, this footage is questionable at best, considering the points outline above.

There was trouble brewing, though, as several theories were published online, which claimed Campos somehow conspired with the gunman. These theories did gain momentum, due to the issues with the timeline revisions, and the fact Campos was proving elusive. However, once it was claimed there was footage that tracked his movements, the media started to move away from stories of Campos being a possible co-conspirator.

Despite this, though, why change his route, as all the elevators have cameras in them. So, irrespective which elevator he used, he would have still been seen on camera. Also, why did it take MGMRI some eleven days to make it known they had this footage. It would be easy to find and would have taken someone no more than an hour, to get to the time on the camera and download it. But they never made it known, they had it, until it looked like Campos was shot some 6 minutes before the attack.

At this stage of the review into the Campos Conspiracy, there were far more questions than answers. Also, it appeared that someone was trying cover something up, which related to some type of negligence. But there was one aspect of the whole event, which seemed out of place.

At around 10:12 p.m., the maintenance manage that Campos spoke to on the phone, while reporting the bracket, arrived on the 32nd floor with one of the armed security managers. In fact, Hendrix, and his armed group, got on the same elevator as Shannon Alsbury, as Alsbury was heading to the 32nd floor 100-wing.

While Alsbury and the armed group were heading up to the guest levels, not only does he tell them about the bracket on the fire door. He also tells them that when he spoke to Campos a short while before getting on the elevator, Campos never mentioned anything about being shot. But why would a maintenance manager head to the guest floors, in the first place?

Granted, the bracket is not an everyday occurrence. But it still does not warrant a manager to head to the floor unless he was removing the bracket. But he wasn't, as that is why Schuck was sent to the floor. Evidently, as Campos did not tell him he was shot, what did he tell him that required Alsbury's presence on the floor?

What is even more bizarre, Alsbury is only mentioned some four times in the final case report. But he was a critical eyewitness and was on the 32nd floor, while the gunman was still firing into the venue. Yet, his witness statement was never summarized. Yet, a sushi bar worker who served the gunman days before the attack, had their statement summarized, when they had no crucial information to give.

The answer lies, in what Alsbury told investigators, when he was interviewed on October 10. He stated that towards the end of the call with Campos on the night of the attack, Alsbury told Campos to stay at the fire door, until a hotel maintenance technician arrived to remove the bracket. This was because, the fire door was an emergency exit, so if any guest should need to use it for any reason. Campos could direct them to another fire door, on the 32nd floor.

After Campos was told to stay at the fire door and wait for the maintenance worker to arrive, he then told Alsbury to hang on, as he could hear a drilling sound. Alsbury asked Campos where the drilling noise was coming from, and Campos claimed from the back of the stairwell door. This would mean he was indicating the sound was coming from the stairwell side of the fire door.

Once Campos made this claim to Alsbury, he was then told to leave the foyer and use one of the other floors above or below, to access the stairwell to catch the person seemingly securing fire doors. Along with this, Alsbury also told Campos he would head up to the 32nd floor, to see exactly what was going on. According to Alsbury, he estimated that the call ended at right around 10:05 p.m.

Basically, the call ended just seconds before the gunman fired his first shots into the concert venue. What is also interesting, had there been any type of drilling sound coming from the stairwell side of the fire door, Alsbury would have also heard it. Because the distance from the house phone to the fire door, was only 5 feet. Yet, Alsbury never claimed to hear the sound.

Maybe this also explains as to why Campos claimed to hear drilling coming from 32-135, after leaving the foyer, which would have been around the start of the attack. Because had Campos been re-interviewed later on, due to what Alsbury stated. Campos could have said he was mistaken as to when he claimed to hear the drilling sound and, was meant to have stated he heard it while speaking to Alsbury.

Again, there was nothing that was making sense, and it was easy to see why the FIT team were getting confused. Because no sooner does it seem like you have a plausible and coherent set of circumstance, then suddenly, something emerges that does not fit into place.

Like the time Campos was wounded. Because there were notes added to the security log that stated it occurred sometime between 10:10 p.m. to 10:20 p.m. Then LVMPD initially placed it happening at 9:59 p.m. and

MGMRI then threw a curved ball, by claiming it occurred around 10:06 p.m. But the only evidence they had, was an inaccurate timestamp on a recording. However, they did give a little breadcrumb as to how to determine when it occurred.

In their October 11 statement, MGMRI claimed that armed hotel security and LVMPD officers responded to the 32nd floor, as a direct result of Campos' radio message. This can only be the armed group Hendrix was leading, who never made it to the 32nd floor. To further confirm this, the security manager that spoke to Hendrix, about the incident upon the 32nd floor. Heard Campos' first radio message about being shot. This is why they told immediately told Hendrix about.

Fortunately, LVMPD officer Varsin who was with Hendrix, was wearing a BWC and had active it just as they walked into the casino security office. Like everything else involving Campos, though. There was an issue with the footage because someone had enlarged the video, so the time and date stamp were not visible. However, just like the BWC footage from the hotel security dispatch office, there is a way to confirm when Varsin's camera starts recording.

To confirm what time Varsin's BWC footage started to record. The radio message that Hendrix broadcast on his patrol radio, about being on the floor below the shooter, will be used to determine the start time of the footage.

According to the CAD log, Hendrix's message occurred at 10:12 p.m. and 59 seconds. By this point, Varsins BWC had been recoding for 5 minutes and 58 seconds. So, by subtracting the elapsed time of the video from the time of Hendrix's radio message, it shows that Varsin's BWC had been recording since 10:07 p.m. and 01 second.

Then, by watching the footage from the start to the moment Hendrix was told about Campos' radio message, 2 minutes and 24 seconds had elapsed. This places Campos wounding at around 10:09 p.m. and 25 seconds.

This shows that both Schuck and Campos, were shot at by the gunman at around the same time, which makes sense. As it has always been questioned how the gunman spotted them, minutes apart, while also focusing on the concert venue. This information also slots another piece of evidence to slot into place.

The guest in 32-132, who was a Vietnam combat veteran, was able to tell what direction the gunman was firing, at various stages of the attack. According to the guest, the first volley down the hallway was very short and amounted to around 6 to 8 shots. Then, around forty to fifty seconds later, there was a second volley of around 20 to 30 shots.

When the guest was asked to give a rough time as to when the shots down the hallway, occur. He stated that the gunman fired the 6 single shots from 32-134, which seemed to be going outside of the building. Then the three short bursts from 32-135, which again, was aimed outside of the hotel. After this, the gunman then fired the two volleys down the hallway. A few moments after firing down the hallway, for a second time, the shooter then returned to firing back outside of the building.

Based on this evidence, it seems that Campos ended the call at right around 10:05 p.m., just as the gunman opened fire, on the concertgoers. Campos seems to have just hung around by 32-135 and the foyer area, until he thought it was safe. And according to the evidence, this was about the time the gunman was moving between 32-134 and 32-135, which was around 4 minutes into the attack. However, the gunman spotted Campos as he was in the vicinity of the room service cart, and then opened fire on him.

So, the question is, did Campos report the shots being fired or didn't he? It seems, though, that he did not notify anyone of shots being fired, until after he was wounded. Unless he did, and they ignored him, and chose not to react. And maybe, this is what MGMRI covered up? But surely, no one would have ignored Campos' call about shots fired from 32-135? The honest answer is no one will ever know for certain.

This is not the only shocking turn of events, though, as there is also an answer to why Campos has always maintained he dropped down a floor, after leaving the fire door. Even after it was claimed he used the guest elevator on the 33rd floor, Campos still maintained he dropped down a floor.

In Campos interview on October 4, 2017, he was asked if he had made any other statements. He stated that he did, to Henderson Police, while at the St. Rose Dominican Hospital in Henderson, while receiving treatment for his wound on his left calf. The interesting part about this statement, is how he describes accessing the 32nd floor, after leaving the fire door. Because, while he admitted that he dropped down to the 31st floor, he claimed to use another wings stairwell to access the 32nd floor.

"On Sunday October 1st 2017, at approximately 2200 Hours I was responding to a HotSOS room using stairwell attempting to open door on 32 floor 100 wing it was blocked of went down a floor to use another wings stairwell approaching room 32-135 shots fired as I was leaving and I got hit on my left calf called for back up and security dispatch sent armed security with shift manager [REDACTED] responded and I was evacuated and went down to baggage area where SWAT cleared area then got medical treatment. Four Metro officers first responded before I was evacuated, then SWAT."

- Jesus Campos, Oct. 2, 2017, at 2:35 am

This partially answers as to why he has always maintained that he dropped down a floor. Interestingly, the FIT had never read Campos October 2 statement, and had they done, their questioning would have taken a whole different path on October 4. To fully answer the question, as to why he admitted to dropping down to the 31st floor and using the stairwell, is because there are three witnesses to this fact.

Although, when Campos spoke to Henderson Police while getting treatment, for his wound. He would have been unaware of the fact that MGMRI were willing to cover for him. So, as he knew he passed at least three people as he accessed the 32nd floor, after leaving the fire door. He had no choice but to tell the truth. Also, should the truth come to light, by reading Campos' statement, it would have been hard to charge him with any crime, such as perjury. Because in key places of his witness statement, he did not lie. He just made it appear that his memory was a little hazy.

Based on a police intelligence report, from a few days after the attack, a husband and wife who were staying on the 31st floor 100-wing on the night of the attack. Claimed to have seen Campos heading down the hallway, in the direction of the core center on the 31st floor, just as the couple were arriving back at their room. They stated that the time was around 9:45 p.m., when they saw Campos.

LVMPD never acted upon this information, as Campos had already admitted to being on that area of the floor, at roughly around that time. Then, by the time that the final version of events was released, which claimed he used the guest elevators on the 33rd floor, this piece of evidence had been largely forgotten about.

The third witness was another hotel employee, who worked as a food server. According to the food server, after delivering food to a guest on the 300-wing of the 33rd floor, he then used the stairwell to deliver the next food order on their list, on the 30th floor. They passed campos stood on the small landing between the 31st and 32nd floors, playing on his phone. The hotel employee claimed this was around 9:50 p.m.

Seemingly, LVMPD never followed up on this second lead, because countless hotel employee's made false and misleading statements. And as Campos never mentioned anything about using another wings stairwell on the 31st floor, to access the 32nd floor. The FIT team did not see a need to follow up on this. However, had they read Campos October 2 statement, they certainly would have followed up on this information.

Let's suppose for a moment that there was no superimposed timestamps on the service elevator footage from the lower levels of the hotel, and the actual timestamp stated he entered elevator 5410 at 9:36 p.m. and 27 seconds. Then let's also say, that he exited on the 200-wing 30th floor service elevator bank at 9:37 p.m. and 21 seconds. This would fit with the log time of 9:35 p.m., where Campos reported heading to the guest levels.

Here is the question, though: if all this was true, what is the earliest time Campos would have arrived at 32-129 and was it enough time for him to still clear his door checks by 9:59 p.m.?

To determine this, I conducted a third series of time trials based on the first and second series. However, this time, I used the 300-wing 31st floor stairwell to access the 32nd floor. Also, I allowed a 5-minute pause between the 31st and 32nd floors, to account for Campos being seen on his phone.

Third Route Time Trial

Route Three – Campos using a Stairwell on the 31st Floor:

Total Route Time = 18 minutes and 39 seconds.

Total Distance = 2,741 feet

When this time is applied to the time it is believed that Campos entered the 30th floor 200-wing service elevator bank, at around 9:37 p.m. and 21 seconds. A rather insightful perspective is gained, as it shows Campos would have been at 32-129 no later than 9:56 p.m. This is roughly around the time the guest stated Campos arrived on the room. This would also have been ample time for him to speak to the guest and, then sign off his room checks, by 9:59 p.m.

Here is where it gets very interesting, though, because everyone has assumed that what ever someone was trying to cover up, occurred on the 32nd floor 100-wing hallway. However, with this new statement of Campos' along with this new timeframe of him arriving on the 30th floor 200-wing. There is a whole new timeline that comes to the forefront.

This new timeline shows that someone was not trying to cover up a single insignificant action, on Campos' part. They were covering up a highly negligent series of events, which shows, had Campos reported certain incidents sooner. Along with, being honest while reporting the bracket on the fire door and telling Alsbury or security dispatch what he really witnessed on the 32nd floor 100-wing. There is a chance the attack could have been stopped a lot sooner than 10:15 p.m., or he could have prevented the attack from even happening. And here is why.

With Campos entering the 30th floor 200-wing at 9:37 p.m. and 21 seconds, after completing his door checks, on the 30th floor. Campos would have been at the fire door, for right around 9:43 p.m. and 33 seconds. Based on the gunman's door lock records for 32-134, he was outside the room from

9:40 p.m. to around 9:43 p.m. Then between 9:44 p.m. and 947 p.m., there was a flurry of activity with the door to 32-134.

It appears, when Campos arrived at the fire door in the stairwell side, he was aware of drilling as he heard it coming up the stairs towards the fire door. Then, just as Campos pulled on the door, at around 9:43 p.m. The gunman was stood on the other side of the fire door, getting ready to insert the final screw into the doorframe, then add another bracket. However, as Campos pulled on the door, the gunman panicked and ran out of the foyer, and back into 32-134.

Then, between 9:44 p.m. to 9:47 p.m. the gunman hastily set up the cameras on the room service cart and placed them outside of 32-134. Once the cart was in position, he then watched the cameras for a few minutes. Because based on his calculations, it would not take long for someone to access the 32nd floor 100-wing hallway, from the floor above or below. But as Campos never used the guest elevator, he was not back on the floor in the allotted time. So, the gunman went forward with his plans.

Campos, meanwhile, assumed that someone from the hotel maintenance department secured the door, because as he was climbing the stairs between the 31st and 32nd floors, he heard a drilling sound. So, he never bothered to report the issue, as no one takes a drill on vacation with them and secures a fire door. Unless, that is, they have ill intensions, just like the Las Vegas gunman.

Assuming that it was hotel maintenance, Campos then took his time to get back to the floor. Because, due to the time of night it was, he did not want to be assigned more duties, so he hid in the 300-wing stairwell for just the right amount of time. Then, after arriving back on the 32nd floor 100-wing hallway, he completed his door check at 32-129.

He then used his hotel radio to clear the door checks, which was logged at 9:59 p.m. After this, he went to the foyer area to see who was working on the floor, for whatever reason. As to whether or not he spotted the camera on the cart at this point, it is not known. But with clearing the door checks, he may have initially paid any attention to it.

Once at the foyer, and after clearing his door checks, he could not see a maintenance employee. Suddenly, he then heard glass breaking, at around 10:01 p.m. Because between 9:59 p.m. to 10:01 p.m., there were no less than ten reports from guests and hotel staff members who either heard glass breaking by their rooms or witnessed it falling from the 100-wing tower, and either break on rooftops close by windows to the guest rooms, or smash on the ground outside the hotel.

Campos then looked around, and as he did, he saw the camera on the room service cart, and he panicked. Because he knew that what was about to transpire, was not going to be good. As at that moment, he saw the fire door secured, he spotted the highly visible camera on the top of the room service cart, and he heard glass breaking.

There was an issue, though, because he had already spoken to the guest in 32-129, who had also seen him head in the direction of the foyer, after leaving her door. So, Campos had no choice but to report something, which would not cause him to be told to check out what was going on, because after all, he was hotel security. So, he opted to tell people about the bracket, as that was out of his scope of work. It seems, though, the only thing Campos did not bank on, was that Alsbury would tell him to wait at the fire door.

After being told to stay at the fire door, he then claimed to hear drilling, as a way to get off the floor. But also, if the person who secured the bracket, that seemed to be in either 32-135 or 32-134 was captured, and they mentioned someone pulling on the fire door. Campos now had a plausible explanation. And he could have said he misspoke when he told Alsbury about the drilling.

After the call had ended, Campos was about to leave the foyer, and that is when the first shot was fired. He knew he could not leave the area, due to the highly visible camera on the room service cart. So, he waited by the door to 32-135, until he thought it was safe to leave. This would be around the time of the seventh volley; however, the gunman spotted him either on the peephole camera or the one on the bottom of the cart.

Based on how the peephole camera was set up, it would be safe to assume that it was the camera on the bottom of the cart that the shooter first saw him. Then, the gunman walked over to the main entry doors to the room and fired his first shot at Campos. At this point, Campos made a run down the hallway, and the gunman fired at him as he was moving away from the 32-135. At this point, he sought cover.

The reason the gunman never spotted Campos sooner, was after he placed the cart in the hallway and watched the cameras for a few minutes, and no one reappeared. He then continued with his plans, which meant he was not fully focused on the cameras. And by the time he did look at them, Campos had slipped by, and into the foyer.

By the third volley, he was more relaxed and into a rhythm, so he did not pay as much attention to the cameras, as he was before. Then, after herding people to the area he wanted them, he took his first shots at the fuel tanks. However, they failed to explode. But just as he was starting to fire back into the venue, he saw movement on one of the cameras, and it distracted him. That is when he saw Campos' leg in the view of the camera, and the gunman chose to fire at him, as he did not want his location exposed.

After firing down the hallway, and Campos taking cover, the gunman then waited to see if Campos would re-emerge from cover. At around this time, Schuck came walking up the hallway, and so the gunman then also fired at him. Knowing that he may not have killed the hotel employees, he knew they would raise the alarm. So, he fired into the venue for another few minutes, then ceased his attack and took his own life. So, by the time law enforcement arrived, he was already dead.

When all the evidence is reviewed in the Campos Conspiracy, out of all the possible variations and scenarios that the evidence could fit. This version, where Campos pulled on the door and waiting around by the foyer area for 4 minutes, before trying to escape. Fits more than any others and makes more sense them all the other variants put together. And this is not just some crack pot theory that has been muddled together, this is how the evidence has presented itself.

Once MGMRI either figured out what really happened, or Campos told them the truth, they knew it was a colossal failure and serious negligence. Both of which, MGMRI were on the hook for, due to how trot law is laid out in the United States. Because employers are responsible for their employees' negligence, while the employee is at work. So, they had no choice but to protect Campos.

Why did Campos go along with it all, as that seems unthinkable when you consider how many people were killed and injured. The truth is, there is evidence to suggest he was not willing to report what he truly witnessed that night on the 32nd floor 100-wing, and he even admitted that after hearing sounds coming from 32-135, he chose to walk away from the room. The only reason he did, was due to the fact he was wounded, and he feared the gunman may come out of his room and finish him off.

But once he knew MGMRI were on his side, and they were willing to protect him. He took full advantage of this fact. Oddly, enough, there is even proof that Campos was going to use the incident to his advantage and get what he could out of his employer. Because in January 2019, a freelance journalist named Doug Poppa was given screenshots by a former member of Campos' family, showing that Campos said those exact words, just two days after the attack. The mainstream media never picked the story up and it was only published in a minor fringe newspaper, called the Baltimore Post-Examiner.

So, while countless victims and their families were suing MGMRI for their negligence, Campos was given his settlement by October 20, 2027. Meanwhile, the victims from inside the venue had to wait close to three years for their settlement, and at one point, MGMRI tried counter sue them. Then, close to the third anniversary of the attack, MGMRI settled out of court for $800 million, and even then, the victims were still owed money.

Why did law enforcement go along with the cover up? The simple answer is, senior commanders in LVMPD saw the case as open and shut. Also, by standing behind the timeline produced by MGMRI, it made their job a lot easier, as it removed Campos from the picture as some type of accomplice, considering Campos had so much time missing from his night, and then the route he took back to the 32nd floor 100-wing. In truth, he never conspired with the gunman or even knew him. But that was hard to prove, due to the level of his negligence.

Even to this day, Campos still gets 'perks' from MGMRI, like VIP box tickets to Las Vegas Raiders games. Also, in the wake of the attack, two go fund me accounts were set up for Campos, which generated nearly $40,000.00 extra for him, along with his undisclosed settlement from MGMRI. Out of this whole tragic event, the only one to truly benefit the most, was Jesus Campos. The man that was once hailed as a hero, but then suddenly become the villain.

Chapter Six:
A Co-conspirator or an Unwitting Accessory

"We are interested in a companion that is traveling with him [the gunman], and her name is Marilou Danley. She is an Asian female approximately 4 [foot] 11 [inches], wight of 111 pounds. We have not located her at this time, and we are interested in talking to her."

- (Former) LVMPD Sheriff Joe Lombardo, 4:00 a.m. media interview on Oct. 2, 2017.

One of the main questions, which continually came to the forefront of the investigation into the Las Vegas Mass Shooting was: did the shooter act alone in his planning and preparation for the attack, or was there a co-conspirator? This question came up on countless occasions because at certain stages of the investigation, there was evidence discovered that suggested maybe someone did assist him. And all the evidence pointed to just one person, his long-term girlfriend, Marilou Danely.

To further cast doubt on how much Danley may have known about the attack and what her role may have been. She exhibit some unusual behavior in the immediate aftermath of the attack, and took some questionable actions. Also, when she was interviewed by law enforcement on several occasions, her answers did not seem to fully match the evidence, they had discovered.

Despite her unusual behavior and countless irregularities with her answers when she was being asked direct questions, regarding specific items of evidence. Nothing could be conclusively proven to determine how complicit Danley may or may have not been, in helping the gunman plan and prepare for the attack. Neither did she give any specific insights, as to how much she really may have known about what he was planning to do. So, by the end of October 2017, law enforcement no longer considered Danley a person of interest, due to the lack of evidence.

Although, privately, while she may have publicly cleared of being a co-conspirator, several members of law enforcement very close to the investigation, still had a firm belief that she had somehow hoodwinked investigators and walked away Scott free. Because to them, there was just too many unanswered questions and a mass of evidence, which on its own did not mean much. But when it was all put together, it showed Danley maybe hiding something. The question was, though, what was it?

Person of Interest

By 11:40 p.m. on the evening of October 1, 2017, Danley was initially classed as a suspect law enforcement. The reason for this, was because her Mlife players card had been found in 32-135 and, room 32-134 was booked under her name. However, when they tried to find her either in the hotel or anywhere within Las Vegas, she was nowhere to be found.

This led law enforcement to one of two conclusions: Either the gunman had murdered Danley and disposed of her body somewhere. Or she was a possible second attacker, who may have been lying in wait to unleash an equally deadly assault, as the first one. The question was, though, which option was it?

When the efforts of law enforcement had failed to locate Danley, they put out a nationwide plea at around 3:30 a.m. PST on the morning of October 2, asking for anyone with information as to Danley's whereabouts to contact either LVMPD or the FBI immediately. Furthermore, if she should be seen anywhere, she was not to be approached. Shortly after LVMPD made their request to the public for help, Danley was finally located.

The FBI field office in Los Angeles received a call, from an attorney named Matthew Lombard who stated that he represented Danley. He told the FBI, Danley was not present in the United States at the time of the attack, as she was in the Philippines visiting family, and had been since September 15, 2017. Her lawyer then told the FBI that his client was set to return to the United States on October 3, 2017. Once she was back, Danely was willing to cooperate with law enforcement, in any way that she could.

Once this information became known, law enforcement first took steps to verify that this information was correct. And after around an hour, it was confirmed by the Transport Security Administration (TSA), that Danley had left the US on September 14 on a direct flight from Las Vegas to the Philippines, and she was scheduled to return on October 3.

After this, LVMPD updated the media that Danley had now been located and she was safe and well in Manila, visiting family. She was also set to return to the US in the next 24-hours, to assist law enforcement with their investigation. Due to this, she was no longer classed as a suspect, but she was still seen as a person of interest.

Filling in the Blanks

On the evening of October 3, 2017, Danley's flight from the Philippines touched down at Los Angeles airport in the early evening. Several FBI agents and TSA officers met Danley on the flight, and quickly whisked her away in a wheelchair. Danley wore a black baseball cap, so that she could pull the peak down over her face to hid it from any waiting news outlets. Once off the flight, several TSA officers took Danley through passport control, then to the arrivals parking area of the airport, where she was picked up by her daughter.

Less than 24-hours after arriving back in the United States, Danley, along with her daughter and attorney attended the FBI field office in Los Angeles, so that she could start assisting law enforcement with their investigation. The first section of her interview focused on how she met the gunman and what he was like as a person.

Danley's response to these questions, covered how she first met the gunman in 2011, while she was a VIP casino host at the Atlantis Casino in Reno. Initially, the relationship was purely professional, but as time went on, it developed into a romantic relationship. Then, by 2014, she had quit her job and became the gunman's full-time partner.

She then went on to reiterate the same information as the gunman's family, that he was never violent, non-political, neither was he religious. However, she did state that while he described himself as an atheist, neither did he have any objections to Danley practicing her catholic faith. He would make comments that her god did not like them, and when she made the sign of the cross prior to gambling, if the gunman lost money, he would blame it on Danley.

This information was a new insight for investigators, and it seems that Danley was the only person who ever witnessed these types of anti-religious mutterings, from the gunman. It is surprising, though, that no one else had ever witnessed these types of displays of negativity towards religion, from the gunman. But considering he was not known to spend a lot of time with his family and had no real friends, there is chance these types of anti-religious sentiments, were never noticed before.

Danley also gave law enforcement other pieces of information, which the gunman's family did not know about. Mainly, the fact that he seemed to be suffering from a general decline in his memory. Then she also told investigators how the gunman was starting to spend increasing amounts of time in bed, due to feeling increasingly exhausted.

This information was insightful, in more ways than one. Because based on Danley's statements, the decline in the gunman's memory occurred at around the time that the casinos began to change machines on him. So, she may have mistaken what was really happening to the gunman. And it may have even been the case, where he believed his mental ability was declining, due to his increasing losses. But there was a reason for what was going on, and it was nothing to do with his memory.

Then there was the fact that she claimed he was spending an increasing amount of time in bed, which does not fit with his overall movements in the months leading up to the attack. Because the gunman's neighbors never noticed the couple spending any increased amount of time at either the Mesquite or Reno properties. Along with this, is gambling record seems consistent, what he rarely missed a trip to the casino. And when he was at casinos, he would gamble from the early evening to the early hours of the morning.

Danley also made reference to his allergies, and how he seemed to be suffering increased symptoms, as he got older. Such as his sensitive skin become even more sensitive, or his sense of smell was considerably heightened. But the odd thing is, while the gunman was known to have worn black cotton gloves and did suffer from headaches due to chemical smells. There does not appear to be any evidence to confirm that his condition was worsening.

Once this round of questioning was over, law enforcement wanted to understand the financial arrangements between Danely and the gunman. Because over $300,000.00 of expenditure was attributed to Danely, between April 2014 and September 2017. The bulk of this money was paid to her between September 16 to 28, 2017, totaling $150,000.00.

According to Danley, after she quit working, they entered into a private agreement where the gunman would pay for all her daily expenses, along with paying her $3,000.00 per month as an allowance. In addition, he would also purchase her a new vehicle every couple of years. On top of this, he would also give her money to gamble with at the casinos.

Nothing seemed to be out of the ordinary to law enforcement regarding these transactions, but they were questioning the large amount of money he sent to her in the weeks leading up to the attack. Because to them, it seemed very suspicious and out of character for him.

When Danley was asked about this, she claimed that she did approach the contact the gunman after receiving the first wire transaction, as she feared he was breaking up with her. However, he claimed that it was to buy her family a house in Manila. This is odd, because $150,000.00 USD would not have purchased any type of house in the Philippines, because at the time, the average house price was around $200,000.00 USD.

In addition, there is evidence that suggests the Danley, and the gunman actually had a written financial agreement, which would be in-keeping with his character traits. In this document, it is believed to contain a death clause, where in the event of his death, Danley would receive $150,000.00 from his estate. It seems law enforcement did not know about this agreement, between Danley and the gunman. However, if this is true, which it seems that it is. How did she not connect the dots, after receiving the exact amount agreed upon, in the event of his death?

After this round of questions, investigators wanted to know how she heard about the attack and what her response was. With this, she claimed that while on the way to have dinner with a member of her family, she had a call from another relative who said they had seen her photo on the news as a person of interest in relation to a mass shooting in Las Vegas. Danley then claimed that after discovering this information, she went back the relatives house to watch the news.

Once back at the house, she saw her picture on the TV, and she immediately called her daughter in Los Angeles. While on the phone with her daughter, Danley instructed her to find an attorney who could represent her, in all matters relating to the gunman and the attack. She then waited until the attorney called her, to discuss the incident. After Danley and her lawyer spoke, the lawyer then called the FBI field office in Los Angeles, to inform them of his clients whereabouts.

Based on this information, Danley claimed that she first learned of the attack at around 7:30 p.m. on the evening of October 2 local time in Manila, as the press conference given by LVMPD, naming her as a person they wanted to trace, occurred on the morning of October 2 at around 3:30 a.m. (PST). To investigators, this made sense, because no one in the gunman's family had contacted Danley to let her know what was going on. So, like the rest of the world, she found out through a news network.

What was confusing to investigators and did not make sense, though, was why Danley immediately called her daughter to inform her that she needed an attorney. Then she spoke to her attorney and then gave him permission to inform law enforcement where she was. To many members of the investigative team working the case, it would have made more sense for Danley to contact law enforcement the moment she found out she was a person of interest, then engage a lawyer and get them to make her whereabouts known.

At the time, though, Danley was only a Green Card holder and due to Trump's new immigration laws, it was surmised that she feared she would not be allowed back into the United States, due to her connection to the gunman. Because there had been various stories in the media, where Green Card holders were being deported for the most minor of infractions.

This does seem logical, when viewed along those lines. However, the attorney Danley asked for was not one that specialized in immigration law, it was one that dealt with criminal defense. Also, Danley was only a person of interest and nothing more, and with her being outside of the US weeks before the attack even occurred. Her reaction to the overall event, would have raised a few suspicious, because it looked like she had something to hide.

Not long after this phase of the meeting, investigators were about to get a glimpse of what exactly it was, Danley maybe trying to hide. Towards the end of the interview, out of nowhere, she suddenly blurted out that her fingerprints would be found on both the ammunition and magazines used by the gunman, in the attack. This statement would shock the investigators, as they were not expecting this. After she made this fact known, law enforcement wanted to know more.

They asked her to explain what she meant by her statement, because they wanted to understand why she made this claim. Danley then stated that around late August or early September, just as they were getting ready to leave their house in Reno and head back to the home in Mesquite. The gunman loaded up several large cases of ammunition and some weapons, he had been storing at the Reno house.

Then, after returning to their home in Mesquite, over the course of several days, she helped the gunman load countless magazines and put them in small roller suitcases and duffle bags. Based on Danley's estimation, she believed it was around 25 magazines per bag, but she was unaware of exactly how many bags they did fill up, as there were a lot. It seems that this was not the only time Danley helped the gunman load magazines, as it seems there were countless occasions between late August 2017 to just days before she left for her trip.

Investigators then asked if she questioned the gunman as to why he needed so many magazines loaded, and Danley replied that she did. According to her version of events, either while loading the magazines or sometime after, she asked the gunman as to why he needed so much ammunition loaded into magazines. He apparently responded by saying that one rifle can fire a lot of ammunition. It seemed that Danley never pressed the matter further, and trusted what he was saying.

Due to Danley making this assertion, investigators evidently wanted to probe a little deeper and asked her if she had noticed anything out of the ordinary while staying at the Mandalay Bay with the gunman, such as, was he taking an unusual interest in the Route 91 concert.

According to Danley, while staying with the gunman for one of the final times at the Mandalay Bay in early September 2017, in room 60-325. She had observed him looking out of the windows in the room, and seemed to be focused on the area where the concert was going to be held. Then she added, that while he was stood there looking at the concert grounds. He also seemed to be shifting his weight, as if he was looking at the venue from the same window, but from different angles.

To determine a sequence of events, investigators asked Danley if the loading of magazines occurred before or after the event, she witnessed in 60-235. Danley responded by saying that this was during that time. Because there were numerous occasions between late August and early September 2017, where she helped the gunman load magazines. This highlighted that some of the gunman's final preparations, consisted of loading magazines with the assistance of Danley. Along with selecting his firing positions.

It later emerged that when the gunman initially reserved his rooms at the Mandalay Bay for the period covering the attack, he asked for a room on the 200-wing of the hotel on a high floor as he liked the view better. However, the day before he checked in, the computer automatically changed his room, based on occupancy of the hotel. At check in on September 25, 2017, he was given 32-135, which again was selected by a computer.

However, a few days later, he spoke to his casino host and asked if he could change rooms to one on the 200-wing, as he did not like the view from 32-135. This request could not be actioned, as there were no available suites on the 200-wing of the hotel. As a compromise, he was offered 32-134 and the accepted, and placed the room under Danley's name.

What is strange, though, is the fact that Danley mentioned what she observed in 60-325. Because it was only her and the gunman in the room, so she did not have to admit to seeing this event. Unless she was genuinely trying to help law enforcement piece together what led to the attack, and how the gunman planned and prepared for it.

Towards the latter stages of the interview, investigators then wanted to learn about what Danley knew regarding the firearm purchases, in the months leading to the attack. This was because between October 2, 2016, to September 30, 2017, the gunman purchased over fifty firearms and countless rounds of ammunition, along with firearm accessories.

Danley started off by telling law enforcement in late September 2016, the gunman moved a large gun safe from the Reno house to the property in Mesquite. And shortly after this, when she went to put some jewelry in there, she only noticed a pistol and nothing more. But she was aware that the gunman had been buying a large amount of ammunition and weapons, and she had also been with him on several occasions when he purchased the firearms and even went to gun shows with him.

However, Danley initially assumed that firearms were a new hobby for the gunman. Because there had been several times during their relationship, where he became interested in a hobby, and emersed himself in the pursuit. Then, a few months later, he would lose interest in the hobby and sell the items he had purchased.

Danley even went as far as to give an example of this type of behavior displayed by the gunman, which related to when he became interested in scuba diving, prior to a vacation they were planning on taking to the Mediterranean. The gunman took countless diving lessons and spent an enormous amount of money on obtained oxygen tanks, diving goggles, wetsuits, and much more. Then once they returned from their trip, he let the diving stuff sit around, then sold it for a lot less than he purchased it for.

The final subject covered in the interview, related to the financial arrangements between Danley and the gunman, because according to the gunman's bank records between September 1, 2013, and September 1, 2017, he had spent over $140,000.00 on Danley. Investigators also wanted to learn more about how the trip to the Philippines came about, along with how she initially viewed the three wires totaling $150,000.00 between September 16 to 28, 2017.

Danley stated by telling investigators that when they first became romantically involved in 2013, the gunman asked her to quit working and be with him full time. However, Danley said that she would be willing to do this, but she did not want to lose her independence and not have to rely on him financially. The gunman agreed that he would pay her a monthly allowance of around $3,000.00 per month, along with covering all her bills and buying her a new car every few years, which evidently, she was happy with the arrangement.

Then she went on to say that, around late August to early September 2017, the gunman began pestering her to take a trip to see her family in the Philippines. Initially, though, she did not want to go on a vacation to see her family. After several days of the gunman continually pushing her to take the trip, she finally relented and told him if he could find her a good deal on the flights, she would go. Then, a few days later the gunman sent her the ticket confirmation for her trip leaving on September 15 and returning on October 3.

Danley then dealt with the three wire transfers of $50,000.00 each, sent to her account in the Philippines, while she was visiting her family. She claimed that when she received the first wire, which was around a day after of her arriving in the Philippines. She immediately contacted him as she thought this was his way of breaking up with her.

However, after contacting the gunman, he told her the money was for her to purchase a house in Manila for her and her family, and nothing more. She then said that after being told this, she believed the gunman was telling her truth, and never thought anything more about this.

Overall, Danley's first interview with law enforcement did offer them some very good insights. More than that, though, it left them with more questions than answers. Mainly because, the explanation Danly gave to many of the questions may have seemed plausible, but there was just something not adding up. For example, how she blurted out about her fingerprints would be found on the ammunition and magazines. Because when she made this comment, it seemed like she was trying to preempt what was coming, more than allowing investigators to lead the questioning.

Evidence Gathering

By the time of Danley's first interview, the evidence gathering efforts were still in their early days, which meant law enforcement, really did not know a whole lot. But all that changed as the days went on, as more reviews of all the evidence could be undertaken by investigators and forensic testing was being completed. Also, the warrants served on companies like Facebook and Microsoft, were now finally being responded to.

The first hint that something may have been wrong in relation to Danley, was signaled by Facebook. Because when they responded to the warrant sent to them by LVMPD, they stated that at 12:30 a.m. PST on October 2, Danley changed her account profile settings from public to private. Then, at 3:20 a.m. PST on the same morning, she fully deactivated her account.

This was significant, as it contradicted Danley's version of events. Because when the times of these events are transferred into the time it would have been in Manila, it shows that these actions occurred before she was officially named as a person of interest. So, the question is, what made he make these sudden changes to her Facebook, before she or the gunman were officially named?

Initially, though, when this information came to light, law enforcement thought maybe someone from the gunman's family altered Danley. Because at around 11:30 p.m. PST on the night of October 2, 2017. LVMPD did contact the gunman's mother and brother, after obtaining the numbers from his cell phone. However, it was later confirmed that neither of them contacted Danley, and they did not even know where she was at the time.

This meant that Danley must have learned of the attack, earlier than she claimed. Then, she somehow made the connection between the incident and her boyfriend. Because how else would she know to change her profile settings, even before either of them was named? Also, how did she connect this incident to her boyfriend, so quickly? As the only information in the public domain by either of those times, was that the gunman fired from the 32nd floor of the Mandalay Bay hotel into the concert venue. No matter which way the evidence was looked at, it seemed Danley knew more than she was saying.

There was also her statement to the media, immediately after she was interviewed for the first time by law enforcement. Because in Danley's statement, read by her lawyer, it was claimed that she was excited to go back and see her family after the gunman found her a cheap ticket online. But she told law enforcement during her interview that at first, she was hesitant to go on the trip, and only agreed when he continued to pester her.

Along with the statement read by her attorney, there was also comments made by one of Danley's sisters that lived in Australia, in relation to the trip she took to the Philippians. And according to these comments, Danley seems to have been claiming to her family that the gunman surprised her with the trip. Because it was claimed in the news article that the words the gunman used was "Marilou, I found you a cheap ticket to the Philippines."

It now seems Danley was being less than truthful, but the question was, why was she? The only answer that makes any sense was that she was trying to hide something. But what, as she admitted helping the gunman load the magazines, and if she was going to try and hide anything, that would be it. Even after her fingerprints were found, she could have simply claimed she helped the gunman move them from one location to another.

Another issue soon came to the forefront though, because while one of the gunman's cell phones was being examined, a chain of emails between Danley and the gunman was discovered. The content of the emails related to the money that the gunman had wired to her bank account in the Philippians, which suggested something other then what she claimed to investigators.

Based on the wording of the message, she seemed to have been fully expecting the money the moment she landed. So, this proved she knew about the money even before she left the United States. But some of the content in the emails in certain places was not very clear, but it did certainly give enough of an impression that she knew he was sending her the money. There was also a hint in the messages that Danley and the gunman were communicating, via another means.

An issue arose, though, because when Microsoft responded to the search warrant from LVMPD, they only submitted partial information from both Danley's and the gunman's accounts. Because it was claimed, there was not much information on either of their OneDrive accounts, pertinent to the attack. With this, the FBI submitted a second search warrant to gain access to Danley's entire Microsoft account, with the claim that she was under investigation as a person of interest and possible accomplice.

When Microsoft responded the second time, they did supply everything from the accounts. However, there was no indication that Danley and the gunman corresponded via another means on Microsoft software, such as Windows Live Messenger. Because this avenue of investigation proved inconclusive, and due to this, law enforcement was not able to obtain a warrant to search Danley's cell phone call and text message records.

There was one ray of hope, which may have been able to prove how Danley and the gunman communicated, and if this line of inquiry proved to be true, then law enforcement had probable causes, for a search warrant.

On the counter of the wet bar, in 32-135, an inexpensive black ZTE Z837VL cell phone was discovered. What was unusual about this phone, was that it was locked, and it had tape covering both the front and black cameras. This was unusual, as the other two cell phones found in 32-135 that belonged to the gunman, were unlocked and the cameras were not covered.

When the FBI Digital Forensic Laboratory tried to access the ZTE cell phone, they were unable to, due it being locked. Even with the specialized systems they had access to, they were unable to access any data on the phone. The only thing that could be determined, was that the phone's operating system was linked to a google account. With this, a search warrant was granted for law enforcement to retrieve the information directly from google.

Disappointingly, though, when google returned the requested information, there was nothing of substance on there. In fact, the usage on the cell phone was virtually non-existent, and it seems he had not placed a call on the phone since March 30, 2017. But he did receive a call on September 17, 2017, from Danley. It appears that the prepaid cell phone was for use when she was overseas.

With very little information to go on, and not enough evidence to prove probable cause, law enforcement was unable to obtain a warrant to access Danely's cell phone. However, just because they could not prove anything of substance, it did not mean they did not have anything to speak to her about. Because with the Facebook activity alone, this was enough to bring her in for questioning a second time. But before they did that, they wanted the forensic tests on the weapons to be completed, to see what that yielded.

Something else came to the forefront, though, from the hotel security camera system, which was rather insightful. It showed Danley with the gunman during one of their final times together, at the Mandalay Bay hotel. What was interesting, is that it showed them entering the main lobby, with a bellman pushing a luggage cart. It appeared that the cart contained around eight to ten items of luggage, which was unusual for Danley and the gunman. Because they normally would only take around one to two bags each.

Another curiosity was what was not found at the Del Webb and Babbling Brook properties. Because there were very personal items of Danley's found, not even any important paperwork or jewelry. It seemed like she had taken everything with her and left only a few items to make it look like she lived at the two properties, which again, baffled investigators.

By October 10, 2017; every single piece of ammunition, magazine, and weapon found in either 32-134 or 32-135 had been forensically tested. As expected, Danley's fingerprints was found on around 200 empty shell casings, countless unfired rounds, and on many of the magazines. But another discovery was made. Some of the weapons found in the rooms, contained a partial DNA profile, belonging to another person.

The second DNA profile discovered on the firearms, was not conclusively proven to belong to Danley. However, nor could it be ruled out that it did not belong to her, as there were several DNA points consistent with her DNA profile. The reason a 100% DNA match could not be obtained, was due to the samples being tainted with gun oil or residue from being fired. This must mean, if it was Danley's DNA, she must have handled the weapons and possibly even fired them.

There was also something else that did not seem to fit, which was found in 32-135. There was a small rolling suitcase by the table close to the window the gunman fired from. Inside the bag were around 20 turquoise magazines. These were out of place because the countless other magazines were either black or coyote tan. And usually, in the firearm's accessory world, turquoise items are aimed at female shooters, not male. So, why did the gunman have these?

What is even more interesting, is that the rounds found in the turquoise magazines, contained mainly Danley's fingerprints and not the gunman's. Whereas the black and coyote tan magazines contained a mixture of both of their fingerprints. Did that mean the turquoise magazines were specifically for Danley? And if this was the case, why would she have her own set of magazines?

It is evident that he was not using these magazines to distinguish between tracer rounds and normal rifle ammunition, as the one-hundred-and-twenty 5.56 trace rounds, he purchased, were still in the Amazon box by the window in 32-134. And the magazines found in the small roller suitcase were already loaded.

There was also something else that remains a mystery, and it relates to his firearm purchases between October 2016 to September 2017. Out of the fifty-six weapons he was known to have purchased during this period, forty-two of them were rifles in various calibers. Out of all the rifles, twenty-three of them were found in the hotel rooms, with fourteen of them being used in the attack. So, it seems he only took just over half the rifles to the hotel.

The remaining firearms that he acquired, were either bought prior to April 2016, where it seemed he was copying the UT Tower and Columbine High School shooters, but then realized shotguns and small caliber weapons were not ideal for his attack. And the remaining rifles were found at either the Reno or Mesquite properties. Then there is the total number of rounds he purchased, for the attack. Because he bough 12,000 round, but only took 6,000 with him.

It seems the gunman was purchasing double of everything, which does not fit his overall suspectology. Because he only acquired exactly what he needed for this attack. That is, unless he changed his plans at a certain point, then those items were put to one side, like the shotguns and pistols. This meant there was forty-two rifles, 12,000 rounds of ammunition, and countless magazines for use in the attack. But he only took around half of everything to the hotel.

It is hardly believable that he would over purchase rifles and ammunition, but not anything else. Because that just does not fit the gunman's method of planning and preparation. That is, unless there was a second shoot, who got cold feet at the last minute.

There was also the fact that the gunman chose to send Danley to the Philippines and not to her daughters' house in Los Angeles, which seemed odd. Because after all, providing it could be proved that Danley was not in the hotel or at any of the houses they lived at in Nevada, around the time of the attack, there should not be an issue with distancing herself from his actions. And then there was the way Danley, and her sister tried to portray the trip in the wider public domain, which was vastly different from what she told law enforcement.

Maybe, though, her daughters' house was just too close, as it was only around four hours south of Las Vegas. Then with Danley and her sister making it appear like she was surprised by the gunman and glad to go and visit her family in Manila, this would make it look like it was part of his overall plan. Because law enforcement was not going to contradict her in the media unless she gave them cause to.

But again, the overall method of planning and preparation has to be examined, as the gunman left very few things to the last moments. And if any aspects of preparation were left to the last moments, it was because the gunman did not account for something. Such as the webcam he put on the front of the cart. Because he found that he needed to hide it, as a further attempt to conceal his location. So, he purchased the vase and fake flowers in the days leading to the attack.

So, why did he only purchase the plane tickets for Danley at the last minute, and not plan for it, months in advance. Because the gunman usually shopped around for several months to find the best deal, before he purchased anything. But getting Danley as far away as possible was only an afterthought. Truly bizarre to the say the least.

With the mass of evidence that was being collected, in relation to Danley. It was inevitable that she would be interviewed again because the facts did not fit her version of events. This time, though, they would focus on the evidence they had collected in relation to her and see how she responded. This would then allow law enforcement to determine what direction they would go from there.

More Blanks to Fill In

The structure of the next round of questioning for Danley, seemed to mainly be focused on the partial DNA evidence, then anything else. It seems that the train of thought was, if she was faced with hard hitting questions from the moment the interview started. This may have been enough pressure to cause her to crack and tell what she really knew.

One of the first questions she was asked, was about the partial DNA marches on some of the rifles used in the attack. It seems Danley's initial response was that this may have been because there were occasions when she did go with the gunman to the unofficial rifle range in Mesquite. And, while she was there, she would not only layout targets at various long distances, but she would also help to move the weapons around.

But when Danley was told that while that explanation was adequate, it did not answer for the partial DNA matches inside of the rifles. Because the only way these could have gotten there, was if she physically touched the inside of the weapons. It also appeared that someone went to great lengths to clean the weapons, as they were nearly spotless.

Danley responded by saying that there were occasions at the gun range, where she would also shoot the weapons with the gunman, because he insisted that she learn how to fire them. And to the gunman, cleaning the weapon was another step in using them. However, it is believed she then stated that she was too afraid to make this known before, as she did not want anyone to think she was involved in the incident.

This response made sense, to a point. Because on one hand, it is true Danley would have been fearing that maybe she could be blamed for something, while on the other hand, if she was not guilty. So, what would she have to fear, by telling the truth? After all, she admitted her fingerprints would be found on the rounds and magazines. But was the statement about the fingerprints, just a ruse to throw law enforcement off the trail?

Danley was then asked about the luggage taken to the room, during one of their final stays at the Mandalay Bay. As evidence had come to light that showed she was with the gunman when he started taking large amounts of luggage into the hotel. Danley openly admitted that she was with the gunman and she knew what was inside of the extra bags, and she even stated where the items had come from.

According to her, after leaving their Reno residence, with a supply of ammunition and several rifles, they stopped off at the Mandalay Bay for a few days. After arriving at the hotel, she claimed that the gunman did not feel they should be left in the vehicle, and they would be safer in the hotel room. Again, this explanation is entirely plausible, and the truth is, the gunman is not the only person to have taken a large supply of weapons to his hotel room.

In 2014, a felon was caught on one of the upper levels of the hotel with around five rifles, and he was arrested for having the weapons in the hotel, which were discovered by a housekeeper. The only reason he went to jail, was because he was in possession of the firearms illegal, as he was a felon.

Also, countless people in Las Vegas take firearms to their rooms, whether it is their everyday carry, or they are going to one of the many gun shows held in Vegas. So, why would Danley have any reason to suspect anything untoward was being planned. The truth was, though, the gunman was in effect loading up on bags so no one would suspect anything in the weeks to come.

After this, investigators then moved onto the email exchange between Danley and the gunman, regarding the wire transfers, while she was in Manila. Her response was that it could have been the gunman who responded the emails, as he had full access to her email account. Or at least, that is what she seemed to imply to law enforcement.

The response from Danley with respect to the emails was one of the most insightful comments she made, while being interviewed. Because there was proof that the gunman had sent emails between two of his own email accounts, which occurred in June 2017. He did this as a counter-surveillance measure. However, other than law enforcement, no one knew about this, until LVMPD released the evidence regarding the mass shooting.

By Danley making this claim, she must have had prior knowledge of him sending emails to himself. So, if she knew that much, what else did she know and what did investigators miss? The FBI did obtain a search warrant to access Danley's personal email account to check the IP address, to see where the email was sent from. However, it seems whoever responded to the gunman's email about the money, used a Virtual IP app to hide their true location.

Once the investigators obtained the answers to these two questions, it seems that they were satisfied that there was nothing more they could have done to pursue the matter. Because unless they had a full confession from Danley, detailing her exact involvement in the planning and preparation of the attack, there was nothing more they could do.

Even if they would have put the matter in front of a District Attorney to obtain an arrest warrant for Danley, they did not have enough concrete evidence to charge her with any specific crime. Had they pushed to arrest her, and the case failed, it would seem that law enforcement was arresting Danley out of spite, because she was the closest person to the gunman. Therefore, as they could not charge him, she was the next best choice.

The truth is, law enforcement made the right call on this aspect, because while there were breadcrumbs and circumstantial evidence to suggest, she knew more then what she truly did. There was not enough unequivocal evidence to prove whether she was a co-conspirator or an unwitting accomplice.

Since Danley's return to the United States in the wake of the attack, she had lived with her daughter in L.A., and despite lucrative media deals, Danley has never spoken to anyone other than law enforcement.

Chapter Seven:
The FBI Report

"To say that this will take a while, is not surprising. So, there is a lot of information that is going to change over time, as we determine more facts. But this is what I can tell you, our resolve is firm. We will get to the bottom of this no matter how long it takes."

-SAC FBI Las Vegas Field Office, FBI Agent (Rtd.) Aaron Rouse. Oct. 4, 2017.

Some sixteen months after the Las Vegas Mass Shooting, in January 2019, the FBI released a brief document title: Key Findings of the Behavioral Analysis Unit's Las Vegas Review Panel (LVRP). The purpose of the three-page report, was to highlight ten key points, which was believed to have contributed or motivated the gunman to commit his heinous act.

The report was primarily authored by the FBI's Behavioral Analysis Unit (BAU), however, there was also civilian experts who sat on the LVRP, to assist the FBI with their findings. Typically, the experts on the panel had a background in either threat assessment, psychology, research, cyber behavior, or were legal professionals. To aid the LVRP reach their ten key findings, they used the wealth of evidence collected by the FBI, during their nearly twelve months long investigation, into the Las Vegas Mass Shooting.

Shortly after the publication of the three-page document, though, various experts with the same qualifications as those that formed the LVRP, blasted the findings in the report. Because they viewed the conclusions as nothing more than window dressing and a whitewash, to reinforce the official narrative surrounding the incident.

In addition, amateur sleuths and even retired law enforcement officers have also criticized the findings. Because to many who have an in-depth understanding of the incident, the report draws on tangible facts in the place of credible evidence. It also seems to force the points that the gunman acted alone, wanted to commit suicide after the attack, and that there were no clear motives for his actions.

Surprisingly, when the evidence gathered by both the FBI and LVMPD is compared against the then key finding, there are obvious issues with the conclusions. So, the main question is, how did a team of seasoned professionals, seemingly arrive at the wrong conclusions? Because it does not make sense as to how they would, considering the fact the LVRP supposedly had exclusive access to the unredacted swaths of evidence, collected by law enforcement.

<u>First Possible Motivating Factor/Key Finding:</u>

The LVRP found no evidence that Paddock's attack was motivated by any ideological or political beliefs. The LVRP concludes that Paddock's attack was neither directed, inspired, nor enabled by ideologically-motivated persons or groups. Paddock was not seeking to further any religious, social, or political agenda through his actions. The LVRP further assesses that Paddock conspired with no one; he acted alone.

Within hours of the attack, ISIS and a group that had ties to ANTIFA claimed the gunman was associated with their groups. However, neither LVMPD nor the FBI could substantiate the claims. Even after both groups made further statements, claiming that law enforcement was wrong, there was not one single shred of evidence found to confirm any connects between the gunman and either of the organizations.

But despite the LVMPD and the FBI confirming that there was no known connection between the gunman and any nefarious organization. There were several media outlets that were being fed information, to state otherwise. However, it later turned out that the alleged evidence to prove the connections, was false and misleading. To a point, someone ceased upon the chance of trying to connect Danely to ISIS, but the information used to try and prove this, was not even based on credible evidence. The evidence was fictitious and fabricated.

The latter finding of the first point, is interesting. Because this related to the persistent claims circulating in the media, and on several websites, which stated that someone assisted the gunman with certain elements of his attack. Unsurprisingly, the two names mentioned the most was the unarmed hotel security guard, Jesus Campos, and the gunman's live in girlfriend, Marilou Danley.

Evidently, the only reason that Campos was ever interjected into the mix of being a possible accomplice, was because the timelines relating to his movements on the night of the attack, kept changing. It was also evident that there was an unknown amount of time missing from his presence upon the guest levels. However, as the Campos Conspiracy chapter confirmed, once his true route from the night of the attack is known, these timing issues are no longer apparent.

Danley, on the other hand, is the enigma in every aspect. Because she openly admitted that she assisted the gunman with loading magazines, firing the weapons he planned to use in the attack, and even helped him set out targets when he was researching how best to use a bump-stock. Then there is the fact that after all of this, she was with him at the hotel when he openly took firearms and ammunition into the Mandalay Bay. Then she observed him planning out his firing positions. Yet, at no time did she ever suspect anything was untoward, despite what she continually witnessed.

In essence, the first point was produced to reinforce the fact that the gunman acted alone and was not connected to any type of organization. So, this point was to try and subdue the rumors and innuendo, more then anything else.

__Second Possible Motivating Factor/Key Finding:__

The LVRP concludes that there was no single or clear motivating factor behind Paddock's attack. Throughout his life, Paddock went to great lengths to keep his thoughts private, and that extended to his final thinking about this mass murder. Active shooters rarely have a singular motive or reason for engaging in a mass homicide. More often their motives are a complex merging of developmental issues, interpersonal relationships, clinical issues, and contextual stressors. The LVRP assesses that in this regard, Paddock was no different.

It has always been maintained by law enforcement that; they were never able to zero in on a specific reason for the attack. Also, there were claims that the gunman went to great lengths to keep his planning and preparation hidden from Danley.

While the first part of this finding may be true, the latter remarks, certainly are not. Because Danley openly admitted that she observed out of the ordinary behavior from the gunman. Such as when she saw him in 60-235 looking out of the window, in the direction of the festival grounds. Then there was the fact she helped him load countless magazines, while also being with him when he purchased many of the firearms.

In this context, while he may have kept any written plans private, from Danley. He never kept physical actions private, which in turn would require him to have thoughts about various aspects of his planning that she witnessed. So, overall, the gunman never went to any great lengths to hide his true intensions. With that being said, though, he did go to some effort to hide the missing hard drive, which was later discovered by a team of researchers, so the evidence for this point is both for and against.

The latter part of the statement is highly irregular because it was confirmed that the gunman did not have any developmental issues, he was also able to maintain interpersonal relationships, and other then being on medication to help him sleep, there was no known clinical issues. However, the contextual issues may have been the driving force behind his attack. Because he was suffering stress due to his losses at gambling. So, this would be classed as a contextual stressor.

Finally, it is apparent that there were certain characteristics and steps taken by the gunman, which were indicative of other mass shooters. Overall, though, he was not viewed as other mass shooters are, due mainly to his advanced aged and financial means. Because these two points alone, places him in the lowest risk category.

Third Possible Motivating Factor/Key Finding:

Investigators found no manifesto, video, suicide note, or other communication (hidden, encrypted, coded, or otherwise) relating to the planned attack or explaining his reason for attacking. However, an important aspect of the attack was Paddock's desire to die by suicide. As he grew older, Paddock became increasingly distressed and intolerant of stimuli while simultaneously failing to navigate common life stressors affiliated with aging. The LVRP assesses that Paddock experienced an objective (and subjective) decline in physical and mental health, level of functioning, and financial status over the last several years of his life. In reaction to this decline, Paddock concluded that he would seek to control the ending of his life via a suicidal act. His inability or unwillingness to perceive any alternatives to this ending influenced his decision to attack.

Although there was no actual physical form of communication left behind by the shooter, stating his reasons as to why he committed his cruel and unprovoked assault, on the innocent concertgoers. It can be argued that the attack itself could be viewed as a way he tried to explain his attack. Because there was ample evidence obtained by bother the FBI and LVMPD, which highlighted how many casinos treated him.

Two examples of this, is the lengths several casinos went to, to make him lose large amounts of money. Such as changing out his preferred video poker machines and keeping the same floor number on the device. Then there was the way that his comp packages were swapped around, with very little or no notice. This proves there was a concerted effort to claw back money from the gunman, due to his unusual win rates.

Based on the evidence found in the aftermath of the attack, it is reasonable to assume that the gunman planned to take his own life, at the end of the attack. This is supported by the efforts he went to, to pay off all but two of his outstanding debts. And the debts he did leave, were the line of credit owed to the Mandalay Bay, which he used in the days leading up to the attack. Along with a final payment to the Nevada court system, for his case against the Cosmopolitan Casino in 2012. In addition, he also took concerted steps to ensure Danley was financially secure, as he wired her $150,000.00 prior to the attack.

The point relating to the gunman becoming increasingly distressed and intolerant of stimuli, while failing to come to terms with getting old, is based solely off Danley's evidence. Because while the gunman had seen a doctor for several medical issues, the gunman refused anti-depressants, but did accept anxiety medication. Furthermore, the symptoms that Danley noted, related to two medical complaints the gunman had suffered from, nearly all his life.

The increased stress levels and anger issues, which started to occur around 2015 to 2016, was at a time when his losses at the casino started to mount up, and he did not have a consistent source of income like he used to when he owned the rental properties. So, based on this information, while it is believed the gunman was getting agitated and stressed due to his memory failing, which is typically associated with getting older. This change occurred at a time when the casinos started to change his preferred video poker machines and alter his comp packages.

This means, while it appeared on the outside to Danley and the gunman that his memory was failing. In reality, his memory was not failing, as there was an external factor, such as the machines being swapped, which was causing his apparent memory loss. Because the gunman knew he had a somewhat robust strategy, so when his win rate decreased and his lose rate increased, he put this down to his memory not being as good as it once was. However, the truth was, there was nothing wrong with his strategy or memory, it was due to the casinos changing out machines.

Along with this, as the gunman wrongly believed that his win rates were solely decreasing, due to his memory failing. This would have caused him to become more agitated and aggressive, because he wrongly believed his memory was failing. Then, once he came to the realization of what was truly happening, this would have caused him to be far more agitated and distressed, as he was powerless to stop the casinos.

In addition, had his memory truly been failing to the extent Danley claimed, there is a high degree of probability that he would not have been able to plan his attack. And if he had, he would have needed an abundant supply of written notes as reminders, but that was not the case as only two notes were found in 32-135. One was the bullet drop calculations; the other was to unplug the phones.

Finally, the later part of the statement that the gunman's reaction to getting old and wanted to control how his life ended, and his unwillingness to adopt any alternatives, which led to his decision to undertake his attack. Is something of an enigma, to say the least. Because why would a man who was known to be non-violent and considerate to other, decide that before he took his own life, he was going to massacre people. It simply does not make sense, neither did the true suspectology suggest that.

The reality is, the gunman's character profile suggests that, had he not figured out what the casinos were up to. He would have simple just taken his own life, if he was afraid of getting old and not wanting to lose his memory. But instead, he decided that his attack was the only way to get back at the casinos for slighting him. And the reason the Mandalay Bay was chosen, was because he saw that they were the ones that really abused him, and clawed back what they lost, and then some.

Fourth Possible Motivating Factor/Key Finding:

The LVRP concludes that Paddock's intention to die by suicide was compounded by his desire to attain a certain degree of infamy via a mass casualty attack. In this aspect, the LVRP believes that Paddock was influenced by the memory of his father, who was himself a well-known criminal Paddock's father created a façade to mask his true criminal identity and hide his diagnosed psychopathic history, and in so doing ultimately achieved significant criminal notoriety.

The fourth point is one of the most bizarre of all the ten points, because the LVRP try and link the gunman's father to a possible reason as to why the shooter committed the attack. It also appears that not only are they trying to reinforce the point that the gunman intended to commit suicide, but he did so to make himself more infamous. As to how they arrived at this conclusion, it is not known.

Because the gunman's aims was not to become an infamous criminal, his goal was to get back at the casino industry, more specifically, the Mandalay Bay. Had he truly wanted to obtain any degree of infamy, he would have done it prior to October 1, 2017. As the attack proved, the gunman could do nearly anything he set his mind to.

In addition, there are documented accounts that the gunman tended to shy away from the limelight, while he was alive. Because he was a private person who had serious trust issues, due to how he was lied to about his father being deceased. Irrespective if his father mistreated him, his mother was the one person in the world he thought he could trust the most, and he later found out she had lied to him for over a decade.

Also, it was a known fact that the gunman could not stand his father, for a multitude of reasons. And one reason may have been because his father could have abused him, at an early age. Because there were suggestions circulating that the gunman's father was some type of child abuser, and this was one of the main reasons Irene chose to cut Benjamín out of the family's life. As to what type of abuse this was, it is not really known, but it is believed to be more mental than physical abuse.

However, there was a theory put forward that as both the gunman and at least one of his brothers, Bruce, was known to have a sickening interest in child pornography, there may have been some elements of physical abuse by the father. This was stated, due to the rumors and the fact that studies have shown that in cases where children are abused, either mentally or physically by a parent. They are between 30% to 40% more likely to become abusers themselves, later in life.

With this, medical evidence proves that when a person is subjected to a form of mental trauma, like one that has happened to them in the past. Any signs and symptoms of PTSD that they have been surpassing, are more than likely to be triggered by the current abuse. Interestingly, the treatment of the gunman by the casinos, can be viewed as a form of abuse, which he was powerless to stop.

So, if he was mentally or physically abused by his father, this could have triggered some type of suppressed memories. Combined with the stress caused by the casinos making him lose, could be enough to trigger flashbacks and nightmares. This may also explain why in the latter stages of his life, mainly in the year to eighteen-months leading to the attack, Danley noticed that the gunman began to suffer from increasing nightmares.

What is interesting, is how the LVRP seem to give Benjamin Paddock Jnr. a certain amount of criminal notoriety. Because while is true that he was once on the FBI's Most Wanted List, he was by no means a master criminal or some notorious gangster. He was a bank robber who got caught. And had the father never escaped from prison, he would never have been on the most wanted list in the first place.

What is even more interesting, when the FBI changed the criteria as to who could be put onto the list, Benjamin was one of the first people to be removed. Because his escape from federal custody was no longer seen as a criteria to be put on the FBI's Ten Most Wanted List.

Also, it is strange that prior to the Las Vegas Mass Shooting, outside of the family, Benjamin Paddock was relatively unknown. And it was only due to the attack, that he did become known outside of family circles. So, had the gunman never committed his attack, Benjamin's one-time minor criminal standing, would have been lost to history. Because unlike other more infamous criminals, Benjamin Paddock was not googled prior to October 1, 2017, nor was he deemed worthy enough to have a Wikipedia page, until after the attack.

<u>**Fifth Possible Motivating Factor/Key Finding:**</u>

The LVRP assesses that Paddock displayed minimal empathy throughout his life and primarily viewed others through a transactional lens of costs and benefits. Paddock's decision to murder people while they were being entertained was consistent with his personality. He had a history of exploiting others through manipulation and duplicity, sometimes resulting in a cruel deprivation of their expectations without warning.

The fifth finding of the LVRP was somewhat accurate, but very overstated. Because while it is true that the gunman did view certain people through a transactional lens. There was never any conclusive evidence that the gunman lacked empathy. This can be proven by how he treated Danley, because even after she had been seen by many to outlive her use to the gunman. He still cared for her, and still showed concern for her wellbeing.

Furthermore, there are also countless documented cases from former tenants, which showed that the gunman was not quick to evict a person for non-payment of rent. Because he would prefer to work with a tenant, until such time, it was seen by him they were not willing to help themselves.

Had he truly lacked any type of empathy, he would never have taken these steps, instead he would have been quick to evict tenants and re-rent the apartment to a paying customer.

<u>**Sixth Possible Motivating Factor/Key Finding:**</u>

Exhaustive investigations by the LVMPD and the FBI yielded no indication that Paddock's attack was motivated by a grievance against any specific casino, hotel, or institution in Las Vegas; the Mandalay Bay Resort and Casino; the Route 91 Harvest Festival; or against anyone killed or injured during the attack. Paddock's exploration of other potential sites suggests that his final selection was based on the identification of a tactically-advantageous location from which to attack. His selected position in a hotel room on the 32nd floor enabled Paddock to shoot at a densely-packed crowd of unsuspecting and vulnerable people. Further, it provided sufficient privacy for Paddock to prepare for and execute the attack, all within driving distance of his residence in Mesquite.

Many of the experts have seriously questioned as to why the LVRP felt the need to put this point into their key findings. Because this basically states that the gunman only chose to attack the Route 91 Concert, as it was the most advantageous target he could find within driving distance of his house, while also affording him the privacy to unleash his attack away from prying eyes.

This is not true, though, because even though the gunman was not tactically inclined, he would have known that the Life is Beautiful concert was a far better target, than the Route 91 concert. Firstly, the crowds were right outside the Ogden, whereas at the Route 91 they were across the street. Also, the Life is Beautiful crowds, were far bigger than the ones outside of the Mandalay Bay.

Secondly, in the sense of security, the Ogden again was the better choice. Mainly because it had a lot fewer staff members, and a lot fewer people upon the guest levels. Thirdly, just like the Mandalay Bay, the Ogden was within driving distance of Mesquite. In fact, the Ogden was closer by some five miles or more.

Finally, from all of the evidence amassed by LVMPD and the FBI, it is clear to see that the other venues the gunman looked at, was nothing more than a smoke screen. So if anyone was watching the gunman, they would be confused as to what his true target was. Hence the reason why he was staying at the Ogden in the first place. Because due to the Life is Beautiful event, had law enforcement been watching him, they would have had no choice but to respond to the Ogden, even if he did not fire a shot.

This is also why he was seen walking around the complex on the morning the concert ended, which was to see if anyone other than guests were in the hotel. As he could not see anyone, which may have been there to arrest him, he knew by this point, he was not under any type of surveillance. This also explains his outburst at the El Cortez on September 17. Because the gunman was nervous that he was being watched, so he became easily agitated and frustrated.

To further support this, when he was at the Mandalay Bay, he showed no outward signs of any type of aggression or fear of being stopped. He was relatively relaxed and not acting out of the ordinary. He may have taken Diazepam in very small doses, when escorting the countless bags to the room with the bellman, as a way to relax him further. But this cannot be confirmed.

Furthermore, based on several statements, the Mandalay Bay not only changed out the machines the gunman favored, like other casinos. They also took it one step further by changing offers on him at the last moments, sometimes at check in, while also refusing to honor points he earned during double and triple point play.

To further confirm this, when all the gunman's player account information is reviewed, which was released by the FBI in mid-2023. It is clear to see that while many of his accounts reflect an average number of wins verses losses. The Mlife information shows the greatest number of loses compared to wins, from around mid-2015 to around the time of the attack.

Initially, when the gunman started to incur the greater number of loses at the MGMRI casinos, he did not seem to be overly bothered. Because that is how gambling goes, you win some and you lose some, and the gunman was fully aware of that. But when his losses started to impact his overall wealth, which was when his income was limited to investments and gambling, and not combined with the influx of cash from his rental properties. This is when the gunman started to raise objections with his casino hosts at MGMRI locations.

When his loses overtook his winnings, which they should not have done as significantly as they did with his strategy. He initially believed his memory was failing him, but when he worked out what was going on, he possible raised concerns about this to MGMRI, and they seemingly dismissed him. Then, when it came to the point where the gunman was not making any positive progress with changing his fortunes at the MGMRI casinos, specifically the Mandalay Bay hotel. He decided that he would fight back.

In essence, what the gunman hoped to achieve by committing his heinous attack, from the Mandalay Bay, was to cost the hotel and MGMRI, more money than they cost him. While this is a blatantly sickening and selfish act because the gunman attacked the innocent concertgoers, for his own sick gain. In his mind, after the attack, he would be the clear winner, by costing MGMRI more money than they could have ever taken from him. The fallout for MGMRI from the attack, was truly monumental on a financial standpoint, and still impacts them today.

The first cost to them, was in the days that followed the attack, as their share price plummeted from $32.59 per share on September 30, 2017, to a low of $29.38 per share on October 2, 2017. While this seems like a very small decrease, as it is only $3.21 per share. The cumulative losses were in the hundreds of millions of dollars, in such a short space of time.

Even to this day (Dec 2023), considering that MGMRI are the worlds largest casino company, their share price is still relatively low, as it averages at around $41.00 per share. When you compare this to a small casino company, such as the Las Vegas Sands Corp. who have an average share price of $46.00 per share. Or even Wynn Resorts Limited, whose average share price is $85.00 per share. It is evident that the ripples from the mass shooting, are seemingly still impacting MGMRI.

Then there was the cost for MGMRI to fight a lengthy legal battle against the victims and pay compensation. These costs alone were close to $900 million, with at least $56 million having to be covered by MGMRI directly and the remainder being covered by their insurance provider. In turn, the cost of MGMRI's insurance policy at the Mandalay Bay also increased, due to the mass shooting.

MGMRI also lost revenue from the guest rooms on the 100-wing 32nd floor and lost revenues from gambling as a direct result of the attack. Because in the aftermath of the attack, the entire 100-wing 32nd floor was closed off, until the lawsuits were settled. This would have cost the hotel over $4 million per year for that the section was closed. Considering it was sealed off for some two to three years, the losses for the company would have been over $9 million.

Along with this, when the quarterly earnings for MGMRI are looked at directly before and after the attack on their global operations, there was a $1.416 billion net decrease in profits. And based on market data, any time that the mass shooting is mentioned, their profits suffer for several days after the publication of news articles.

Finally, there is the loss of revenue from 32-134 and 32-135, because even after the 32nd floor 100-wing was reopened to guests, both rooms were closed off, for good. While these room losses will be small, the cumulative losses over years will mount up. Along with this, when MGMRI sold thirteen acres of the fifteen-acre plot where the concert was held, in late 2021. It is believed that they took a heavy hit on the sale price, due to the attack and the fact that two acres of the site are going to house a permanent memorial to the victims.

When you review the evidence relating to how MGMRI seemingly treated the gunman, and the wider impact on their operations due to the actions of the gunman. It appears, in a sick and twisted way, he felt that he never needed to leave a manifesto or suicide note explaining his actions. Because the evidence, attack, and impact on MGMRI after the fact, should speak for itself.

<u>Seventh Possible Motivating Factor/Key Finding:</u>

Throughout his life, Paddock displayed an ability to devote significant time, focused attention, and energy to specific hobbies or projects of interest. Once Paddock decided to attack, he characteristically devoted time, attention, and energy to the

shooting. Paddock engaged in detailed preparations for the attack, including a year-long burst of firearms and ammunition acquisition. The planning and preparation – in and of itself – was likely satisfying to Paddock as it provided a sense of direction and control despite his mental and physical decline. He engaged in significant, methodical, Internet-based research regarding site selection, police tactics and response, and ballistics. Paddock conducted in-person site surveillance and engaged in end-of-life planning. Despite Paddock's research, planning, and preparation, the LVRP found no evidence that he communicated his intent to commit an attack to others or that anyone was aware of his objective. This finding is consistent with Paddock's personality and private nature.

It was true that the gunman was driven and highly determined to obtain his end goals, in any tasks that he truly wanted to succeed in. Also, it is true that the evidence reflects that he spent up to a year or more, planning his attack. Furthermore, he did plan for his suicide, by ensuring that nearly all his debts were settled and Danley was taken care of financially.

However, no one can be certain as to how much Danley truly knew about the attack. Because while there is no written communication determining this and no physical evidence to say she was going to be a co-conspirator. No one truly knows about their private conversations, which were never known to have been recorded.

And yes, initially, Danley could have ignored the increased firearm and ammunition purchases for the attack. She could have also ignored placing targets at long distances at the unofficial gun range. And she could have even ignored the fact that the gunman started to take weapons and ammunition into the Mandalay Bay when they stayed there.

However, the questions arise as to why she never suspected something when she witnessed his actions in room 60-235. Because now, there are countless signs that something was not right, and she seems to have dismissed them. Then you must account for how she acted upon her return to the United States, and how she portrayed her trip to see her family, in the public domain.

Then there was the fact that when both the Mesquite and Reno properties were searched, very few items of Danley's were found in the aftermath of the attack. And the only items that were found, seemed like they were disposable.

Combined with this, when you account for the email exchange between her and the gunman, regarding the wiring of money to her account overseas, which seemed she was fully aware of. Then how she tried to cast doubt on who responded to the emails, which implies she knew about the few emails the gunman had been sending between his two email accounts in June 2017. By this sage, the benefit of the doubt is gone, and serious questions can arise.

As for his target surveillance, the gunman had stayed at the Mandalay Bay on countless occasions, since 1999. So, he was well versed in the operations of the hotel, and how lazy certain hotel staff truly were. He was also aware, if you gave a very generous tip, the staff tended to not notice anything you were doing wrong. Even if that was taking weapons into the hotel.

<u>Eighth Possible Motivating Factor/Key Finding:</u>

There is no evidence that Paddock planned for or sought to escape the Mandalay Bay hotel room after the attack. Further, the LVRP assesses that Paddock took multiple, calculated steps to ensure that he could commit suicide at a time and in a manner of his choosing. This included the use of surveillance cameras to alert Paddock to approaching police responders and his decision to bring one handgun (a .38 caliber revolver) which he used to commit suicide. The LVRP assesses that Paddock accelerated the timing of his attack on the Route 91 Harvest Festival based on his perception that a security/law enforcement response to his room was imminent.

The first section of this point was mainly added into the findings, due to several statements made in the aftermath of the attack, by Sheriff Joe Lombardo. Because there were several occasions where he claimed the gunman planned to escape the scene at some point. However, none of the evidence found at the hotel, supported this theory.

What is interesting, is the latter part of this statement, because there was evidence that the gunman accelerated his timeline, but no one has ever been able to definitively prove what caused him to do this. However, when you consider Campos pulling on the fire door, as the gunman was securing the brackets, this would have been enough for him to advance his plans.

<u>Ninth Possible Motivating Factor/Key Finding:</u>

Prior to the attack, Paddock maintained interpersonal relationships and was not completely isolated. He appeared to demonstrate authentic concern and responsibility for his girlfriend and certain family members while sustaining amicable relationships with previous intimate partners. Paddock's declining mental and physical condition, stressors, and concerning behaviors in the years leading up to the attack were observed by others although not interpreted as indicative of preparation for a mass casualty attack.

This point drawn up by the LVRP contradicts their earlier finding in point five, which suggested that the gunman had no empathy and he only used people. However, now they are showing that after all, the gunman did have at least some human qualities. Because he did show concern for Danley and several members of his family.

<u>Tenth Possible Motivating Factor/Key Finding:</u>

The LVRP's Key Findings illustrate that Paddock was, in many ways, similar to other active shooters the FBI has studied. Research conducted by the FBI indicates that active shooters typically experience an average of 3.6 stressors prior to an attack and display an average of 4.7 concerning behaviors to others. Additionally, 21% of active shooters studied by the FBI had no identifiable grievance or the grievance was unknown prior to their attack. More than half lived with someone else and 48% had suicidal ideation or engaged in suicide-related behaviors at some point prior to the attack.

The final key finding/motivating factor was primarily inserted into the document, to show that while in certain respects the Las Vegas gunman was different to other mass shooters. Such as his age, financial means, time spent preparing for his attack, and the method of his attack. Overall, he did fit the profile of a typical mass shooter, based on the evidence that the LVRP had reviewed.

It also appears, that again, anyone, such as Danley and Campos who may have been a key witness to certain events that would suggest something was not right. They were given a 'free pass' because there have been documented cases where other mass shooters have displayed certain types of behavior or even allowed people to see certain elements of their planning phase. But the people that observed unusual behaviors or witnessed key events and did not respond, usually do not associate these actions or events, until after the attack.

<u>LVRP Key Findings Conclusion</u>

After reviewing the ten key findings and comparing them against the known evidence, released by both LVMPD and the FBI, along with reviewing a more accurate suspectology of the gunman. It does appear that most of the experts that blasted the findings of the LVRP, were justified. And overall, it does appear that some of the conclusions drawn-up, do not make much sense or match the evidence relating to the attack.

One example of this, are the findings in point four, where it was claimed, the gunman was partly inspired to commit the attack by the memory of his criminal father, and he also wanted to be more infamous than his late father. However, contemporary evidence proves that the gunman had no interest in his father, let alone wanting to be just like him. Also, everything the gunman did in his life, up until the time of the attack, was the complete opposite to what his father did.

Such as building a successful real estate business and being able to gamble large sums of his own money, without having to steal it from a bank. Because that is the life his father wanted, he just could never achieve it. And neither did the gunman commit his attack, to be more infamous than Benjamin Paddock. Because prior to October 1, 2017, Benjamin Paddock was an unknown has been.

It is also an amazement how the LVRP claimed that Benjamin Paddock was some type of criminal mastermind and infamous outlaw. Because he was nothing of the sort, and the only reason he was on the Most Wanted List, was due to the fact he escaped from federal prison. And the circumstances of his escape are not very spectacular either, because he literally walked out of an open door on News Years Eve 1968, after a group of drunken prison guards had left the door open.

The only reason Benjamin remained on the run for so long, was because he was seen as a minor criminal and, when the FBI did undertake efforts to find him, they were looking in the wrong place. Because they believed he was somewhere close by his wife and kids in L.A. However, he was 855 miles north in Eugene Oregon, living under an assumed name. Then when the guidelines were reevaluated for who could be on the Most Wanted List, he was one of the first to be removed.

Furthermore, had it not been for the actions his eldest son, history would largely have forgotten him, and he would have been lost to the sands of time. But due his son's actions, he was brought to the forefront by the media, as it created more of a mystique around the gunman. Also, there was not a Wikipedia page for Benjamin Paddock, until two days after the attack, when information resurfaced about him. And the information on the page is not as in depth as other pages related to infamous criminals.

It also seemed that continually, the LVRP wanted to reinforce the point that the gunman acted alone, and he never gave any indication of his attack, neither did he allow anyone to knowingly help him prepare for what he was planning. It was also found that even though several casinos had taken advantage of him, he did not seem to care about this. He was just more concerned with getting old.

Yet, there were at least eight separate aspects of evidence known to law enforcement that not only highlight how casinos were treating the gunman. But also, how he felt and what his reactions would be when he discovered he was being abused and taken advantage of. And look at what the end result truly was, it cost 60 people their lives (58 people were killed during the attack or shortly after, and two further people died as a result of their wounds several years later) and left hundreds of others with mental and physical scars.

Overall, it is clear to see why so many people do not hold the LVRP report in any type of high regard. Because like most things connected to the Las Vegas Mass Shooting, when you scratch away at the surface, the reported facts quickly fall apart.

Chapter Eight:
The Gamblers Last Hand

"Human behavior flows from three main sources: desire, emotion, and knowledge."

-Plato

Anyone who has ever been to Las Vegas, a casino, or even gambled, knows how the system works. You place your bet and hope beyond all hope, that you can beat the odds and win against the house. But as any seasoned gambler knows, just like the Las Vegas Mass Shooter was fully aware, gambling is not that simple. Because no matter how good you are at your game of choice, the odds are never in your favor, because in the end the house always wins.

The truth is, the only way a gambler truly beats the house, is not only by mastering their game of choice. It is by developing a strategy that enables them to limit their losses and play to a level, so casinos offer them outrageous comp packages. Then, at the end of the year, when they add up their winnings, rooms, food and beverage packages, and anything else they can get for free from a casino, that is how much they have truly won.

In the case of the Las Vegas gunman, who was a little smarter than your average person and good with numbers. He not only developed a strategy that gave him a small edge over the house, but he also took full advantage of what casinos had to offer him. This meant, by the end of the year, he was usually $50,000.00 ahead of the casino.

The trouble is, though, casinos don't stay in business for very long when high rollers like the Las Vegas gunman are always ahead. Because when a whale, as casinos call high rollers, takes the house for more than the house takes from them. The casino starts to lose money, which is never good for them.

Casinos have a variety of methods they employ, though, to limit their exposure to whales. Typically, the casino will allow the whale to have a 'good run of luck', then they will change the odds on them. Like altering the comps, they give them, or changing their room offers. Even denying them double or triple points, during promotions. This is usually enough to drive away a high roller for a few months.

Then, after several months, when the casinos have recouped their losses from tourists and low-level players. They will then send an exclusive offer to the whale, encourage them to come back and play, at their casino. This cycle will go on, and on, for as long as a high roller is willing to risk their money.

The Las Vegas gunman was a little different, though, because his gambling system not only gave him a small advantage, but he would also continue to frequent casinos, for as long as the numbers made sense. Then when they did not, he would rely on his trusted negotiation skills to secure an outrages comp package. But after entering the deal with the casino, he would not stick to his side of the bargain. Usually, he would indulge in the comps and not gamble as much as he agreed to.

This resulted in the casinos losing hundreds of thousands of dollars, in a very short time. In response they would ban the gunman for a short period, maybe a year or two, until they thought he learned his lesson. Then all would be forgiven, and he would be allowed back to play. However, when he went back to the casino, he played the system to his advantage, and took more from the house than they took from him.

It came to a point though, that something had to give. Usually, the casinos would play him for a fool and take far more than they should have done. And the worst offenders seem to have been the Mandalay Bay. So, at the point where the gunman had had enough of being taken advantage of and being made a fool of. This caused him to snap, and unleash a mass shooting, the likes that had never been seen before.

Not only did he have the drive and determination to make the casinos pay for their miss treatment of him, but he also had the money to make the attack as deadly as he desired. All with the aim of costing the Mandalay Bay and MGMRI, more money than they could have ever dreamed of taking from him.

The true losers that night, though, were the victims inside the venue. In the months that followed the attack, they tried to sue MGMRI for unimaginable amounts of money. Because they had medical bills, loss of earnings, and so much more to cover. But MGMRI were not going to settle that easy.

Over the course of nearly two years, the victims would have to endure a treatment like no other. First, MGMRI tried to claim the mass shooting was a form of a terrorist attack, which meant they would not have to compensate the victims, due to the laws enacted in the wake of 9/11. However, no matter how hard MGMRI tried, this tactic did not work.

Then they tried another legal step, which they claimed, was a normal progression. They countersued the victims of the attack. Even going as far as to sue a 9-year-old child who was the beneficiary of an estate from one of the decreased victims. Again, though, this legal challenge was quickly dropped when the media got involved and shed light on the matter.

After this, MGMRI chose to enter mediation with the victims, to try and keep the matter out of court. But this would lead to more issues for MGMRI and the mediation team.

At the time of the mass shooting, the head of MGMRI security was George Togliatti, who was a former FBI Agent and Directory of Public Safety, for the State of Nevada. However, in January 2019, George Togliatti stepped down from his position as head of MGMRI security and returned to his former position as Directory of Public Safety. At around this time, George Togliatti's daughter, Jennifer Togliatti, stepped down from her position as Senior Judge in the Eight District Court in Nevada.

A few weeks after these events occurred, Jennifer Togliatti then took the role as one of the two mediators in the case against MGMRI and the mass shooting. Several legal experts questioned this, because based on the Model Standards for Mediator Conduct, any person who has a connection or had a connection to anyone associated with the case, should not be acting as mediator. However, despite the concerns, Jennifer Togliatti accepted the position as mediator.

It was later claimed by countless victims, that when they agreed to Jennifer Togliatti's being appointed as mediator, they were unaware of who she was and the fact that at the time of the mass shooting, her father was head of MGMRI security. Irrespective, though, just shy of the first year of mediations, the victims and MGMRI settled out of court for $800 million. Then started the arduous and horrible task, of putting a dollar amount on pain, suffering, and emotional trauma.

In a news article published around the time of the settlement being announced, a prominent and highly experienced lawyer of mass tort cases, Katherine Feinberg told USA Today, " In my experience, justice, fairness, satisfaction, happiness, none of it enters into this equation. The idea that money is an adequate substitute for loss or horrible injury is a fallacy. This is mercy, not justice. You do the best you can. And whoever's handling this should brace themselves for a lot of emotion and anger."

Ms. Feinberg was not far wrong, because what was to follow would add just another twist in the drawn-out saga, of the quest for justice. Because many victims felt that the amount of money there were offered, was not adequate. Mainly because when the settlement calculations were drawn up, in some cases, the money the victim was paid was not even enough to settle their medical bills from the night of the attack, and the ongoing care they still needed.

Then there were other victims who had preexisting conditions, such as Post Traumatic Stress Disorder (PTSD). These people were told that as they were already suffering from PTSD, then there was a chance that the attack was not the cause of their issues. Even though many of these people had been managing their PTSD reasonably well before the attack. Then after that fateful night in Vegas, their conditions worsened.

Then, came the more obvious questions, mainly on Facebook groups and in the media. How was it that so much questionable activity could take place in relation to one incident, yet law enforcement or State authorities never seemed to step in. The truth was, based on countless media articles from the time. Many of the people that had the power to do something, who were the elected state and city officials, were past or present recipients of political donations from MGMRI.

For example, when Joe Lombardo ran for the position of Sheriff in 2014, two of his biggest donors were MGM Grand and MGM Resorts, contributing a total of $20,000.00. Then when he ran for the position of Governor in 2022, MGM Resorts International donated $10,000.00 to his campaign.

Even more shocking, was Steve Sisolak, who at the time of the mass shooting was running for the position of Governor and was stood next to Joe Lombard at countless news conferences relating to the mass shooting. Just two months after the attack, MGMRI or companies associated with them, donated $20,000.00 to his campaign funds in December 2017.

The truth is, had it not been for the casinos, Las Vegas would possibly not exist today. Because prior to gambling being legalized in Nevada, it was only a small rail depot town, at the midway point between Salt Lake City and Los Angeles. Then, once gambling was legal, Vegas become the first internal hub for gamblers and has remained being the gambling mecca of the world, even after the Las Vegas mass shooting. In short, casinos are the life blood of Vegas, and without them, sin city would not survive.

So, it seems that as the case of the mass shooting was relatively open and shut, senior commanders and key state and city officials wanted a quick end to the matter. They had the perpetrator, there was no co-conspirators, and the motives of the attack were seen as a minor aspect of the incident. All that mattered to many, was give the victims some closure and get back to business as normal.

Because from October 2, 2017, until the investigation into the mass shooting officially ended in January 2018. The gross revenue generated from tourism and gambling in Las Vegas dropped by nearly 10%, which to Vegas was a big hit. This is why pressure was applied from all sides to close the case as fast as possible. And truthfully, who was going to be convicted for the attack, because the person that unleashed hell on innocent concertgoers, killed himself once he knew his position was exposed.

So, in a sick and twisted sense, by allowing Vegas to flourish and to continue the endless streams of cash coming in from gambling, the Las Vegas gunman is being denied what would have been his ideal outcome, to hurt Las Vegas. But he was not aiming at destroying the whole industry, that is evident. He just wanted to bring an end to MGMRI's mistreatment of him and those like him.

But what about the level of negligence showed by Campos on the night of the attack, and then the apparent cover-up by MGMRI. Should they not be punished for this? In an ideal world, yes, they should have been, but how do you punish a non-physical entity or a person that has nothing really to give, and seems like they would not care? The only answer is, expose them for what they did and show the world what really happened.

Because in truth, Campos has gotten of light in all of this. Not only was he the first victim that got their settlement, but also, even to this day he is still reaping the rewards of his newfound lifestyle. As there has been many occasions where he has been spotted entertaining people in VIP boxes at Las Vegas Raiders games, which has even been published in the media. And also, he is set for life, while MGMRI continue to protect him.

The truth is, though, he is the one that has to live with the fact that he could have at least prevented the deaths of maybe twenty people, and saved hundreds of others living with the pain and suffering they now have to endure. To many that know his story, they have started to refer to him as a modern-day Judas, as he willing accepted his forty pieces of silver and then some, to betray innocent people.

Chapter Nine:
Revised (New) Timeline

"Physical evidence cannot be intimidated. It does not forget. It doesn't get excited at the moment something is happening–like people do. It sits there and waits to be detected, preserved, evaluated, and explained."

-Herbert Leon MacDonnell, The Evidence Never Lies, 1984.

The revised (new) timeline has been constructed using viable and firm evidence.

TIME (HH:MM:SS)	EVENT
8:40:00 p.m.	The HotSOS system received an open-door notification for room 32-129.
9:18:00 p.m.	Jesus Campos is assigned 4 open door checks on the 30th floor, and 32-129 on the 32nd floor.
9:35:00 p.m.	Campos informs security dispatch he is heading up to the guest levels to start the open-door checks. Due to the location of the door checks on the 30th floor, Campos uses the 200-wing service elevators.
9:36:26 p.m.	Campos enters the 200-wing service elevator on the lower levels of the hotel. Also at this time, the shooter closes and deadbolts the door to 32-135 for the final time.
9:37:21 p.m.	Campos arrives on the 30th floor 200-wing to start his guest door checks.
9:40:00 p.m.	The shooter opens the door to 32-134 from the inside and engages the deadbolt, which will prevent the door from closing as he goes into the foyer area to start attaching brackets to the fire door, which is only 11 feet across the hallway from the door to 32-134.

9:42:31 p.m. — Campos has completed the 4 door checks on the 30th floor, with the final one being on the 100-wing, and he is entering the foyer area that leads to the 100-wing stairwell to access the 32nd floor to check 32-129.

9:43:33 p.m. — As Campos was ascending to the 32nd floor from the 30th floor, he could hear short rapid bursts of drilling. He initially believes that it is maintenance working in one of the foyer areas. Campos arrives at the fire door on the 32nd floor 100-wing stairwell, and as he tries to pull on the door, he finds it secured. Unbeknown to Campos, it is not maintenance worker who is the other side of the door, it is the shooter. The shooter is about to put the final screw in the first bracket, just as Campos pulls the door.

9:43:55 p.m. — After trying to get the attention of the person the other side of the door, Campos decides to use another route to access the floor. As it is coming close to Campos finishing his swing shift and it is a Sunday night, he decides to use the 300-wing stairwell on the 31st floor to access the 32nd floor.

9:44:00 p.m. — The shooter reenters room 32-134 and locks the door behind him. He is now wondering what to do, as he thinks someone has discovered his plan. For the next 2 minutes he hastily attaches a black webcam to a white plate with packing tape and places it on the top of a room service cart. He then attaches a wireless camera to the bottom of the same room service cart.

9:46:00 p.m. — After not seeing anyone coming up the hallway towards his room, the shooter decides to place the room service cart outside 32-134, which has the black Logitech webcam stuck to a plate on the top of the cart, and the camera is in full view of anyone that walks past. On the bottom of the cart is the wireless camera stuck to the bottom supports.

9:47:00 p.m. — The shooter opens and closes the door several times to adjust the view of the cameras. When he is satisfied with the view, he is getting of the hallway down to the core center, he locks the door to 32-134 for the final time and engages the deadbolt.

9:55:51 p.m. — Campos arrives at the core center of the 32nd floor, after using a stairwell on the 31st floor to access the 32nd floor. He now starts to head up to room 32-129 on the 100-wing.

9:56:01 p.m. — Campos arrives at 32-129 and speaks to the guest to see why the door is open. The guest tells Campos that she is a nanny looking after a child who is asleep in 32-130 across the hall, whose parents are at the concert over the road, because the father is a DJ performing at the event. She also tells him that her door will be remaining open for a while to come, as the parents are not expected back until later that night. He is asked to tell his security dispatch that if another door alarm should be trigged before midnight, please do not respond.

9:58:30 p.m. — Campos has now finished talking to the guest in 32-129 and calls down to his dispatch to inform them that he has completed his door checks on the guest levels. The dispatcher assigned to the HotSOS system that night, likes to add detailed notes on each open-door notification. As Campos is talking to the dispatcher, he begins to walk slowly to the foyer area of the 100-wing, some 41 feet away from 32-129 up the hallway towards the shooters room. Many of the door checks Campos completed does not warrant many notes to be added.

9:59:00 p.m. — Campos has now finished speaking to the dispatcher and is stood outside the door to the foyer. He has passed within 3 feet of the room service cart. Meanwhile, the HotSOS log relating

	to the door check at 32-129 is closed out and timestamped.
9:59:30 p.m. to 10:00:58 p.m.	It is believed that Campos is stood in the foyer area of the 32-floor 100-wing, responding to text messages.
10:01:00 p.m.	Campos looks around for the maintenance worker, he hears suspicious sounds coming from 32-135 and 32-134, which is the shooter breaking the glass out.
10:01:30 p.m. To 10:03:00 p.m.	After briefly looking around and being unable to find a maintenance worker, Campos calls down to security dispatch to ask if they know why the fire door is secured. The person who answered the phone knows that it is Campos, because the caller display shows it the house phone 100-wing 32nd floor calling, and Campos is the only one that floor. The security dispatcher is unaware of the bracket. Campos call is transferred to maintenance dispatch. Again, Campos is told that maintenance are unaware of the bracket, but tell him to hold the line, as they speak to a manager.
10:03:10 p.m.	Campos is transferred to the on-call maintenance manager and asks him if he knows why the fire door is secured with a bracket. The manger states he does not, and as the door is an emergency egress, it should not be secured at all. The manager then asks Campos to describe the bracket, to which Campos replies it is an 'L' shaped metal bracket screwed into the fire door and door frame with three screws.
	The manager tells Campos to wait there, and he will send an engineer to remove bracket. Just as Campos and the manager are about to end their call, Campos states he can hear drilling coming from the stairwell side of the fire door. The manager then advises Campos to access the stairwell from either the floor above or below and try and catch whoever it is securing the doors.

	However, the manager never heard drilling. The manager also tells Campos he will come up to the floor to see what is going on.
10:05:10 p.m.	The manager and Campos end the call. Immediately the manager contacts Steven Schuck who is on the 62nd floor fixing a water leak and tells him to head to the 32nd floor 100-wing, to remove the bracket from the door. Before Campos exits the foyer area, it is believed he received a text message on his cellphone, which he responds to.
10:05:30 p.m.	Just as Campos is about to leave the area outside of 32-135, he hears a strange sound, which sounded like a gunshot coming from inside of 32-135. He then hears several more, and he dives back in the foyer. Campos is apprehensive to leave the foyer, as he has seen the two cameras attached to the cart, and he knows if he is spotted, he will be shot at and possibly killed.
10:05:31 p.m. to 10:09:10 p.m.	Campos remained hidden in the foyer area, until he believes it is safe to escape from the 32nd floor 100-wing. The gunman spots Campos on the camera secured to the bottom of the cart, and heads to the entry way of 32-135 to fire at Campos and try to kill him.
10:09:12 p.m.	Just as Campos walks next to the cart and in front of the bottom camera, the gunman fires at him, though the doors to 32-135. Campos then runs down the 32nd floor 100-wing to try and escape, while the gunman fires several more shots at him.
10:09:13 p.m. to 10:09:24 p.m.	Campos makes it as far as 32-122 and 32-124 and dives into the doorway alcove, for cover. He then uses his hotel radio to inform security dispatch that shots have been fired from 32-135 and he has been hit in the left calf. Hotel security dispatch seemingly do not hear the radio call.

Campos' radio message is heard by a hotel security manager who is responding to the attack in the concert venue, along with several other hotel security managers and two LVMPD officers. The security manager tells the lead LVMPD officer about the security guard wounded on the 32nd floor 100-wing. The officer asks to be taken to the floor.

Campos calls his dispatch from his cellphone, and the dispatcher sees Campos number on the display and picks up the phone, and in a very abrupt tone asks Campos what he wants. Campos then tells the dispatcher that he has been shot with a pellet gun from 32-135. The dispatcher asks Campos to confirm what he just said, and
10:09:26 p.m. then the dispatcher relays the information to other people around him.

Meanwhile, the shooter is watching the monitor for the camera on the bottom of the cart, to see if Campos comes back out from the door way alcove.

Campos has been on the phone to his dispatch for close to a minute, when he hears someone coming up the corridor, so he pops his head out and sees it's a maintenance guy (Schuck), and
10:10:15 p.m. Campos yells to him to take cover.

The gunman is still watching the hallway, and he sees Schuck walking down the middle of the floor, towards 32-135.
Schuck stands in the middle of the hallway confused for a second, then jumps into the alcove of 32-117 and 32-119, just as the shooter starts shooting down the hallway, for a second time.
10:10:16 p.m. Schuck immediately uses his hotel radio to tell maintenance dispatch that someone is firing down the hallway. The gunman fires a total of 25 rounds, at Schuck. Campos ends the call with his dispatch, who fear the worst, as they hear gunfire in the background of the call.

10:10:20 p.m.	The gunman is now refocused on firing into the venue.
10:13:00 p.m.	Schuck and Campos have been in their respect alcoves for 3 minutes, while listening to the continued volleys being fired into the concert across the street.
10:13:25 p.m.	Campos and Schuck make it to the core center and run into the maintenance manager and an armed security manager. The armed security manager takes up a position looking down towards the shooters room, while Campos and Schuck tell the other manager what has been happening.
10:15:30 p.m.	The sound of firing ceases and the floor goes quiet. The armed security manager, Campos, Schuck, and the maintenance manager wait to see what is happening. But nothing does.
10:16:16 p.m.	The maintenance manager who has remained at the core center of the 32nd floor, hears a subdued popping sound. It would later turn out to be the shooters suicide shot.
	2 LVMPD officers arrive on the 200-wing 32nd floor via the service elevators. As they head to the core center, they see Campos leaning up against the wall with his left pant leg pulled up. Once they get close to Campos, he shows them his wound.
10:17:00 p.m. to 10:19:00 p.m.	The LVMPD officers then walk into the core center and one of them looks down the 100-wing towards the shooters room. They suddenly notice a suspicious room service cart, close to the area where the shooter is located. They ask the manager if he knows what it is there for, and he says he has not been down there, but he asks Campos if he knows what it is doing there. Campos claims he never saw it down the hallway when he was at the far end.

	More offices arrive on the floor, and Campos shows them his wound. The LVMPD officers then begin to formulate a plan to get to the shooters room.
10:28:16 p.m.	Campos is told to use the 200-wing service elevators to go and wait down in the baggage area at the lower levels of the hotel.
10:29:25 p.m.	The LVMPD officers enter the 32nd floor 100-wing hall, to evacuate guests and get to the gunman's room.
10:54:31 p.m.	The group of LVMPD officers now stop ¾ of the way down the floor and have cleared the rooms to where they hold their position and wait for the SWAT team to breach 32-135.
11:21:10 p.m.	The LVMPD Assault Team enter 32-135. Within seconds of being in the room, they find the gunman dead on the floor, close by the window he was firing from.
11:26:57 p.m.	Rooms 32-134 and 32-135 have been officially cleared, and the incident comes to an end. Now the LVMPD start their investigation into America's deadliest mass shooting.

Printed in Great Britain
by Amazon

44763238R00118